INCUBUS AWAKENED

FATED MATES 2

KITTY THOMAS
ZOE WINTERS

INCUBUS AWAKENED

KITTY THOMAS
ZOE WINTERS

FATED MATES BOOK TWO

INCU BOOKS

Incubus Awakened

(C) 2011 Zoe Winters, (C) 2021 Kitty Thomas

Printed in the United States of America

ISBN-13 978-1-938639-73-9

Published by IncuBooks

Contact: kittythomas29@gmail.com

For Mrs. Speight. When you told me I'd better dedicate a book to you someday, it was just what people say. But I remembered. Sorry about all the sex, violence, demons, and profanity. You weren't super specific in your request.

1

The house on Cranberry Lane breathed and had a soul. Black shutters glared ominously down at Anna, watching her like fresh prey as she regarded it from the front yard with a mixture of fear and fascination.

It was a white two-story monstrosity with plantation-style columns and rocking chairs that beckoned from the expansive front porch. She imagined the porch had hosted many a lemonade drinker as they'd fanned themselves, praying for relief from the sweltering Georgia sun. The generous lawn was shaded by peach trees that lined the drive like sentinels.

A realtor stood before Anna, her hand outstretched, a vision of professionalism in a powder blue suit and gray pumps. She smiled broadly as if she hadn't kept Anna waiting for the past twenty minutes.

"Ms. Worthington. Hi, I'm Cathy Lindley."

"Please, call me Anna," she said, her eyes never leaving the house.

She hadn't been back to Golatha Falls in years. Her father had been so cold when she'd left. *He's much colder now.* She shook that morbid cobweb from her mind.

Her mother had passed when she was still very young, and Quinton Worthington had left her everything. His business, his money, and a house she couldn't live in and equally couldn't bear to part with. The plan had been to leave immediately after the funeral. She'd been almost free of the cloying southern town until she made the mistake of detouring down Cranberry Lane.

The *For Sale* sign had teased her from the edge of the lawn. And although she would happily ignore her father's house; *this* house she couldn't ignore. It had been as if an unseen force had guided her hands to turn the wheel and pull into the driveway.

Anna took a deep breath and followed Cathy inside. She'd expected a hollowed-out cavern, but the place was filled with priceless antiques as if it were still inhabited.

Her black heels click-clacked over the hardwood floors as she shadowed the realtor. The hair on her arms rose with each echoing step. They were alone in the house. Of course they were, but she still had to turn around to make sure.

No one.

As she stood in the foyer trying to look like she wasn't having a mental breakdown, she realized the house felt sad. No, she was sad. There was no sense projecting buried emotions onto an inanimate object, imposing though it was. A house couldn't emote.

"These are the original fireplaces . . . " Cathy's voice droned on, blending in with the buzz of a bumblebee that had slipped inside the open front door.

The entryway flowed into the living area, one unbroken room with a door leading off to the kitchen. Rich drapes framed the windows, while lace curtains dripped down to end in a puddle of fabric on the floor. An antique burgundy sofa and chairs sat comfortably around a cherry coffee table.

The kitchen smelled of freshly baked bread. No doubt a ploy by

Mrs. Lindley to make the house more inviting to prospective buyers. It had been touted as industrial-sized. Anna didn't have the heart to tell Cathy that her version of cooking was reheating take-out.

"Do the furnishings come with the house?"

"Oh, yes. No one ever seems to want the furniture. It's been here from the beginning." She lapsed back into her sales pitch then. "It's believed a relative of Margaret Mitchell once lived here, and this staircase was the inspiration for the house at Twelve Oaks."

"Mrs. Lindley, not to be rude, but somehow I really doubt Margaret Mitchell was ever inside this house."

Cathy's cheeks flushed a shade of pink that would have been adorable on anyone but a real estate agent. "Um, well, that's what they told me. Shall we move on to the library?"

Yes, please. Maybe if she could distract herself with books, she wouldn't feel so watched.

The library was a dark cave of a room, a place for drinking brandy and having philosophical conversations into the wee hours of the night. There were high ceilings and shelves with books that stretched to the top and a rolling ladder attached to a railing that went the full circumference of the room.

Anna's inner voice wouldn't shut up. *What are you going to do with this house? Throw parties? Or maybe you can be the pathetic cat lady. Yes, get a hundred cats to fill up the place.*

She'd loved the house as a child, but she was twenty-nine now. And no matter how much money they had, twenty-nine year old women didn't go around buying real estate based on a prepubescent fantasy life.

"The master bath has been updated," Cathy said when they reached the second floor. "You could fit five people in this tub."

"I'll be sure to do that when I have my orgies," Anna deadpanned.

"What?"

"Nothing." Now that the image of several brawny men in a tub filled with bubbles had entered her mind, she couldn't seem to shake it free. *Bad Anna.*

"Well, what do you think?"

She hadn't heard half the presentation as Cathy pranced around, lovingly stroking each piece of furniture like a game show hostess. She'd instead been trapped in the internal fight not to buy the house. What harm could looking do? Clearly a lot if she was considering moving into a throwback from *Gone With the Wind.*

Buy the house. The thought flowed through her mind like a whisper, and she turned once again to see if someone had spoken.

"I'll pay the asking price," she heard herself say.

"Wonderful! I know you won't regret it." Cathy pumped her hand with all the vigor of a slick, used car salesman, and Anna wondered if she was buying a lemon.

ANNA PLACED A HALF-EATEN CARTON OF CHINESE FOOD ON THE coffee table. Scarlett looked up from the nearby chair with interest, a happy little purr interrupting her previous activity: upholstery clawing.

Sweet and sour sauce trickled down the side of the carton and onto the cherry surface. The cat hopped onto the table and sniffed at the contents as if it might be a biohazard. Satisfied it was safe, she began to lick up the sticky sauce.

"That's fantastic," Anna said. "You decide to broaden your horizons *after* I buy a fortune of that gourmet cat crap."

"Mrarrrr." Scarlett blinked innocently.

Anna was going insane. Talking to your house cat was the first step. She was pretty sure it was in a warning signs pamphlet somewhere. Probably right above hearing voices and below swatting at imaginary flying insects.

She peered out the front window. A couple of elderly ladies

stood on the sidewalk, whispering and pointing. Knowing Golatha Falls as she did, Anna thought it best to face the firing squad before it got any bigger and uglier. She slipped into a pair of daisy-covered flip flops.

Scarlett meowed again, drawing Anna's attention from her mission.

The food carton sat on the floor several feet away, while the cat perched on the tabletop complaining loudly. A frisson of fear crept up the back of Anna's neck.

Scarlett couldn't have moved the food that far on her own. Not without making a mess. And yet the white box sat upright, and was even closed, the cardboard tab neatly curved into the slot.

A childhood memory bubbled to the surface without warning.

SHE WAS TEN, SITTING ON THE BACK TERRACE AT CECELIA TOWNSEND'S house, drinking lemonade. Cece was the only old person she was friends with. She was something like fifty. Anna always came to her house after school.

This afternoon Cece was teaching her how to cheat at poker. Occasionally, Anna looked out through the sparse grouping of trees to see the empty house on Cranberry Lane. There had been stories.

"Do you really think she's in there?" Anna whispered, afraid the house might hear her if she talked too loud. It was up for sale. "Again" Cece had said, though Anna wasn't old enough to remember the last time.

"I don't know, I've never been inside." Cecelia shuffled and cut the deck before dealing five cards to Anna. A bit of long black hair had come loose from her bun, and she swept it back behind her ear.

"Not even when she was alive?" She thought Cece had been friends with the woman who'd lived there, and found it weird Cece had never gone over to her house to play.

"Beatrice's father didn't approve of me. I acquired my money later when I married."

Anna didn't understand that, but didn't ask more questions, her thoughts too focused on the fact that the house was finally empty. She jumped up from the chair, tossing her cards onto the table. "Let's go over there and check it out." If there was a ghost, maybe they could see something.

Cece stared at the house, her eyes going distant as if she were remembering something sad. "Maybe some other time."

Anna turned from the window to look again at the food carton. Little old ladies or potential ghost? When framed that way, it was a tough call, but she chose to go outside and brave the elderly.

She'd barely reached the sidewalk when one of the women squealed.

"Anna Worthington, my dear child. I thought that was you. We're so happy to see you back in Golatha Falls. We just knew you couldn't stay away forever."

"And we were so sorry to hear about your father. He was a good man. I'm glad you finally got over your pride and decided to live like he would've wanted you to."

Anna gritted her teeth. Perhaps she should have taken her chances with the ghost. Bitsy and Mimi Baker were two of the most trying old women she'd ever come in contact with. If her driveway wasn't so damned long, she would have recognized them and stayed inside where it was safe.

The twins were dressed in matching dark raspberry suits, their knee highs rolled all the way down to the ankles, ending in orthopedic shoes. Bitsy wore a hat with a feather in it. Mimi also wore a hat, but instead of a feather, she'd opted for a matching berry-colored veil that went over her face. Probably for the best. Both hid their wrinkled hands inside pale pink gloves and carried an overstuffed handbag looped over one wrist.

Mimi's little black poodle yapped at their heels. Anna took a whiff of the air, at first thinking she was smelling Bitsy and Mimi's perfume. If only that were the case. It was the dog. They'd smothered him in *White Diamonds*. The sisters themselves had opted to slather on a too-sweet vanilla lotion.

Bitsy snaked an arm through one of Anna's, while Mimi flanked her other side. "Tell us, dear, what made you buy the Johnson house? Why, the house has been on the market forever and a day. Surely you heard about all the troubles they had."

"Um . . . no?" It wasn't as if the goings on of a small southern town routinely made their way to Atlanta.

Bitsy got a rabid gleam to her eyes, looking like some rogue squirrel had gotten hold of her. "You haven't heard?" She lowered her voice as if the house itself might overhear. "They say it's been haunted for fifty years now. But it's just gotten more angry recently." She shivered.

Anna thought there should be a wolf howling in the distance, but the only ambiance was the Baker sisters' poodle, still on high alert.

"Poor Caroline," Mimi said, in reference to the previous owner.

Her sister nodded. "Yes, poor Caroline. You're a very brave girl living here. But then, you're a Worthington." She clapped Anna on the back with more vigor than a woman her age should have been capable of.

Anna changed the subject. She wasn't about to let Bitsy and Mimi scare the crap out of her with embellished bedtime stories. She didn't believe in ghosts. Well, not since she was ten, anyway.

"So, what has the town been up to while I've been away?"

The sisters exchanged a glance, conveying an entire telepathic conversation in mere seconds. "All right dear," Bitsy said. "We'll leave you alone about the house . . . for now. But when you need answers, you know who to come to."

Anna smiled weakly as they guided her down the sidewalk, intent on involving her in their ritual morning walk. They chattered on for the next seven blocks about Old Widow Saunders' unfortunate tooth incident, and a series of house toilet paperings that the Sheriff was taking *very* seriously. They didn't stop talking until they'd herded her into the Java Junkie.

The coffee shop sported a tattered *Grand Opening* banner over the doorway. It was a big step up from the diner on State Street which had always smelled of tuna fish and day-old grease. In contrast, the Java Junkie smelled of cinnamon rolls and mocha. After Bitsy and Mimi had placed their orders, they maneuvered Anna to a corner booth, fully intent on getting every last detail of her life in the big bad city of Atlanta.

"Caroline!" Mimi's arm shot up in a sudden wave as a leggy brunette with a mane of dark curls entered the coffee shop.

Caroline Johnson wasn't the same person Anna had met years before. Her eyes looked drawn, worn around the edges, as if the life had been sucked out of her.

"You've met Anna, I'm sure," Bitsy said when the woman reached their table.

Caroline's eyes shifted nervously as she turned to Anna. "I've been meaning to speak with you. Your number isn't listed yet, and I couldn't come by the house."

The Baker twins exchanged another of their cryptic glances.

"Of course you could have come by," Anna said.

"Would you mind if we spoke privately?"

When they'd moved outside, Anna gestured toward the window. "They don't mind being obvious about it, do they?"

Bitsy and Mimi were staring directly at them, trying to learn the fine art of lip-reading on the fly. But Caroline wasn't listening. She was busy self-consciously twirling a strand of hair.

"I feel just awful. I never would have done it. We knew your father and we would never intentionally . . . I'm sure you'll be able to find a buyer as long as you don't make the mistake I did and talk too much about the occurrences."

Anna gaped, trying to figure out what Caroline was babbling about, when it hit her. "I'm not selling the house."

"Oh, but you have to! You can't live there."

"Caroline, traditionally people buy houses to live in them."

"But you just can't." Her eyes were wide and just a tinge too caffeine-addled. "It started out little things, but the longer we lived there, the more apparent it became, like something was feeding off us. I had dreams . . . "

Anna noted the redness that came to Caroline's face as she trailed off, but chose not to comment.

"You see, we're very religious people, and I don't want to say . . . demon . . . but . . . Well, anyway, my daughter, Sara, was only seventeen. She's in an institution now. I'm telling you the house is possessed. I should have burned the vile thing to the ground rather than let someone else buy it. But we needed the money."

Anna shivered, but then quickly got herself together. She'd gone her whole adult life without believing in the supernatural. Why ruin that track record now?

She smiled kindly at Caroline to diffuse the situation. "I'm sure you believe something happened in the house, but I'm not superstitious. And I'm not willing to part with it now that I have it."

The horn of a red sports car blared impatiently. "I have to go. Please consider what I've said. If something were to happen to you, I'd never forgive myself." When the car rolled up to the curb, Caroline slid into the passenger side and was gone in a gust of hysteria.

Anna sipped her rapidly cooling coffee and stared after the car. She tried to remember if Caroline had been that high strung the last time they'd met. Definitely a woman who should prayerfully consider switching to decaf.

Anna's mind wandered back to the Chinese food. There was no way in hell she was getting freaked by misplaced takeout. If Cece's ghost stories were true, Beatrice was going to have to do a lot better than that. Maybe float the box around like it was being operated by a pulley system.

Back inside, there was a new addition to their table. Sandwiched between Bitsy and Mimi with a trapped expression on his face, was Marshal Crust. He smiled up at Anna with genuine relief.

She'd once had a crush on Marshal when she was a teenager, but she'd gotten over it. Now, it appeared he was finally noticing her existence. If his eyes' refusal to wander far from her cleavage was any indication.

"Anna." His voice was a little more breathy than was attractive for the average male.

"Marsh." Well, this was getting off to a great start. If they'd hooked up at sixteen they surely would have set the world ablaze with their clever banter.

"Marshal is recently divorced." Mimi couldn't have been more obvious if she'd said *hint, hint, wink, wink.*

Anna smiled politely, wondering if Marshal had been more attractive in high school or if she'd been less discriminating. She remembered herself in high school, so she suspected the latter.

"We were thinking you two should go together to the Peach Festival this weekend," Bitsy said, ever the little matchmaker.

The Peach Festival was the event of the year in Golatha Falls. Tragic, but true. It was a quaint little festival where everybody knew everybody. Anna was beginning to miss Atlanta, where nobody knew anybody and she could sit for five minutes without hearing: 'Anna, my, how delightful it is to see you!'

Three faces turned expectantly toward hers as her inner monologue ran out of steam. "I hadn't really planned on going."

"But you have to." Mimi's lip jutted out into a pout that must have driven the men wild in her younger days. "Everybody's dying to see you again."

Anna could see she was going to lose the battle. Her powers of resistance failed her in the face of pouting old people. They were her kryptonite. She might be able to buy herself some peace until the weekend if she just caved now.

"I suppose I could find a few hours in my schedule." *As if my schedule isn't TV, Chinese food, argue with the cat, surf the net*, she thought.

"Splendid!" Bitsy said.

"I could meet you by the courthouse." Marshal looked up at her from underneath thick, blond lashes, working the shy guy angle. Anna hated when men did that.

"That'd be great. Listen, I'd love to stay, but I'm not finished unpacking." She took the Baker sisters' smug smiles and nods as her cue to flee.

The moment she got home she set the security code, sank to the floor, and peered out the window. The sidewalk was empty of threats. Scarlett approached her, meowing and bitching and rubbing up against her legs. The cat's nose turned up at the lingering smell of *White Diamonds.*

Great. In the space of two short weeks, Anna had managed to elevate old people and blind dates to exciting life events. Vince hadn't been her long haul guy, but it didn't mean it hadn't been fun while it lasted. At least until he couldn't commit and she was sharing him with half of Atlanta. She'd been his *casual every other Friday* girl.

It hadn't been all bad. He'd included her in his social circle. She'd had a job. Maybe working in the mail room of the *Journal-Constitution* wasn't the height of glamor, but it was something. She had no idea what she was going to do with herself now. Get a job? Join committees?

Her brow scrunched at the idea of being one of those bored town committee women arguing over floats for the annual Christmas parade. Then a part of Anna's ten-year-old self came through as she imagined finding prince charming, having a whole passel of kids, and throwing fabulous parties.

Snap out of it. Don't go there. The town might be having an odd effect on her, but she wasn't about to go all damsel-y. She wasn't waiting for a man to come along and make her life complete. *Gag me.* It was the house. It was possessed with Margaret Mitchell's ghost.

Anna picked herself up off the floor and settled onto the sofa with her laptop. Within moments she was inside the archives of the *Golatha Falls Gazette.* She wondered if they ever just printed an edition that said, "Sorry kids, no news today . . . check back tomorrow."

The *Gazette* sported a general archive, as well as archives for categories of special interest. The sun was dipping behind the peach trees when she found a web of interconnected links on her house. Leave it to the fine journalists of Golatha Falls to think ghost stories were newsworthy.

The paper seemed to have a sort of obsession with the house, archiving articles on it far past what they'd saved and uploaded to the Internet for any other topic. The oldest article was dated August 18th, 1959. A beautiful fair-haired girl with bright eyes stared back at her from a black and white photograph. The caption read: "Beatrice Stone found dead in her home the morning of August 17th, circumstances unknown. Foul play suspected." Anna felt the hair on the back of her neck stand up.

Beatrice had been found in the parlor, which Anna suspected was the room now known as the living room. Where she was sitting. *Lovely.* She clicked to the next link. September 26th, 1969. The article rambled on about how the Stone Estate had sat empty for several years. A few neighbors reported hearing female screams at night. Blah blah blah. Weird occurrences, blah blah.

For a ghost, Beatrice was boring. No wonder Anna hadn't remembered the stories. Clicking through several links brought more of the same until she got to the Johnsons. After trying unsuccessfully to exorcise what they believed to be a demon, they'd moved. A link to an interview transcript showed Caroline Johnson using the phrase *just awful* to an extent that should have been punishable by law.

Anna closed the browser window. Pretty wimpy for a ghost story. She flipped on the television and heard a crash in the kitchen.

"Damn cat."

"Mrarrrr?"

Anna's eyes shot to the overstuffed armchair where the cat was regally sprawled. She got up and edged toward the kitchen, her heart hammering in her chest so fast she couldn't count the beats.

I'm not superstitious. I don't believe in ghosts.

As she inched forward, her skin crawled, and it occurred to her that not only was she being silly thinking something supernatural was at work, but she hadn't considered the very real danger of a possible flesh and blood intruder.

Her gaze darted around the room until she spotted her keys and pepper spray in the candy dish on the table. She held her breath while she tiptoed over and snatched them, then returned, holding the spray at the ready as she entered the kitchen.

Shards of blue glass from her favorite cereal bowl were scattered across the tile. She distinctly remembered placing that bowl in the back of the cabinet. Her last logical explanation was ripped to shreds when she looked up to see the panel by the back door showing the security system still armed.

---

2

*A*nna was wasted as an heiress. She should have been in surveillance. Or stalking. She'd quickly determined that Bitsy and Mimi started their morning walks at precisely 9:45 am. Soon after, Sir Franklin, the perfumed poodle, relieved himself in Mr. and Mrs. Sedgewick's rhododendrons. Depending on the dog's diet the night before, the three were passing in front of Anna's house between 10:00 a.m. and 10:05.

The doorbell rang as the grandfather clock began to chime out the dreaded hour. Anna assumed crash position. Whoever was on the other side was repeatedly stabbing the bell like an impatient sugar-high child on Halloween.

A full minute passed before she gathered the courage to peer out the front window. She was relieved to find a perky blonde with a pixie cut. No blue hair or poodles visible for miles. She'd forgotten she'd asked a friend to come by. Anna flung the door open.

"Tam, get in the house!" she hissed.

"Um, okay." Tam glanced around her as if she expected to find snipers hiding out in the peach trees. "Is there some special reason we're reenacting a *Charlie's Angels* episode?"

"The blue-hair brigade will be by here any minute. Oh wait. On second thought, go hide your car around back. If they think I have company, they'll know I'm home."

Tam quirked an eyebrow. "Don't you think you're being a bit over the top on this Bitsy and Mimi thing?"

Anna thought maybe her friend didn't understand the seriousness of the situation. "They set me up with Marshal Crust for the festival. These women are a force of nature. God only knows what other chaos they can create between now and then."

Tam shrugged but went to move the car. When she returned, Anna was at the kitchen table reading *The Wall Street Journal* and working on her second cup of coffee.

"I thought you had a crush on Marshal."

Anna shot her friend a look intended to convey exasperation and disgust. "When I was sixteen. I'm a grown-up now."

"Yes, because grown-ups always insist their friends engage in covert car hiding missions to avoid the elderly."

"Shut up," Anna said, moving the coffee mug to her lips to hide the smile. She hadn't seen Tam in years, yet they'd picked up as if they'd never been separated.

"You got cream and sugar?"

Anna waved a hand indicating the side pantry. "I still think you're a sissy for not drinking it black."

"I'm just going to let that slide on by." Tam poured her coffee then hefted two heavy-duty garbage bags onto the island counter top. "You really do have the best kitchen for this. If you hadn't said yes, I had no idea where I was going to make this stuff."

"So the truth comes out. You're using me for my kitchen."

Tam smirked. "Yes, our entire friendship has been building to this moment."

Anna watched as Tam pulled out huge blocks of white wax in plastic wrapping along with wicks, molds, dyes, fragrance vials, and decorative paper.

"This looks potentially complex." She was beginning to have second thoughts about the whole candle-making enterprise. The most crafty thing she'd ever done was order a crochet magazine for a charity drive. She still didn't know how to crochet.

"You'll get the hang of it. I'll start you out dipping tapers. A trained monkey could do it." Tam pulled out several pots and metal containers, meat thermometers, and two hammers. "This is the fun part." She tossed the slabs of wax onto the floor and started vigorously beating one.

"Where are you planning to sell these?" Anna hoped she wouldn't be enlisted in distribution as well as manufacturing. She grabbed a hammer and set to work on the other slab.

"Sally said she'd be glad to have our stuff in her shop. She's got all that herbal bath crap and soaps but no candles. She's gonna clear off a wall for us." Tam started a pot of water boiling. She placed another pot inside the first and dropped some of her wax chunks in. "Okay, let's watch TV while this melts."

Anna followed her and collapsed on the couch, frowning when she noticed the television was on the cooking channel. That wasn't what she'd been watching. "Scarlett, did you step on the remote again?"

"Mrarrr?"

"Well did you do it, Rhett?" The newest edition, a gray-haired tabby, looked offended as he put his tail high in the air and sauntered off.

"Fine. Whatever."

"Two cats now? When we spoke on the phone you said you had one," Tam said.

"I don't have to explain myself to you." She wasn't going to be the crazy cat lady. She wasn't. Two cats in a house this large was not excessive. Anna swatted Scarlett off the couch and switched to a movie. As soon as she set the remote down, the television flicked back to the cooking channel.

"Maybe the TV is trying to tell you to learn to cook," Tam said, trying to keep a straight face. She stretched her arms in front of her like a zombie and wandered around the living room making *woooo* noises.

"That's not funny. The house isn't haunted. There's a reasonable explanation."

Tam stopped, her hands planted on her hips. "The house *is* haunted. I can feel it."

Anna had to work to hold onto her patience. They were about to get into dicey territory. "I thought you got over that phase."

"My beliefs are not a phase," Tam huffed. "I could read your cards if you wanted."

Anna ignored that. Tam knew how she felt about Tarot cards. She flipped the channel back only to have it change again.

"Dammit!" Undeterred, Anna took the batteries out of the remote and flung it against the wall, then changed the channel manually. She returned to the couch, feeling smug.

The television clicked off.

"It's not haunted," Anna said.

"It's not? So there's a reasonable explanation?"

Anna hauled herself up off the couch, latching onto the only diversionary tactic at her disposal. "I think it's time to check the wax." She went to the kitchen without waiting for Tam to reply and peeked over the vat.

A chair scraped across the floor.

"It's melty, now what?" Anna turned, expecting to find Tam in the chair, but the kitchen was empty. A chill skittered down her arm, causing goosebumps to prickle out over her flesh. She let out a slow breath.

"Okay. Fine! I have a ghost. Aren't you cute? I know who you are, Beatrice. And I'm sorry about your death and all, but really, get the *fuck* out of my house!"

The back door flew open and slammed against the wall, shattering the glass.

"Thank you." Anna crossed her arms in front of her to hide the faint tremor in her hand.

"Who broke the glass? The ghost or you?"

She turned to find Tam standing in the doorway with a velvet bag, surveying the damage. "Where did you go?"

"Sorry, had to get something."

Anna sighed, tired of denying the obvious. "The ghost. Are you happy?"

"Yes. Now let me read your cards." Tam opened the velvet bag and removed an elegant deck of tarot cards wrapped in red silk.

"I said no." The last thing Anna needed right now was to see her fortune spread out on the kitchen table of her haunted house.

Tam ignored her and shuffled the cards, laying them out in a Celtic cross spread.

Anna glanced at the table, immediately wishing she hadn't. "Put them away, now! I don't want to know."

"But ... "

"I said put them away. I saw the death card in there. I don't need to know about that shit. I don't believe in it, and I don't want to see it."

"The death card doesn't always mean death," Tam said defensively. "In fact, normally it doesn't. It just means a big change."

"Yes, and death is a big change. There is somebody dead *in* my house. Let's not tempt fate."

"But most of the spread isn't that bad, really."

"Tam, what part of *I don't want to know do* you not get? If you want to figure out my future, do it on your own time, in your own house, and never ever tell me about it."

"Sorry." Tam wrapped the cards back up in the silk. "I shouldn't have pushed."

"Why won't she just show herself, or tell what she wants? See, this is why I've never believed in ghosts. It's ridiculous. Moving things around, changing the channel on the TV. Why not communicate with me directly?"

Tam shrugged. "Maybe she can't."

"Or maybe she just likes messing with me."

ANNA STOOD IN THE DOWNSTAIRS BATHROOM, WRAPPED IN A TOWEL, exhausted from spending all day decorating candles. Her hand swiped out to clean the steam from the mirror. She stopped herself in time. A single word was smeared in the moist fog.

Leave.

Anna felt a tightness curl in her chest. She gripped the pedestal sink, taking a few deep breaths, knowing the ghost was watching and waiting for her reaction. If she were sane, she'd flee the house, do not pass go. But she'd left sane about three exits back when she'd bought the house to begin with. She wasn't giving it up to a ghost.

Anna wrote her own response on the mirror with her finger, just underneath the first message.

No.

It had taken all her concentration to keep her hand steady, but she'd accomplished the feat. She opened the mirrored cabinet and took out a comb to untangle her hair. When she closed it again, another word had been inscribed.

OK.

Anna didn't like the sound of that. Somehow it didn't seem like Beatrice was agreeing to be her roommate. The fear wrapped more tightly around her. She took another, slow breath. After about a minute of being a spaz, she became both angry at herself and exasperated with the ghost.

"Oh good lord! Do you go to a special drama school after you die? I mean, really. Could you possibly whine more? Oh whaaa, I'm a ghost. My life is so hard. This house is plenty big enough for both of us. It's not like I had plans to put down tacky avocado linoleum. What exactly is your problem?"

A hot breath puffed out over her neck. Her knees buckled, and she gripped the edge of the sink to keep from landing on the floor. She'd spent all her courage on sarcasm and now couldn't bring herself to look in the mirror again, afraid if she did she'd see the fuzzy outline of Beatrice reflected back to her.

"Scarlett, Rhett, come on," she said as she left the bathroom. Two furry little heads poked out of the towel rack.

Anna turned on every light on the way up the stairs. Now wasn't the time to prove she wasn't afraid of the dark. The score was: Beatrice: 1, Anna: 0. She was freaked, and she had no trouble admitting it.

The cats followed her to the bedroom weaving in and out of her legs the entire way, clearly as bent on her destruction as Beatrice. As soon as she was settled under the covers, Scarlett shoved her head up underneath Anna's chin while Rhett curled around the back of the pillow, his paws resting on her head. Normally, Anna would toss them off the bed, but tonight she didn't want to sleep alone.

She spent an hour staring at the back of her eyelids, occasionally opening her eyes to see the green LED numbers mocking her as the time dragged on. Once when Anna looked, the clock had miraculously sped up ten minutes. She must have drifted off.

Now she was awake again. Soft, female cries drifted up the staircase. Then the moaning started. What the hell did Beatrice have to moan about? And could she come up with a bigger cliché? Would chain rattling be next? She closed her eyes, trying to shut out the muffled groans and fell into a fitful sleep.

. . . A MASCULINE CHUCKLE PIERCED THE SILENCE. DARKNESS crowded around her. Had the power gone out? The mystery of the lighting situation left her as strong hands skimmed down her body and a honeyed voice whispered in her ear. "Just let it happen, Anna. You know you want it."

Her breath hitched in her throat. She should be screaming right now. She wanted to, but everything felt too wispy, like a dream. It couldn't be real. If it wasn't real, it was okay. Wasn't it?

The hands on her skin felt right, soothing. It had been so long since she'd felt this with anyone. She pressed herself against him, soaking in the comforting feeling of strong, steady hands on her.

Her own voice, sounding nothing at all like it belonged to her, whimpered out, "Yes." His wicked hands set to work, kneading her breasts with expert finesse, wrenching a strangled little whimper from her. Then his hand slid downward to grind between her thighs.

She stared out into the blackness, hoping for a form to take shape. Nothing greeted her vision but a bottomless void. Her hips responded, bucking against his hand as a tongue flicked up the side of her neck. Then he started to nibble, his hot, wet mouth sending her into a tailspin of erotic need . . .

ANNA BOLTED UP IN BED. *IT WAS JUST A DREAM.*

Why did she have to wake up right before something interesting happened? *Easy to think that now that I'm awake.*

She leaned against the pillows, allowing her hand to trail down the path his had traveled only moments before. The need for release was suddenly overwhelming. Her mind pushed replay: his hands on her, his voice in her ear. She arched off the bed as she made herself come for the first time in as long as she could remember.

Anna lay perfectly still, panting, listening to the silence of the house. When her heart rate finally calmed, she could feel it. She didn't know why she hadn't felt it before.

Someone was watching. Maybe she should have puzzled that one out before she'd engaged in masturbation theater.

Her voice cracked a little when she said, "Ghostly voyeurism is *not* cool. I have the spice channel. Go watch that." Anna watched in horror as the door opened, and she sensed the presence slip from the room. Whatever was haunting the house could have simply gone through the wall. But where was the fun in that?

3

---

*T*he Peach Festival took up a single block of downtown Golatha Falls with brightly-striped and colorful tents circling the three-story brick courthouse. A stage was set up in front for the day's entertainment, and there were barrels full of peaches from Mayor Walsh's orchard beside every booth. The peaches were free. It was an election year.

Anna stood next to the stage smoothing down her pale yellow sun dress for the tenth time, as her eyes drifted back to the clock in the courthouse tower. Marshal was late. Charles and Cecelia Townsend had already been by to invite her to Thursday night dinner, followed by Tam who'd steadfastly refused to wait with her, saying three was a crowd.

As if it was a real date. It wasn't a real date.

When Anna woke that morning, there had been a dearth of scary. No writing on mirrors, no breaking glass or scraping chairs or moans and groans. No Chinese takeout being creatively rearranged. Things had been so quiet that part of her wanted to dismiss it all as products of an overactive imagination. But then she'd felt the cool breeze blowing through the broken window in the kitchen.

Maybe Beatrice was taking a nap.

All that haunting and voyeurism must have taken a lot out of her. Maybe ghosts needed to sleep during the day to recharge their batteries. Anna had turned the coffee pot on, allowing the rich smell and drip, drip, gurgle to comfort her. While it was dripping, she'd gone to wipe the bathroom mirror, only to find it already clean. Beatrice was definitely an odd little duck. The whole Mommy vibe didn't seem to go with watching people masturbate.

When Anna left for the festival, Stan the window man had been crouched in the doorway, measuring for the glass and promising it would be finished by the time she got home. *Better than new, no extra charge.* She'd averted her eyes from his backside. The famous plumber crack had unfortunately spread from plumbers to all handymen everywhere. Window men not excluded.

She was jolted from her thoughts as the Baker sisters approached.

"Anna, darling, you look wonderful. Marshal called. He's on his way," Mimi said, winking at her.

"Twirl for us, dear," Bitsy said.

"Huh?"

"You know, twirl." She revolved one wrinkled, yet well-manicured finger. "We want to see the dress."

Anna felt ridiculous, but she obliged them and spun around once. A breeze flew by and picked up the dress, causing her to have to smooth it down for the eleventh time, a la Marilyn Monroe.

"We'll get you married off yet," Bitsy whispered.

She hoped the old woman was referencing the dress itself and not the near-pornographic display the weather had just caused. Anna had become their pet project. Didn't they have Bingo night in Golatha Falls?

"Speak of the devil . . . " Bitsy said.

Anna looked around quickly, thinking perhaps the dark lord

himself had shown up to congratulate the old ladies on a job well done. It was only Marshal.

Her date held a bouquet of wildflowers. At least it wasn't roses. Roses spoke of seriousness and undying affection. Wildflowers said, *I like you. Do you like me? Check yes or no.* Not wanting to be unkind, Anna decided to create a *maybe* box. After all, Marshal cleaned up better than she'd expected.

He took her hand and led her from the gawking sisters into the throng of townspeople. "I'm really glad you decided to meet me here," Marshal said. He wore the shy persona so well Anna wondered if he truly believed in it.

Twenty minutes later he still hadn't let go of her hand. She started to wrench it away, but he held on, not taking the hint. She finally relented in the silent battle. Something low in her gut twinged in warning, but she quickly dismissed it.

The festival was everything a small southern festival should be. Ponies, cotton candy, peach cobbler, arts and crafts. A tall clown teetered on stilts, with a handful of balloons. Anna did a double take.

He was supposed to be giving the balloons out to the kids, but this year the festival was headed up by Mary Walsh, the mayor's daughter. And she hadn't thought about the logistics of stilts and handing balloons to small children.

A couple of hours in date claustrophobia had passed when Marshal squealed. "Oh look! The cloggers!" It was severely disturbing to hear that sound coming out of a grown man. "I love these guys. You know they've won awards, right?"

"Is that so?" There was no way she would carry on a relationship with a man who actually liked to watch grown women clog dance.

He started to clap his hands like a big goon, then a little toe-tapping action got into the mix. She was ready to slink away. "Hey Marsh!" she shouted over the din of bluegrass music.

"Yeah, babe?"

She cringed at the endearment, but he seemed too oblivious to notice.

"I saw Tam over there, and I need to talk to her for a minute about the business we're starting." Anna was still talking in that over-loud bar voice she'd picked up in Atlanta.

Marshal stopped clapping, his attention drawn away from the clogging as his brow wrinkled in confusion. "But you've got plenty of money. Why should you work?"

Anna gritted her teeth. Her voice took on a harsher clip. "Marsh, not to be rude, but it's really none of your business what I choose to do with my time."

He shook his head indulgently before waving her off. She practically ran to the other side of the courthouse to find Tam sitting on a hay bale next to the door prize table.

"Soooo, how's it going?" The lilt in Tam's voice expressed that she expected there to be hot and heavy kissing and groping the moment the sun went down.

"Oh God, save me, please save me."

"You're too picky. He's a nice guy. And he's trying."

"He's overbearing and pushy and annoying. And he likes clog dancers."

Tam's eyes widened. "Not clog dancers! I believe the sheriff's around somewhere. Would you like to file a report? I bet he'd love to investigate that over the toilet-papering scandal."

"I'm serious. I don't like him. I just want to go home and forget I ever had taste that bad."

Tam snorted. "The festival's over in half an hour. Let the poor man walk you to your door. Then let him down easy."

"I need bitchier friends who will support me in my villainy. Come get peach cobbler with me."

Tam stood, brushing stray bits of hay from her jeans. "You haven't gotten cobbler yet? It was the whole reason you were putting up with today."

"I know, but Marshal decided you eat cotton candy at fairs, not cobbler, and two desserts will spoil my dinner. If he thinks he's taking me to dinner ... That's two lame dates in the span of twenty-four hours, and I'm not going through with it."

Tam held up her hands in surrender and followed Anna to the dessert table.

The peach cobbler was everything Anna knew it would be, warm, gooey, and rich. Homemade vanilla ice cream melted on top of it as she tried to eat fast enough to keep alive the lovely contrast between hot and cold on her tongue. She'd almost finished her second plate when Marshal sidled up.

"You'll spoil your dinner. I was going to take you to the bistro downtown. Golatha Falls has really grown up since you've been gone."

Anna bit back the overwhelming urge to snark and smiled up at him. "I'm really sorry, Marsh, but I can't possibly go to dinner. I've got people to call, and I need to get some stuff done for Tam."

His face fell, and *shy guy* was replaced with *pathetic puppy dog face*. "Oh." Marshal wasn't to be thwarted for long. His eyes lit up. It was clear he had something brilliant to say. "Well, I'm sure Tam will let you slack off for one night."

Or maybe not.

Tam took the cue and rescued her. "No, she won't." She cast a sympathetic glance at Anna, which was returned with an *I told you so* look.

"Well, at least let me walk you home." He'd quickly run out of his list of sly overtures and was grasping for anything to prolong the experience.

Anna sighed. The sooner they started walking, the sooner this day would be over. It was only a few blocks, then she'd be safe and sound in her evil haunted house with her voyeuristic ghost. Yay, good times.

When they arrived at her house half an hour later, Anna walked around to the back, Marshal trailing behind her.

"I'm really okay back here, Marsh. I'm just checking to see that the door got fixed."

"It's dark out. I can't just leave you alone." So gallant. So brave. "Why couldn't you just wait til you got inside to check it?" So whiny.

"I don't know, Marsh. Idle curiosity. I'm a wacky kind of girl like that." When Anna was satisfied with the door, she went back around to the front.

"Why couldn't we just go in that door?" he asked, pointing toward the kitchen entrance.

Anna didn't like him tacking *we* onto that sentence and sincerely hoped he didn't think he was coming inside. She turned to face him, reigning in her annoyance.

"Because, I have to disarm the security system from the front, not the back. I needed to walk around the back so that I could look at the outside part of the door."

She didn't feel she owed him that in-depth of an explanation, but if she didn't give it to him, he'd be asking her *why this* and *why that* for the five minutes it took to get him off her property.

"I had a really nice time," she lied when she was finally standing in her open doorway. She was on the home stretch now.

He leaned in. Anna leaned back. A grotesque dance of unrequited love.

"What? Don't I get a little goodnight kiss?"

"I don't kiss on the first date. It keeps the pressure off." That wasn't strictly true, but what Marsh didn't know wouldn't hurt him.

"We've known each other for years. You can't make an exception?" He was easing in again, going for his second attempt.

"No, not really." Anna was becoming irritated. He'd gone from annoying bad date to general all around clueless ass.

Marshal tried to look past her into the house. "All right. Can I have the ten-cent tour at least? I've always wanted to see the inside of this place."

"I'm sorry, but the ten cent tour only covers the outside of the house." When he smiled that goofy shaggy dog grin like he thought he was flirting, she decided to play it straight. "I've really got stuff to do."

She was caught off guard when he pushed his way past her, causing the wildflowers she'd carried all day to scatter in all directions. The warning bells that had been gently tingling all afternoon, started to sound more like a loud cymbal.

The door clicked ominously behind him, causing Anna's anxiety to climb higher. *You're being silly. This isn't a Lifetime movie. He doesn't realize he's coming off this way.* Despite her inner monologue, her hand itched for something heavy to beat him unconscious. Forcing his way into her home was crossing the line. Actually it crossed federal lines, being a felony and all.

"Marshal, I would like you to leave now. You're pissing me off."

He smiled. His voice came out a smooth purr as if he were seducing her instead of planning an attack. "No, I'm scaring you. You know, you always were such a tease, Anna. I would have asked you out when we were kids, but I thought surely Quinton Worthington's daughter wouldn't give me the time of day. It wasn't until much later I heard you had a crush on me."

"Get out." The words were said between clenched teeth. She'd started to back away from him.

The smile didn't leave his face; he only moved closer. *Shy guy* had left the building. "It's pretty ironic. I'll bet there were nights we both touched ourselves thinking of the other, and yet we never got together. Let's find out if our reality lives up to our fantasies."

Anna reached for a lead candlestick off the mantel, only to have it batted away as Marshal pressed her against the wall. He trailed a finger down her cheek, then dipped to capture her mouth in a kiss.

"All you had to do was give me one little kiss. You didn't have to be so uptight."

Anna leaned forward as if to kiss him back. Instead, she bit his lip and kneed him in the groin. His eyes widened as he reflexively doubled over, cupping the family jewels too late.

"Ow, you stupid bitch!" His tongue crept out to lick away the thin trickle of blood. His eyes filled with renewed purpose as his face rose to meet hers.

She knew she should have run for the door, but panic can make you retarded. Now she was the *dumb horror movie chick* running up the staircase. If she got out of this alive she'd never mock *dumb horror movie chick* again.

She'd made it to the landing when Marshal's hand wrapped around her ankle. She let out a hiss of pain as she hit the stairs. He flipped her onto her back and started dragging her roughly down. She struggled and kicked at him, the adrenaline surging through her system.

A terrifying growl reverberated through the house, and it sure as hell hadn't come from Marshal.

Her date was flung across the front entry hall, smashing into the wall and breaking a picture frame. She watched in fascinated horror as Marshal slid up the side of the wall, choking as an unseen hand gripped his throat.

The growls continued; the only audible speech was Marshal begging for his life. Clothing ripped at the seams as if by magic, and he started bleeding. Then he fell with a thud as if whatever had been holding him just stepped back and let go.

Marshal half-crawled, half-dragged himself to the front door, letting out a pathetic whimper as his hands and knees crunched over broken glass in his desperation to get away.

Anna snapped out of her daze as she tried to grasp what she'd just witnessed. She was still shaking as she descended the steps, too emotionally numb to fully feel the pain of her injuries. But she knew it would hurt like a bitch later.

She paused, staring at her potential date rapist as he crawled over the threshold to safety. She didn't want to have to run past him, but he was in no condition to hurt her now, and she needed to get outside. She picked up the candlestick, her hand far from steady. The thing in her house suddenly posed a bigger threat than the bloodied pulp on her porch.

Before she could reach the door, it slammed shut, the deadbolt clicking into place of its own accord. Anna tried to turn it back, but it wouldn't budge. She raced for the kitchen to find the back door had been locked down as well. She slammed the candlestick against the window pane, quickly losing the rest of her grip on calm.

"Fuck!" she shouted as she attacked the glass. Stan had spared no expense with the window strength. *Better than new* wasn't just idle talk. She grabbed the phone off the wall. The silence on the other end didn't surprise her, but she was grasping at any hope of escape.

"No!" She looked frantically around the kitchen, backing up until she was in a corner. She held the candlestick out in front of her, as if it could protect her against the invisible foe that had just shredded Marshal like paper.

"Please, let me out," she whimpered, hating the desperate begging coming out of her mouth. "I'll go. I'll leave like you asked. I'll never come back. Please."

A kitchen chair scraped against the tile. She was beginning to hate that sound. Anna could feel the pain tighten her chest as she gasped for breath, tears streaming down her cheeks. She slid to the floor, her legs unwilling to support her anymore. And then she fainted. Exactly like *dumb horror movie chick.*

4

*A*nna woke disoriented. She was tucked into her bed in that strange, mummified way mothers do with children. Beatrice clearly had some issues. Anna wriggled her arms out from underneath the covers. The room was dark except for the numbers on the alarm clock that read 2:15, and a tiny wisp of light filtering under the crack of the bathroom door.

She lifted the blankets and ran her hands over the smooth material against her skin. It was the satin chemise she'd worn under her sun dress. The dress had been too sheer by itself. Anna noted her bra was absent and decided she wasn't going to think about that for the moment.

Her back hurt like hell, triggering memories from before she'd passed out. She could feel bandages covering the small wounds and didn't know what to make of it.

As she lowered the bedspread, the bathroom light went out, casting the room in the eerie glow reserved for scary movies and bad dreams. Her throat began to constrict as she scooted against the headboard. Before she could gather the courage to speak, the floor lamp across the room snapped on.

Instead of Beatrice, it was about the best looking man Anna had ever laid eyes on—airbrushed magazine spreads notwithstanding. Dark hair fell around his face, framing an olive complexion and cold, bright green eyes that appeared to burn with a light of their own.

They seemed to pull her in, hypnotize her. They were eyes that had known violence. Whether as the victim or the perpetrator, it was too hard to tell, but she suspected the latter.

His lips were as full as any man's had a right to be, and Anna had to stop herself from imagining nibbling on his lower lip. He had the kind of cheekbones sculptors spent a lifetime learning to chisel into stone. Rather than sitting in the chair, he seemed to drape. Casually. Sinfully.

Shirtlessly.

She closed her eyes and raised a hand to her head, feeling for bumps. After what she'd just experienced the last thing that seemed normal was lusting after a hot stranger in her bedroom. Maybe she was dreaming again.

The next words to fly from her mouth were so stupid she would later blame a mild concussion. "You should know this house is haunted, and the last guy who tried anything got beaten bloody for his trouble. So you should ask yourself if it's worth losing your good looks over."

His deep, familiar chuckle slid into her, too fluid to be human. Anna vaulted out of the bed, taking the sheets with her, wrapping them around her frame as she went.

"I've seen it all," he said waving a hand away as if he could never be moved by such banal things as nudity.

Not while I was conscious, Anna thought. She backed farther away as he stood and advanced on her. "Um . . . so Beatrice isn't here?" Diversionary tactics weren't her strong suit.

There never was a Beatrice. It was him. Her throat tightened again as that thought slammed fully into her brain. She tried to shut out the memories of all the times she'd been a little too naked in the house, either ignoring the ghost or thinking it was a woman.

A slow smile spread over his face. "I'm the thing that killed her." Fear pulsed through her at his words, and he seemed to savor it like wine. "Beatrice went to Heaven where all good girls with intact souls go when they die. Tell me, my dear, do you think *your* soul will be intact when I'm finished with you?"

Anna wasn't sure what was required to keep her soul intact, and was even less sure she could manage to follow whatever the rule was. Especially since she found herself simultaneously repelled and attracted to him.

Again, the thought that she shouldn't be feeling anything toward this person, or any person right now, danced across her mind, but then evaporated into nothing.

"W-what are you?" She maneuvered around the edge of the room, moving toward the seat he'd just vacated.

"Haven't you guessed yet? A dirty old demon that slips into your dreams and watches you touch yourself?" When no recognition lit her face, he sighed, exasperated. "I'm an incubus."

He seemed very put out about it. "You women know all about werewolves and vampires, but the concept of an incubus escapes you. I don't know why I bother sometimes."

Anna reached the chair. His self-pity over not being listed on the *top ten list of most seductive villains ever* was enough distraction for her to grab the floor lamp. She swung it out in a wide arc.

The lamp felt awkward in her hand, but wasn't too heavy. Yet it went through him as if he wasn't there and crashed to the floor, causing Anna to lose her balance.

The room was once again cloaked in darkness as his hand shot out and stopped her fall. She pulled away when she was steady, grabbing at the sheet that had slipped partially off her body. Her eyes darted around the dark trying to readjust and determine where the threat had moved to.

She worked to make her breathing and her heartbeat quieter, as if the demon wouldn't hear them anyway. As if he couldn't see her somehow in the darkness trying to keep from pulling another fainting act.

Demon. The idea was so ridiculous, and yet . . .

The lamp had gone through him. She'd seen it. How could he touch her if she couldn't touch him? Was she dreaming again? *God, I hope so. Please, let this be a dream.*

The silhouette of the demon moved swiftly in front of her, and she found herself backed against the wall. Anna struggled, her arms flailing out to protect herself.

"Feisty," he growled, pinning both of her small wrists against the wall with one hand. The demon's lips grazed her ear, and his hot breath sent a wave of unexpected pleasure through her stomach. "I like feisty in a girl."

His free hand roamed over her side, causing the satin material to slide up against her flesh. She remembered those hands, only now it wasn't a dream. God help her. She couldn't stop the little mewl from leaving her mouth. Then her struggling resumed. She couldn't let him do this.

"You'd save me from Marshal just so you can finish what he started?" Her voice came out flat, as if the odds against her had stolen all her energy.

He'd protected her, carried her to bed, tended to her wounds, watched over her. Now she was to be his victim, instead? She ignored the voice in her head that said being this man's *victim* didn't sound like a bad deal.

He growled softly, then pushed himself away from the wall. The door opened and light from the hallway spilled in. His back was to her, every muscle held in tension when he spoke.

"Put on some clothes, and meet me in the living room in five minutes." *Or else* was left unspoken. "We have to talk."

Anna didn't ask why they couldn't talk here. She preferred getting the sex demon away from her bed. Thank you very much.

When he'd gone, she gingerly stepped around the broken glass and reached for the light switch. Her hands wouldn't stop shaking as she fumbled through the dresser drawer. Caroline's tight-lipped response about what had been going on made sense now.

The house shook as the demon in her living room expressed his displeasure at being kept waiting.

"I'm coming!" She pulled a Ramones T-shirt over her head. *What am I doing?*

When she got downstairs, the demon was on her sofa doing the draping thing again as if he hadn't just rattled the house like an impatient ass. He stroked Scarlett's back while she arched and purred more obscenely than if she'd been in heat. Rhett was crouched on the floor by his feet, hissing and scowling up at the interloper.

"Ah, there you are," he said. "Have a seat."

His lord of the manor attitude grated, causing her to forget for a moment that he was the big scary that had at least one, and possibly several murders under his belt.

"Fuck you," she said. But she sank into the chair he indicated.

"That offer was on the table when you had a histrionic fit a few moments ago," he replied, still petting the animal on his lap. Scarlett looked up at her and offered a soft, reproachful, "mrarrr", informing Anna she was quite stupid.

"Oh really? Cause the way I remember it, you confessed to murder, and then were moving in to attack me."

"I didn't attack you. I was going to seduce you."

"You're out of practice, asshole. Seduction attempts work best when you don't mention one of the women you murdered, just an

FYI for future reference." She crossed her arms over her chest, her stare glacial. If she could just stay angry she could keep the panic from consuming the last of her sanity.

She watched as Scarlett wantonly rubbed her little cat body against his sculpted chest, and for one crazy second, she imagined it was her.

"I do apologize. I'm hungry and moody. I shouldn't have taken it out on you."

Anna goggled at him. Did he really believe apologizing made it all better? What century was this relic from?

"I offered you a chance to leave," he said reasonably.

Of course, he'd believe he was being magnanimous. She was sure he felt that by staying in the house she'd given him express permission to do whatever he wanted with her. She shivered at the thought of what that could mean, as well as her shrinking revulsion over the idea.

She wiped those thoughts away. "No. Writing on my bathroom mirror with your finger like somebody just out of haunting school is not offering me the chance to leave. You could have just talked to me."

"I'm talking to you now."

"Fine. We've talked." She crossed the room and picked a protesting Scarlett up off his lap, unable to watch the disturbing display any longer, then moved to the chair farthest from him.

"I'm Luc," he said.

"That's nice. I'm Anna. Get the fuck out of my house."

He observed her quietly for a few moments, his eyes twinkling with amusement. "You have quite a dirty little mouth, which I'm sure we can put to better use later."

Anna flushed as Scarlett clawed down the sides of her arms, making blood well up. She shoved the cat onto the floor, and Scarlett scrambled back over to Luc, primly resettling herself on his lap. She meowed up at him, giving permission for him to continue his ministrations. He laughed but went back to petting her.

"Traitor," Anna said. She turned her attention back to the demon on her couch. "First of all, unless you intend to force me, my dirty little mouth isn't going to be put to any better use you could think of. And secondly, you can and you will leave. Or I'll make you leave." She was feeling doubtful about her abilities in that department, but once her mouth started running she had a hard time stopping it sometimes. This time it might get her killed.

His eyes hardened as they met hers, and he smiled, seemingly satisfied when she shrank under the power of his stare. "I won't force you. I can't feed unless you are more-or-less willing. But I'm not worried. You'll eventually succumb to my charms like everyone else."

Anna snorted, unable to believe this fossil.

Luc glared. "I hope you are successful. I would love to leave this house."

His pronouncement shook her out of her conflicted emotions. "You can't leave?" She hadn't considered he might not want to be here.

He drew a hand to his chest in mock shock, the portrait of a true southern belle, had he been female and in a big froufy dress. "You've decided to graciously give me the floor so I can explain my predicament?"

"Yes, speak! Get it out so I can go back to sleep."

"Very well. I've been trapped in this house for over fifty years. I was old enough to know better, but I fell for a woman I was feeding from. Beatrice, as you may have guessed." He spoke the name as if the word tasted rancid in his mouth. "She was upset I was feeding from others, because to you humans, that's cheating. I offered a way for us to be together forever where I would feed only from her, but she wouldn't have it."

Anna raised an eyebrow. "What was the way?"

Luc suddenly became interested in the upholstery. His response came out muffled. "She had to give me her immortal soul."

"Oh, well I can't imagine why she'd turn you down." She got up to go to the kitchen. She'd had about all of the happy demon nostalgia she could take just then.

"Where do you think you're going? I'm not finished." Luc pushed the cat off his lap and stalked behind her.

"This sounds like a potentially long and boring story, so I'm making coffee." She rifled through the cupboard. "And I've got some biscotti around here somewhere," she said, more to herself than to him.

"I'd like a cup. With cream if you don't mind."

"You're a demon. You don't need food. I thought you ate sex."

"I do not *eat* sex. I feed from sexual energy. But I find eating and drinking pleasurable. Strictly speaking, you don't need sex for your individual survival, and yet you do it because it feels good."

"Whatever." She'd do anything to get him to stop referencing her and sex in the same sentence. It made her mind go places it shouldn't, especially considering he was a killer.

"At any rate, when Beatrice would not take my offer, and I couldn't remain faithful only to her, she cursed me."

"She what?"

"Oh, yes. She was a witch. An evil, dirty little witch, and she cursed me. And now she's frolicking around in Heaven because, as it turns out, you can curse a demon and never hurt your shiny little soul."

"I sense bitterness," Anna said.

"I could kill you right now."

"Charming. I can't begin to imagine why someone would curse you." She turned away to continue the biscotti search, unwilling for him to see her fear.

He growled. "I was simply expressing that I don't need you. You seem confident I won't kill you now that I've told you I can't fuck you unless you want me. Your safety is not as guaranteed as you'd like to think."

Anna looked up from the cabinets. "If I die, won't you starve?"

"Let me finish!" His eyes glowed for a brief moment, and she thought she might have pushed him too far. "She trapped me so I couldn't cheat on her."

"And you killed her." Some poor woman didn't want him to cheat, and he reacted by killing her? She was on Beatrice's side.

"I couldn't help it. She'd cut off all other feeding options. I didn't mean to kill her. I just couldn't stop. I was hungry."

"So, if we had . . . " Anna waved her hands frantically, unable to verbalize what could have happened between them upstairs. " . . . you would have killed me?"

"No. It's not like that now. My clan brother managed to find me after a few weeks. I was driven almost mad by the hunger. I was so weak I couldn't shift from my physical form by that time. He brought me women."

"And you killed them."

"The first two, yes. I was starving. They were food. Stop trying to make me feel bad about this."

Anna had managed to find the biscotti at the back of the cupboard. "Oh don't give me that crap. You're a demon. You don't feel bad about it."

The fear ebbed more the longer they talked. What had happened between him and Beatrice had been personal. As long as she didn't sleep with him, she'd be fine. Theoretically. Her eyes drifted to the finely-chiseled lines of his chest. She tamped down the flutter in her stomach. *Yeah, sure. No problem.*

Luc flopped into the nearest kitchen chair. "Normally I would say you're right. But she did something to me. I don't want to kill anymore." He put his head in his hands. "I'm pathetic."

"No argument here." She poured the coffee into two mugs and placed a jug of milk beside Luc's.

He scowled up at her, but continued. "My brother delivers my dinner at night. He just hasn't been by yet."

"Is he as charming as you?"

Luc's face darkened, and the lights flickered for a moment. His eyes grew colder than she'd seen them all evening, causing her to take a step back from him.

"When Cain gets here, you will be locked away in your safe little bed."

The back door flew open then. Apparently demons were not stopped in any way by locks or alarm systems or really strong glass.

"He's here," Cain said, stepping through the back door with a drunk, blonde co-ed. "This one is a very dirty girl, Lucien. You'll like her."

"Leave her and go."

"But how will she find her way back without an escort? It's dark out. Just anything could come by and grab her." Cain licked his lips as he let his eyes rove over the blonde.

She smacked him on the shoulder then leaned unsteadily against him, oblivious to the danger she was in. "Don't be silly, silly. I'm good. I have a cell phone." She waved a pink flip phone in his face.

Cain stepped to the side and watched as the girl slid to the floor, unable to support her weight without assistance. He turned to Anna and smiled.

"So, what do we have here, Luc? You didn't tell me you had a live-in meal again. How nice for you." His gaze swept lasciviously over her. "Is our boy Lucien not getting the job done? Because I could oblige you."

Anna blushed as she felt a warm wetness flood her panties. She wanted to fuck him. It didn't matter that Luc and some unknown blonde girl were there to witness the act. She wanted him to bend her over the kitchen table and screw her right there. Delightful pornographic images flashed in front of her face.

She whimpered and reached out to him. "Please . . . "

"Back OFF!" Luc growled, moving to stand between Anna and Cain.

"But she wants me. She's practically in pain from it." Cain extended a hand toward her, as she craned her head around the big obstruction that was Luc.

Her body reacted more strongly, and she started to cry. "Please . . . "

Cain shook his head, a mask of pity pulling his features. "Someone has to help her. The poor darling. I think I'm just the demon to do it."

"It's because you're cheating!"

Cain pierced Luc with a sharp glare. "Yes, and demons cheat. They don't try to honestly seduce like insipid humans. You forget what you are. Of course, you always were a little soft, even before the witch."

He stepped closer to Anna, his hand reaching out to caress her cheek. She sighed in relief as she pressed up against him, a soft moan leaving her throat. *Yes, more. Don't stop touching me, please.*

"You'll be delicious. All that emotion and passion."

Anna nodded her acquiescence, leaning harder into his touch. She felt bereft when his hand was pulled away and looked up, disappointed to see Luc had him pinned against the wall.

"I SAID leave her alone!" he roared.

Cain laughed. "So you want her for yourself, then? Fair enough. Just don't make the mistake of falling for your food again. We all know the path that leads down." Cain arched a brow, studying him for a moment, a light suddenly dawning. "You've been hiding her from me. She's been here a while."

"A couple of weeks."

A sinister smile lit the other demon's face. "So, either you've decided to try to convince her to help you break the curse, which I can tell you just from looking at her, won't happen. Or . . . you're already falling for her."

Luc remained silent.

"Fine then. You work it out yourselves. Just don't expect to see me again until you've sorted out your issues."

Cain dematerialized. Only his laughter remained, echoing off the walls of the kitchen. As soon as he was gone, the sexual possession left Anna, replaced by a feeling of revulsion. She couldn't shut off the vivid pictures that continued to spin through her head. She'd felt mindless. The only thing she'd been able to think was how desperately she wanted Cain's hands on her body and how she'd do anything to make it happen. Crawl, beg, plead, kill. Anything.

"Oh God," she said, sliding to the floor. She sat huddled, her hands wrapped tightly around her knees as the shame washed over her. How many hours had it been since she'd been eating peach cobbler and mocking clog dancers? That was her life. Not this.

She was barely conscious of Luc crouching next to her, taking her hand in his. Anna thought at first he was there to comfort her. She didn't have the presence of mind to push him away, though she resented him taking advantage of her moment of weakness.

She looked up in time to see the knife and jerked her hand back, her eyes filling with tears. "What are you doing?"

"I'm protecting you." Luc cut a thin line down the center of his palm. "Expecting Cain to honor verbal tradition is like expecting the sun to set backwards. He thinks because he's the boss, he's above the law." He took her hand gently, his thumb caressing her skin.

"I'll leave. I'll leave the house," Anna said, the panic seeping back into her voice. "Just don't do any creepy blood rituals."

"It's too late for that. Do you want him to get into your mind like that again? Do you want to feel what you just felt and have no control over it?"

She shook her head. The idea made it feel like something dirty and slimy was slithering underneath her skin. She thought she might throw up. "Why do you care? This is what you are, too."

Luc avoided her eyes and made a matching cut down the center of her palm. She hissed as he clasped her hand in his, mingling their blood.

"Are you stealing my soul?" She couldn't believe that was her voice, that dead, hollow sound. Ten minutes ago she'd been *feisty* as Luc put it. Well, if he liked that in a girl, at least she was off the menu now.

"Of course not. I can't steal souls. That's one thing we can't coerce. This will bind you to me temporarily. Cain can't feed from you or control your mind, and neither can any of his minions."

Luc stood, his wound already closing and forming a scar as he crossed the kitchen and took a hand towel from the drawer. He ran it under cool water and returned to wrap it around the injury he'd inflicted.

"Anna?"

"Yes?" She cradled her bandaged hand.

"I have to feed."

She tensed and cringed away. "No."

Why was she saying no? It wasn't like he couldn't just do what Cain had done. He could make her want him. Somehow she knew if he got hungry and desperate enough, he might. Had this happened to Sara Johnson? Was that why she was rotting away in a padded cell right now?

Why didn't I leave when I had the chance? She'd been so cavalier about the whole thing. Scarlett and Rhett slipped into the room then, wrapping their small, warm bodies around her, offering silent support.

"It's not a yes or no proposition. I must feed."

"You guys are majorly weird. I'm just gonna go back to my dorm now."

Anna looked up to see the blonde wavering on wobbly legs as

she tried to get herself re-oriented to her surroundings. Anna and Luc exchanged a look. They'd forgotten about her.

"No," Anna said, "I can't let you do that. She's drunk and . . . "

"I won't harm her or do anything she doesn't want to do. Of her own free will."

Anna shook her head.

"And how exactly will you stop me? Do you really want to stand between a trapped demon and dinner? You can either stay or leave, but you have no power to prevent this. And further, I won't let you. If I don't feed, you won't be safe."

She wouldn't be able to listen to the moans again knowing what was causing them. She wondered how she could have ever thought it was a female ghost making those noises. Noises which now she couldn't mistake as anything but a woman crying out in the throes of passion. The French called the moment of orgasm, *la petite mort*, the little death. Anna wondered if there was a large incubus population in France.

Her eyes welled with unshed tears as she met his gaze. "Please don't hurt her."

"Never."

She couldn't stay there, couldn't listen to him fucking someone else in her house. She needed to get out, get some air. Be somewhere that wasn't here.

Anna was afraid Cain might still be lurking nearby, but she was going to trust in whatever Luc had just done because she had to escape the way her universe had shifted sideways to become a place where magic and demons lived.

Outside in the dark, the peach trees looked threatening, like they might break free of their roots and chase her down, dragging her kicking and screaming into some hell where Cain would have his way with her, and she'd writhe and moan in his arms while he did it.

The moon lit the sidewalk as she ran the ten blocks to Tam's house. She banged on the door, panting and trying to catch her breath.

"Anna, what on earth . . . it's 4 o'clock in the morn . . . " Tam took a closer look at her. "I'll make tea," she said, stepping out of the way so Anna could get inside.

She sat at a bar stool in Tam's tiny kitchen filled with herbs, sipping the soothing Earl Grey brew. She told Tam everything, starting with Marshal, all the way to Luc and the blonde co-ed. "He could kill her, and I just left her there. I'm going to Hell."

"Hon, you don't believe in Hell." Tam stroked her fingers through Anna's hair. Anna shot her a dirty look. "Sorry. Now probably isn't the time for jokes. But from what you just told me, I'm not sure I believe he'd kill her."

"Really?" She looked hopeful. "Still . . . I can't . . . What if she didn't want to sleep with him and he . . . What if . . . "

She'd never forgive herself if that girl got hurt. The blonde might have been a stupid, drunk little twit, but Anna was pretty sure that wasn't a reason to aid a demon.

"Listen," Tam said, "I know this probably isn't the part to focus on, but I'm sorry I encouraged you to go out with Marshal. I had no idea he'd ever . . . "

Anna placed her hand over Tam's and laughed. She wouldn't have believed it a few hours ago, but in the grand scheme of things, Marshal Crust was barely factoring into her night.

LUC STARED OUT THE FRONT WINDOW LONG PAST THE POINT HE COULD see Anna. He'd been tempted to stop her. But what would he do? Chain her up? She was already scared to death of him.

He needed her to break the curse on the house.

You sure that's why, buddy? his inner voice taunted.

No, it wasn't why. He'd spent the past two weeks working up the nerve to show himself and have a conversation with her. Somewhere during that time, an infatuation, perhaps even an obsession, had started to build.

It was the little things about her. The way she twirled her long, chocolate brown hair while she read. The way she talked to characters on the television saying things like 'Don't go in that room!' Her antics hiding from those crazy old biddies. The way she talked to her cats like they were people.

And of course there were those delicious, soft curves she revealed far too often because she thought she was alone. He'd finally entered her dreams, promising himself he'd just take a little. Just enough to satisfy his curiosity.

But it wasn't just all of that. Her loneliness called out to him. He watched her when she looked in the mirror, brushing her hair at night. His chest tightened at the sad, wistful look in her eyes. He knew that look. The feeling that the emptiness could eat you away. He'd experienced the same thing for so long he felt a kinship with her.

He should have just shown himself, talked to her. But every time he worked up to it, he lost the nerve and instead did some stupid, ghostly thing to see what she'd do with it. He might never have introduced himself at all if that dickhead hadn't forced his hand.

Luc had quietly seethed when he'd seen she'd brought a man home. He'd shut himself off in one of the upstairs bedrooms, pacing until he was sure he'd wear a hole in the carpet. He'd been angry over the fact that he was jealous of the man, that he hadn't been able to bring himself to talk to her in all the time he'd lurked in the house. And now someone else had beat him to it.

Her scream of pain and terror had been all it had taken to unleash the demon.

And then he'd had to show himself.

He turned back to the blonde, peering at him with fascination and undisguised lust from the kitchen, like she'd won the sex lottery. Well, that made it easy at least.

Cain really did know how to pick them. Luc wouldn't have to convince her sleeping with him was a good idea. He could tell from the look in her eyes that she was already halfway to mentally undressing them both. And mental undressing came about thirty seconds before the actual undressing. In his experience.

---

5

*A*nna traced a finger over the scar the next morning. Whatever Luc had done had caused her hand to warp-speed through the healing process, skipping the scabbing stage altogether to leave a long, reddish line. The remaining mark seemed ominous and permanent, as if it sealed some yet-to-be-revealed fate between her and the demon in her house.

Tam walked in then, her cropped hair already gelled into little spikes that only she could make look feminine. She poured a cup of coffee, ruined it with cream and sugar, and perched on a stool beside Anna.

"I just talked to Bitsy and Mimi. They were outside when I went to get the paper. Marshal's in the hospital, in ICU. They don't know how he made it there alive." Off Anna's expression she said, "News travels fast here. You've been away too long. Story is wild dogs attacked him."

Anna took a moment to process that, wondering if it was a random rumor or a lie Marshal had fed the orderlies in his last moments of consciousness. She glanced back at the scar. "Can you drive me home?"

Tam's eyes narrowed. "I'm not sure that's such a good idea."

Anna wasn't sure it was such a good idea either, but it was what she was doing, regardless. She was feeling much braver in daylight. "I'm getting him out of my house. I'm not giving up. He'll have to kill me first, and you don't think he will so . . . "

"Hey, I'm not a Magic Eight Ball."

"Just take me home."

Tam took one look at her and sighed.

When they pulled into Anna's driveway, her friend made one last attempt to dissuade her. "You don't have to prove anything. Just put the house up for sale."

Anna shook her head, determined. "This is *my* house. I'll get him out. And then I'll throw a party. Remember to be here tomorrow at ten. We have to work on more candles if we're gonna get something into Sally's by the end of the week."

"I'm coming in with you," Tam said.

"No, you aren't. This is my mess, and I'm cleaning it."

"But . . . "

"Just go. He's had two weeks. If he hasn't hurt me yet, he's probably not going to. Okay?"

Tam looked uncertain but finally backed out of the driveway. Anna turned toward the house. She'd be damned if some freaky sex demon was going to screw up her Barbie Dream House.

The dream house loomed over her, dark and foreboding even in the morning sunlight. She took a deep breath and marched purposefully through the yard and up the front steps. The door banged against the interior wall as she shoved it open.

"Honey, I'm home!" Anna sang out, not expecting a response.

"In here, Sweet Pea," a deep voice called back from the kitchen.

She gritted her teeth and followed the sound of his voice. The scene that greeted her arrival was unexpected to say the least. Luc, wearing nothing but a pair of faded blue jeans, was padding around the kitchen. Cooking.

"Have you had breakfast?" he asked, flipping an omelet like a pro. Anna was beginning to understand his whole cooking channel fixation. He seemed to fancy himself the *Emeril* of the demon world.

She crossed her arms over her chest and was about to respond when Malibu Barbie decided to make her presence known.

"I thought you broke up with her!" the blonde accused in a pouty whine that made Anna's head hurt. The tart was fully alive and way too perky to have just spent the night having wild monkey sex with darkness personified.

"You didn't kill her," Anna said, unsure why that irritated her. Some of his evil must have seeped into her through the blood exchange.

"I didn't think you would like it." He turned to the blonde. "Be sure to drink your orange juice, Rachel. You need to keep your energy up."

Rachel kissed him on the cheek and went to the table with her plate.

"What? You're planning on going at it again after she eats?" Anna whispered.

"Of course not. Even if I wanted to, I couldn't. Not for a couple of days. I might drain too much. I don't do that anymore, remember?"

Anna latched onto the *even if I wanted to* part, not sure why she cared one way or the other. "So, you don't want to . . . um sleep with her again?" *Could I sound more like a desperate twit? It must be some kind of demon mojo.*

He raised an eyebrow and grinned. "God, no. She's a simpering moron. They must just be letting anyone into university now. I'm sorely disappointed in this thing you call higher learning."

Anna turned away to hide a smile. Luc handed her a plate of food along with a small glass of juice. "You should drink your orange juice, too," he said.

Was that innuendo? Her eyes slid over his stomach, her gaze lingering at his waistband until he cleared his throat. She snapped out of it and went to the table, trying not to think about how awkward it was sitting across from Rachel. Not that it should be awkward.

"So, if you guys are broken up, what are you doing here?" Rachel had decided not to bother with pleasantries like 'good morning, did you sleep well?'

Anna speared the other girl with a glare. "Well, see, this is *my* house. Luc just doesn't know when he's overstayed his welcome."

Rachel's eyes went to the demon. "I thought you said the house belonged to you." She seemed annoyed she wasn't getting a nice big house with her newly-acquired sex god.

Luc smiled at Anna. "I've been here a bit longer than you, dear. And possession is nine tenths."

"You'd know all about possession, wouldn't you?" Anna shot back. She tried not to be affected by his warm smile. "What? Why are you looking at me like that?"

"Nothing," he said. "You really are remarkable. I've never met a woman faced with what you were faced with last night who could be so together the next day." He seemed embarrassed suddenly and turned away to load the dishwasher.

"Excuse me!" Rachel said. "It looks to me like you two are still very much together. I don't have to take this." She pushed herself up from the table and flounced toward the door.

Luc grabbed her faster than Anna could track. He placed one hand on either side of her face and stared deeply into her eyes. Anna thought for one sick moment he was going to kiss the blonde, who, judging from her look of breathless abandon, thought the same thing.

"Sleep," he said.

"But I'm not sleepy . . . " Rachel slumped unconscious to the floor.

He turned to Anna. "You've got thirty minutes before she wakes. I suggest you get her into the car and far away from here before then. She'll be disoriented and have the barest recollection of me. Anything she remembers, she'll believe to be a dream."

"What? Are you kidding me? Clean up your own mess. I'm not your minion or your pimp." She almost backtracked and apologized when she saw the hurt look on his face.

"Fine. Leave her. We'll have a house guest. I can start building a harem. Rachel can be my number-one harem girl."

Anna glared at his retreating back and pulled the blonde up by her arms. Jesus. People weren't kidding when they talked about dead weight.

She flung Rachel into the car, slammed the passenger door, and went to retrieve her keys. Half an hour later found her driving aimlessly on the outskirts of town.

Rachel stirred beside her. "It must have been some party, huh? I'm sorry, you look familiar, but I can't place you."

"Anna."

"Right. Anna. So, um, thanks for driving me home. Where did we end up, anyhow?"

"Some cabin out by the lake," Anna lied.

Rachel scrunched her nose. "I don't remember." The visor of the passenger side flipped down to reveal a small mirror. She pulled a tube of lip gloss from her pocket and swiped the wand over her lower lip.

"Yes, well, you were drunk," Anna said, not hiding her disgust.

"Did I do something to piss you off?"

"No, I'm sorry." She didn't know why she was being so hostile. If anything, Rachel had been a victim. One Anna had aided the demon in attaining, she reminded herself. She had no right to be so mean.

Rachel rolled down the window and looked out at the passing blur of trees. She seemed all right. There were no marks on her, and she was happily oblivious. She'd been fully in control of her senses during breakfast and had seemed possessive of the man she'd spent

the night with. Then again, what sane woman wouldn't be possessive of a man that looked like Luc?

Demon. Not man. Remember that if you want to continue breathing.

Anna pulled the car into the parking lot of the college adminis-
tration building. Rachel looked like she might complain about not
being delivered to her dorm, but thought better of it. She got out a
little awkwardly and bumped the door with her hip before leaning
back down to look in the window.

"Um, thanks for the ride, I guess."

"Don't mention it." She pressed the power lock button.

"Hey. How come I'm not hungover?"

Anna peeled out of the lot.

Luc had cleaned the kitchen counter three times. He should
have washed the dishes by hand to give himself something to do,
but they were all happily whirring away in the dishwasher.

He finally dropped the washcloth into the sink and went to flop
in front of the television. He'd worried Anna wouldn't come back or
that she'd run into Cain and the ritual wouldn't be strong enough.

Cain was the head incubus, after all. Maybe it was hubris to
think blood magic would work against him.

Luc's relief at seeing her in the kitchen that morning, alive and
well and in one piece, had made him want to enthrall her. Just a
little. Just enough to break down the wall she seemed to have put up
to keep him out.

He could see it behind her eyes, the need and attraction. But she
was wound so tightly. He knew he was just the demon to
unwind her.

Why am I so obsessed with this woman? What's so special about her?
There seemed to be no rhyme or reason to why he was so drawn
and felt the need to protect her. He might have been imprisoned for

half a century, but he had a steady stream of beautiful women brought to him nightly. Cain had fantastic taste when it came to that.

And yet, with Rachel last night, it had been just that—feeding. The past two weeks it had always been Anna in his mind. He needed to screw her to get her out of his head. It was just a case of wanting what he couldn't have, right?

Luc tensed at the sound of the car door slamming, then muted the television and turned on the closed-captioning. He set his features into a look of nonchalance.

"How'd it go?" he asked when she breezed through the front door.

"What do you mean, how'd it go? I took your dinner back to her dorm." Anna tossed her keys into the candy dish on the end table. "We need to get something straight. I'm not your partner in crime. We are not the Bonnie and Clyde of the underworld, and this isn't going to be a regular zany caper because I'm getting you out of this house."

He took his eyes from the television to give her his full attention. It required all his willpower to focus on the issue at hand and not think about enthralling her to get her bent over the coffee table. "Yes . . . We need to discuss that. Last night I meant to tell you, but things got a little out of control."

"Tell me what?"

"We figured out how to get me out of the house a few weeks ago. But you won't like it."

6

*L*uc went back to flipping the channels on the television. He was seconds from ditching his self-control and just taking her right here. Cain was right, he was a demon. He should just fucking enthrall her. Since when did he have such tight morals?

He looked up to find Anna standing with her arms crossed over her chest, tapping her foot on the hardwood floor, still waiting for him to drop the bombshell. He sighed.

"Yes, well . . . you see, we knew we had to reverse Beatrice's spell to get me out of the house."

"We?"

"Cain has been helping."

"That's like saying the Lord of Darkness has been helping."

"He may be a demon, and we may not see eye to eye on everything, but he's the leader of my kind. On this he can be trusted. He's been searching for years for a seer who could tell us the exact wording of the spell so we could determine how to break it. The problem with seers is that few of them are as good as they think they are, and most of them see into the future rather than the past. The past is harder."

"Why?"

Luc got distracted for a moment by the adorable way her brow scrunched in confusion. He recovered quickly before he could make a fool of himself. "With the future you only have what will be, or what can be. With the past you have not only what was, but what other people remember of what was. Then you can add to that every time the story got told to someone new. Memories are always edited. Without realizing it or intending to, you often lie when you retell a story, whether to preserve someone's feelings, or to entertain them. It takes a very good past seer to be able to separate all the threads to see the true event.

"A few weeks before you purchased the house, Cain found someone. He checked her out, and we believe she is the genuine article." Luc hesitated, gathering steam. "She said I won't be free until the owner of the house burns it to the ground. It's something to do with the wording of the original curse."

"WHAT?"

"I need you to set the house on fire." Luc smiled at Anna in a way that was supposed to be disarming, but from the look on her face, probably wasn't quite coming off.

"Are you kidding me? Absolutely not. I love this house. Why couldn't you have bought it yourself and burned it down?"

"We researched that possibility first. The spell was too specific."

"Did you try just lighting a match and seeing what would happen?"

As if he wouldn't have thought of that. Did she find him mentally deficient? "Yes. I also used kerosene. The magic snuffed it out."

"This has got to be the stupidest thing I've ever heard. We'll find another way."

"But ... "

"There is no *but*. I've dreamed about owning this house since I was ten. We'll find another way."

Luc dropped the remote on the couch and stood, moving into her personal space. He smiled when she backed up a little. He knew he was intimidating her, and he didn't care. He'd had enough. Just because she was doing something weird to his emotions didn't mean he'd lost all sense of what he was. He certainly wasn't going to let her housebreak him.

"I knew I should have stuck with my original plan with you," he said, allowing the eerie glow to come into his eyes.

She took another couple steps back, getting perilously close to the wall that would block her in. He was impressed when she didn't scream or run from him, determined to stand her ground.

"And what exactly was your original plan?"

"To drive you from the house. I knew you were trouble the minute I saw you." Of course, that hadn't stopped him from influencing her to buy the house in the first place.

She was pressed against the wall, trapped like an animal, and far too flushed. He lowered his head toward her, his mouth mere inches from hers. What would she taste like?

"I'm going to church," she blurted out.

Luc was the one who took a step back then. He tried to sort through the conversation up to that point to figure out how they'd gotten from where they were to church.

"Why?" he asked suspiciously.

Anna arched a brow as if quite possibly he was the stupidest demon to ever walk the earth. "You know why."

He nodded and flopped back on the couch. He'd indulge her this once and let her try to get him out on her own. He'd already been here half a century. What was a few more days? It would give him more time to get a taste of her. If she thought she was coming out of this innocent and unscathed, she was crazier than he was.

❄

ANNA IGNORED THE POUTING DEMON DOWNSTAIRS. HE HAD TO BE OUT of his mind if he thought she'd burn her own house to the ground. Why couldn't he have been trapped in her apartment back in Atlanta? She would have gladly committed arson on that eyesore. But this house? Not on her life. Or his for that matter.

This house, after all, had inspired Margaret Mitchell. Okay, so she still wasn't really buying that, but it was like a historic monument. You didn't burn them down just so a demon with cabin fever could take a stroll around the park.

It wasn't even an issue of money. With her inheritance, which included a controlling share in Worthington Paper Products, she could have bought the house three times over without denting her bank account. No, it was simply a matter of principle.

She'd loved this house as far back as she could remember. She used to tell Cece she was going to buy it some day. She'd said it looked like a fairy tale. And she still had that opinion. She wasn't going to destroy it to free some guy she hadn't even known a full forty-eight hours.

It was a quarter to noon and raining heavily when Anna arrived at St. Francis. Late morning mass was drawing to a close, but the smell of incense was still thick on the air. She sat on the back pew trying not to draw attention to herself. It had been awhile since she'd been to a Latin mass. They only had them one Sunday a month. It was her lucky week.

She could listen to the peaceful droning without having to buy any of the actual content. With Latin she didn't have to spend the entire service dividing everything into categories of *this makes sense, but that's crap.*

Henrietta Baker, the younger and less pleasant sister of Bitsy and Mimi, turned in her pew at the front to give Anna the evil eye. This was no doubt because Anna had arrived late and wasn't wearing her head veil.

The veil was optional, but it didn't mean you didn't have a few nutty traditionalists who thought you were possessed by the devil himself if you weren't wearing it. Perhaps Luc was punishment for her veil rebellion. Henrietta made a disgusting sound halfway between a curse and a snort, and swiveled back around, waiting for her row's turn to receive the Holy Eucharist.

Anna had been an official heretic for the past five years, although the pope hadn't sent her a certificate or anything. She'd just come to the conclusion that she and religion were not mixable. She'd tried to buy the dog and pony show, but there were too many ideas that didn't make sense to her. And while questions had always been welcome in her parish, even that policy had started to falter under her constant queries.

Despite her lack of faith, she could no longer deny there was an actual bona fide minion of Satan living in her home. She wasn't too proud to ask for help.

The mass was wrapping up as the last of the stragglers went up to get the thin circular wafer and wine. Despite her intentions not to, Anna found herself becoming nostalgic.

St. Francis had high, gothic spires, stained glass, and the most spectacular hand-carved wooden pews. The interior of the sanctuary was all rich, dark wood. It made the candles appear to burn more brightly. The bluish light streaming in from the windows made the sanctuary feel like a safe haven to hide in.

Anna was ashamed she'd once used her cousin's pocket knife to carve her and Marshal's initials on the underside of one of the antique pews. She wondered if she'd have to admit to that in confession before the priest would help her.

The reverie was interrupted by a heavy hand on her shoulder. She turned in her seat to find Mimi standing behind her, smiling like an avenging church pew angel.

"I knew it was only a matter of time before you came back to the fold," she whispered.

For some reason, after sharing living quarters with Luc, Mimi was seeming less scary. Maybe it was the whole *he could suck your life right out of your body while having sex with you* thing, and Mimi could only talk you to death.

No, Mimi was still scarier.

Bitsy came to stand on the other side. Anna was beginning to wish she'd taken a seat anywhere but the back row.

"*Dominus vobiscum.*" The priest made his way down the center aisle as the congregants stood to sing the benediction.

There was a shuffling of hymnals and bags. Anna made a beeline to the door before she could get caught in the imminent bottleneck as people began to file out the single door that led to the fellowship hall. The priest had taken a separate exit in order to head off the crowd and greet his parishoners.

"I'm Father Jeffries," he said, taking Anna's hand in his to shake. "I'm so glad you're joining us today."

"Anna Worthington. I was wondering if I might speak with you privately, when you have a moment."

"Can you stay for lunch?"

She wasn't about to turn down free food. Religious people made the best potlucks, and the Sunday afternoon lunch at St. Francis was no exception. It was especially true in the middle of summer when potato salad was the dish *du jour*. Who would turn down a choice of fifteen different delicious versions of potato salad? Not her.

When they'd gotten through the buffet line, Father Jeffries led Anna down the long hallway to his private office. He closed the door and sat behind a large, oak desk. "So, what can I do for you? You're Quinton's daughter?"

"Yes, that's right."

"I was sorry to hear about your loss."

"Thank you." Anna picked at her food as she tried to think of the best way to broach her request. She settled on blunt honesty.

"Have you heard anything about the house on Cranberry Lane? The big white one with the columns?"

"Such as?" His voice was guarded.

"Such as anything supernatural going on. I'm having some problems."

"I'd heard Mr. Johnson believed there was a demon and had my predecessor try to exorcise it." He began to pick at his own potato salad.

"Well, he was right, and I was wondering if you might come by and try again."

The priest started to cough. Anna thought she'd have to come around and do the Heimlich, but he managed to get a sip of water and a moment later he looked at her, red-faced. "I don't really do exorcisms. I mean we have the book, and I've been trained. It's just . . . I don't do them anymore."

There was a long period of silence. She waited for him to explain why exactly that was, but the answer wasn't forthcoming.

"I don't want to put you out. I just thought I'd come to the church first."

"And we're glad you did." More awkward silence. "When were you needing . . . "

"I was hoping as soon as possible. Today."

Father Jeffries thumbed through the date book on the desk, his face desolate when he found the day empty of previous appointments. He looked up at her, helpless resignation in his features, and sighed. "How's three o'clock?"

"Perfect." She ate the last bits of her lunch and dropped the paper plate into the wastebasket.

The priest removed a crucifix from the wall and passed it to her along with a bottle of holy water. "Take this for protection. And sprinkle the water over the threshold."

"Father, he's already in the house."

As if it would help, he handed her a couple more wooden

crosses. Did he just stockpile them in his office like Van Helsing? "Hang these on the wall. I'll see you at three."

When Anna returned home, Luc was on the couch, still watching the cooking channel. She doubted he'd moved an inch since she'd left.

"The priest will be here at three."

She couldn't tear her eyes from his bare chest. It was just wrong. The way he was stretched out, his jeans riding low on his hips, with the beautiful indentations which were only sculpted into the flesh of a truly sleek specimen.

He smirked up at her. "Like what you see? Want to take a ride before our holy man comes by to exorcise me? He might kill me you know, and then you won't get the opportunity."

Anna's mind immediately jumped out of the gutter. Alarm threaded her voice. "Kill you?"

Luc got up and moved smoothly to her, kissing the shell of her ear. "I knew you cared," he whispered.

"I don't." As if to prove her point, she pulled the largest crucifix from her bag and pressed it against the skin of his forearm.

"That hurts . . . my feelings." He laughed. "I'm not a vampire, Anna."

"Then I guess this won't have an effect, either." She unscrewed the cap on the holy water and threw some in his face. After the crucifix, she knew it wouldn't hurt him, but his closeness freaked her out.

"It has the effect of pissing me off." Luc stalked off to the kitchen and patted his arm dry with a towel. "You're such a child."

"I am not!" She couldn't wait for the priest to get there and get him out.

"Yes. You are. I'm five hundred and twenty-six. You are a child."

"You're five hundred and twenty-six and you let some human girl trap you with a two-bit spell?" Anna couldn't help it. She started laughing. His eyes glowed, but she worked hard to ignore him, busying herself with the priest's instructions. She took one of the other crosses out of the bag and went to retrieve the hammer and nails.

Luc followed her back to the living room as she started to hang the first cross. "Just what do you think you're doing?"

"Putting crosses on the wall," she said, flashing him a *duh* look.

"I don't think so."

"I thought they didn't affect you."

"They don't, aside from being tacky."

Anna continued to hammer while Luc glowered at her, his irritation practically taking on physical form of its own.

"You are putting holes in the wall."

"Yeah, so?"

"Don't you care that you're destroying the integrity of this wall? This is a historic home."

"What does it matter? If I burned the house down, the wall would be destroyed anyway." She turned her attention back to hammering. "I think you should put on a shirt before the priest gets here." *If for no other reason, than to keep me from drooling all over you in front of Father Jeffries.*

Luc growled then disappeared from the room without another word.

*a*nna opened the door to find Father Jeffries looking much more pallid than he had at lunch. Maybe he'd picked the wrong potato salad.

"Come on in, Father." She stepped to the side and made a broad, sweeping motion that was meant to be welcoming, but from the expression on the priest's face, must have instead conveyed impending doom.

"Um . . . yes . . . thank you," he said as he shuffled into the house.

He looked official enough, still wearing his priestly garb. His arms were weighed down by a cardboard box filled to the brim with a bible, crosses, holy water, candles, and a big black book that Anna presumed held the secret and mystical exorcism rituals of the Catholic Church. The cover read, *De Exorcismus et Supplicationibus Quibusdam.* Yep. That would be it.

His pale blue eyes scanned the room. "Where are the crosses I asked you to hang?"

Oh boy. Here we go. "The demon threw them out the back door."

"Oh, dear." Father Jeffries put the box on the floor and made the sign of the cross. He appeared disturbed Luc had been able to touch the crosses without immolating on contact. He muttered something like, "at least the demon feels threatened."

Anna decided not to disabuse him of that quaint notion. Better that he think Luc was intimidated and afraid than to know the truth that he'd simply found them distasteful.

The poor man already looked ready to bolt. He might not be much to look at, but right now Father Jeffries was all Anna had in the demon-banishing department.

"Could you tell me please where the most activity in the house has been?"

For her, the most activity had been in the living room, what with Luc hogging the TV. Or else the kitchen. Then again, he was an incubus. In his career he'd probably spent most of his time in a bedroom getting laid or slinking into people's dreams. Anna tried to push that thought away.

"There really isn't any one hot spot, Father. He's been all over the house."

The priest sighed. "That's what I was afraid of."

Anna had no idea what difference it made where Luc had been. They weren't cleaning up demon residue here; they were trying to get him out. "I don't know if it changes anything, but he was cursed by a witch." She didn't think the priest's eyes could bug out any further.

"Do you mean to tell me you've been in communication with the demon?"

Anna shrugged, inexplicably feeling guilty. "It's not like I held a seance or did any spooky chanting or anything. He just showed up and started gabbing at me. It's like *True Confessions* in this house."

Father Jeffries busied himself, arranging a circle of white pillar candles on the foyer floor. "Are you not afraid of him, child?"

The truth was, Luc scared the crap out of her. She could banter with him until doomsday, and for brief moments at a time she could pretend he was just a quirky human or friendly ghost, but those moments were fleeting. If she wasn't so stubborn, she would have fled the house already or put it back on the market.

She found herself less afraid he might kill her and more afraid she might invite him into her bed. Which, with him being an incubus, just raised the odds that he might kill her. She blushed when she looked back over to the priest, realizing she'd gone off on a tangent in her head.

"You must not converse with him. It only gives him a stronger connection to you. If you must speak to him, say the Lord's Prayer or the Hail Mary."

Anna nodded. She didn't want tell the priest it was impossible not to talk to Luc, but Father Jeffries was right. Nothing good could come of communicating in any way with a demon.

He pressed a small bottle of olive oil into her hand along with a white handkerchief, instructing her to make a sign of the cross with the oil over all the doors and windows while saying a Hail Mary and an Our Father.

She dutifully went through the house, doing as he'd asked. The kitchen was her last stop. Anna drew the cross on the window pane with the oil and began:

"Hail Mary, full of grace, the Lord is with thee. Blessed art though among women, and blessed is the fruit of thy womb . . . "

Luc materialized beside her. "This isn't going to work."

"Jesus!" Anna nearly jumped out of her skin.

"Blasphemy during a ritual to rid yourself of me? Naughty, Anna." He wagged a finger at her.

Luc's chest and feet were still bare. Shoes were probably excessive for someone who couldn't leave the house anyway, but something about him running around barefoot, humanized him and made her forget what he was.

He was also eating chocolate chip cookies straight out of the bag.

"Give me those!" She swiped the bag and put it on the table. "You don't need food."

He shrugged. "I'm a nervous eater."

Anna rolled her eyes, a retort ready on her lips. Then, remembering the priest's advice, she turned back to the door and started muttering the prayers again.

"It's not that I don't want out of the house, but this is a waste of time. I can tell you it won't work."

"How do you know?" She'd been halfway through the Our Father, but it was hard to concentrate while someone was talking to her. She was amazed she remembered the prayers at all.

"A priest was already by here, remember? Besides, this priest is dirty. He's been diddling a couple of his married parishioners. If anyone is going to get a sex demon out of the house, it won't be someone enmeshed in his own sexual sins. Anyone could tell you that."

"You couldn't possibly know that. He's a nice guy, he would never ... "

The look he gave her made it clear he thought she was naïve. "Everyone in this town talks. With Cain bringing my dinner, I know more than you think. The priest is human. He's weak. He's a member of a religion that expects celibacy, something no human should have to or be able to give. I can smell an impure soul, and I'm telling you, it's not going to work." He picked up the bag of cookies, his interest shifting to the activity going on in the other room.

"Leave him alone," Anna said.

"Relax. I'm just going to watch the show. Also, if you want someone pure, someone who actually has a shot at this . . . look outside the church." With that final bit of wisdom he disappeared into the living room.

When she'd finished with the doors and windows, she joined

Father Jeffries. The candles were lit, and the exorcism book was lying open on the hardwood floor. The priest stood in the center of the circle, flinging holy water to all corners of the room while he chanted fervently in Latin.

"*Domine, exaudi orationem meam. Et clamor meus ad te veniat . . .*"

Apparently it was impossible to get rid of an evil thing without the aid of a dead language. Anna had a feeling ancient Sumerian might have been just as effective. And maybe it *was* effective. Despite no windows or doors being open, a wind started to howl. Stray papers rose from the coffee table and swirled through the air as if they had lives of their own.

His voice grew louder and stronger. "*Exorcizo te, immundissime spiritus, omnis incursio adversarii, omne phantasma, omnis legio . . .*"

Luc stood in the corner with his arms crossed over his chest, his patented bad boy smirk firmly in place. She crossed the floor to him and lowered her voice.

"That's not the priest's doing is it?"

Luc chuckled. "It's me. It seems to encourage him, though. Don't you think? Look at how much more into it he is now. God, humans are fun to play with."

"I thought you wanted out of the house!"

"I DO! And I've told you there is only one way to make that happen. This isn't working, and it's frustrating."

"We will find a way!"

"There is ONE way."

"NO!"

The priest, believing Anna was fighting with the demon in more of a *fight for your soul* way than a *you are annoying the hell out of me* way, started flinging holy water in Luc's direction. His chanting became even more intense as beads of perspiration popped out over his forehead. " . . . *per omnia saecula saeculorum . . .*"

Anna was sure if not for the curse, Luc would be out of there. It was an impressive show. The exorcist's alleged impurity aside.

Moments later, the front door banged against the wall as the wind rushed out in one violent burst. Father Jeffries wiped the sweat from his brow with his sleeve, a satisfied smile on his face as if he'd single-handedly resurrected the bad-ass reputation of the Catholic Church. He said final prayers in Latin and began snuffing out candles and packing the holy items back into the box.

"Why did you do that?" Anna whispered to Luc, careful not to draw the priest's attention.

"Because it was just sad. Pathetic. It was like watching a woman try desperately to orgasm and not being able to. Eventually they just have to fake it."

Anna tried not to let the images he'd evoked affect her. "At least try to get out of the house again."

Luc let out a put-upon sigh before making the obligatory effort to leave. As expected, he bounced off the barrier.

"If you have any more trouble, let me know," Father Jeffries said.

"He's still here."

"Oh that can't be. I felt his presence leave."

"No, you felt a wind that he created, fly out a door he opened with his magical mind powers. That's it. Can't you see him? He's standing right there." Anna pointed to the spot the demon now occupied.

The priest squinted as if Luc was a *Magic Eye* poster, and if he just looked hard enough the image would appear. A troubled expression creased his brow. "No, I don't see him."

"Look, I really appreciate your help. I'll just have to find another way."

Father Jeffries got a strange look in his eyes all of a sudden. He gripped Anna's hand and unfolded her palm. She tried to jerk away from him, but he held on. Every hair on the back of her neck stood at attention as he ran his index finger over the length of the raised scar.

"He did this, didn't he?"

She looked away. "Yes."

"Oh, this is worse than I thought. He's tied you to him. You'll have to be cleansed." Anna could see him going through a mental checklist as he rattled on. "You'll have to come to confession and get reconfirmed. And there's a convent a couple of hours from here, where they can . . . "

A savage growl tore through his litany of *how to clean up Anna's filthy soul.* Judging from the startled look on the priest's face, he'd heard it too. Luc picked Father Jeffries up by the throat, marched over to the door, and flung him outside.

"What are you doing?" Anna shouted, suddenly very aware of what was trapped inside her house.

"I'm taking the trash out."

He picked up the cardboard box and threw it onto the lawn, the candles and books spilling out everywhere. Anna stood at the window, unable to brush past Luc and not wanting to mess with him right then. A wave of fear flowed over her in response to Luc breaking out the *big scary.*

He growled again and shouted to the priest to stay off his property.

The color drained from Father Jeffries' face. His eyes met Anna's as he made the sign of the cross, then turned and ran. His exorcism kit remained in the grass. Anna jumped as the door slammed, and Luc rounded on her, fury blazing in his eyes.

In spite of herself, she backed away. "Calm down. Why are you acting this way?"

He gripped her hand. "You belong to me. You understand that, right?" His eyes were glowing that scary bright green. It was as if whatever humanity he had, had receded, and his darker nature was fully in control.

"No . . . " Her voice came out too breathless. She didn't know how much more of this Jekyll/Hyde routine she could take. "You said you didn't take my soul."

"Yes, that's true. I've told you already I can't take it without your permission. Goddammit, Anna, your soul isn't the only thing in danger from me." As if to prove a point, he brushed his lips against her throat while his hand caressed one breast.

She melted against him, the side of her that was terrified losing to the side of her that was aroused. He was too male, too attractive, too completely visceral. Was he doing this to her? Like Cain? She didn't know. She couldn't think straight.

"Stop it right now." The voice she'd meant to sound forceful and commanding, came out strangled.

She could see the fight going on within him as he backed up, allowing her the opportunity to move farther from him. Her eyes kept going to the door.

When he spoke, his voice was calm. "Run from me, and I'll have Cain hunt you down. He doesn't have the same handicaps I have at the moment."

Tears slipped down her cheeks. She couldn't help it; she felt too betrayed by his outburst. Even though he was a demon and she knew it was silly to be indignant that he was behaving like one. She wiped her face angrily with the back of her hand.

"I thought you were protecting me from him, and you said he couldn't . . . "

"He'd bring you back to me."

"What is wrong with you?" Anna wasn't sure if she was more disgusted with him and what he was or with herself for wanting him in spite of it. Why couldn't he behave in some way approaching the human mask he wore so easily?

"He touched you. He had no right to touch you." Luc's voice was harsh.

"Who? The priest?"

"He touched what's mine."

Her stomach fluttered at his words, even as he still terrified her. She inched toward the door. The afternoon had gone from banter to life-threatening far too quickly. She didn't feel safe alone with him anymore.

"Anna, what did I just say?" Wrapped in his tone was a reprimand.

"Please let me go. I'll come back, I just have to get out of here for awhile." *Away from you* hung on the air unspoken.

8

*W*atching Luc peer at her from behind the lacy curtains, Anna knew he'd never let her go. Not even if she burned down the house. Mingling their blood had clearly crossed some primal demon line for him.

The scar on her hand twinged as she moved to where the exorcism kit lay strewn over the grass.

The bond was starting to get pissed off when she wasn't with him. She ran a finger over the red, raised mark, and her palm started to tingle. It wasn't an altogether unpleasant sensation, but it made her think of Luc in a warm, fuzzy way. And that scared her.

She bent to put the spilled items back in the box Father Jeffries had abandoned. She didn't need a bunch of Catholic ritual items littering her front yard. And the neighbors didn't need more gossip material. Once the box was packed, she loaded it into her car.

She wondered if she could just leave town and never come back. Could Cain really find her? Maybe the scar was like some sort of homing beacon. If she ran and Luc sent Cain after her . . . what then? She wanted to be alone with Cain even less than she wanted to be alone with Luc. With Luc, there was something almost human there. Most of the time. Cain's eyes didn't have that. They were just empty. A monster with a pretty face.

Anna stopped off at the hospital on the way to church, needing a captive outlet to unload some of her anger and fear, as well as a target that deserved it. The receptionist at the information booth gave her directions to Marshal's room.

She didn't bother knocking, just barged right in. After all, he had barged in. It seemed only fair. He'd been moved from ICU to a regular room, but he still looked like shit.

Under the fluorescent lighting she could see the entire right side of his face was purple and puffy. One eye was swollen shut, and a neck brace kept him from being able to lie back on his pillows. One of his arms was in a cast. A couple of people had already been by and written on it in bright pink and green magic markers.

He turned from his television program, his good eye going wide when he saw her. He looked like he might be sick.

"Hello, Marsh. I just wanted to drop by personally and thank you again for the lovely date. You left so soon last night. I was having such a wonderful time. You know what with you trying to *rape* me and all."

"I . . . I didn't mean to . . . "

Luc had damaged Marshal's throat enough that speech was a struggle. She wondered how he'd ever gotten the story out about the wild dogs, or if it was all just so much Bitsy and Mimi gossip.

"Sure ya didn't, Marsh. It was all just innocent. I wanted it, right? Had it coming? If I hadn't been wearing that alluring dress like some slut that wanted it . . . "

"No . . . that's not . . . " His eyes were wild and panicked.

"No? So I must have hearing problems. You didn't comment on how you were scaring me? Your face didn't light up while you were doing it? You didn't try to force yourself on me?" She was greeted with silence as the protests died on his lips. "If he hadn't stopped you, you would have raped me. Assuming I wasn't able to knock you unconscious first. I still think I could have managed it."

She had his full attention now.

"Who . . . what . . . "

"It's none of your business who or what he is. Just know if you ever come near me again, he'll kill you, slowly and painfully." Anna said it to scare him, to take back some of what he'd tried to take from her. But as she spoke the words she knew they were true.

Luc would torture the life slowly from him and enjoy the whole sordid affair, if his freak-out with Father Jeffries was any indication. Luc would protect her from anyone. But who would protect her from Luc?

She rubbed her palm against her jeans in an attempt to get the bond to settle down.

Marshal struggled to nod. "I won't bother you again."

"Good. I heard you said you were attacked by wild dogs. I can't believe anyone bought that."

Marshal used his good hand to rip the hospital gown away from his chest. Savage claw and bite marks covered his flesh. Anna tried to think back to the night before. All she'd been able to process at the time was that her date was getting his ass kicked. It wasn't like she'd been shooting a documentary of the event.

Still, the injuries came as a shock. Luc looked human, and humans didn't have claws or teeth like that. She schooled her features into the hard line they'd been set in before.

"I think it would be very wise if you stuck by that story. If I were you, I wouldn't tell anyone what really happened." She started for the door and paused, turning back. "Oh, and Marsh? If you ever see me again, I don't care where you are or what you're doing. You turn and walk the other direction. 'Kay?"

He nodded as well as he could, and Anna closed the door softly behind her.

LUC STOOD IN THE LIBRARY, PORING OVER BOOKS CAIN HAD BROUGHT him years before from the demon dimension. There had to be something to explain what the hell was going on. He was still shaken by his behavior. He'd never felt this mindlessly possessive of another person before.

He'd scared the shit out of her, and with the curse in place, he had no power to make her stay with him where she'd be safe.

"Yeah. Safe," he muttered, taking another drink. He'd love to be drunk right now. It was possible, but a demon needed a whole lot of hard liquor. All Luc had at his disposal was a wine cellar. Not nearly good enough.

Maybe it would be best for both of them if she didn't come back. He'd only heard about bonds like this. He'd never actually done one.

After Cain had gotten near her, the only thought on his mind was doing something to protect her. His instincts had kicked in and taken it from there. He hadn't thought there would be consequences. Or side effects.

It took searching through three different books before he finally found one that offered any information on the bond.

"Fuck me." He slammed the book shut and put his head in his hands. He still hadn't found the details he needed, only one book with a brief mention in a footnote of the type of blood mingling he'd performed. It could be used as a first step to a mating. No wonder he was feeling so possessive and sappy about her.

Luc tamped down the voice in his head that said he'd been fixated on her for weeks. That it wasn't the bond. He wondered if the ritual was having an effect on her as well.

He thought back to how he'd begged Beatrice to give him her soul and wondered if something like this would have let him keep her forever. When he'd originally researched mating, he'd missed it because it was a strategy that had been lost in the lore of their people, buried in unrelated books for centuries. He'd been looking in the wrong place. He should have dug deeper. If he had, he might not have ended up trapped in the house in the first place.

THERE WAS NO EVENING SERVICE AT ST. FRANCIS, BUT THE DOOR WAS kept unlocked for those who wanted to come pray or have a quiet, peaceful place away from the world to escape to. Anna carried the box in and put it down by the altar, then lit a candle in one of the red votive holders at the front. Gregorian chants emanated from a speaker in the balcony.

She curled up on a pew and allowed herself to relax as the music washed over her. Surely Cain couldn't come inside a church. It seemed the church was one of the few truly safe places for her. Seeing Marshal had provided some closure, but it also made the threat of returning home seem too great to seriously consider yet.

But you will go back, a voice in her mind whispered. She wanted to deny that thought, but recognized the truth of it. As insane as it was. The mark held some sort of power over her now.

Luc had been threatened when the priest sensed the bond. That was enough to let her know Father Jeffries wasn't just some random boob with a shiny prayer book. Whether it came from a god some-where or just an inner sense, he had a gift. Maybe untapped and underdeveloped, but it was there. If she allowed him to help her, what then?

Hours passed in the stillness of the church while Anna tried to think through her options and tried not to have naughty, wrong thoughts about Luc. That was definitely a bad idea.

It was almost sunset when her hand started to burn. Was the demon doing something with the bond? Using it like a magical leash to reel her back to him?

In the sanctuary, she'd slipped into an almost trance-like state, floating somewhere inside the soft, comforting candlelight and chanting. Faced with the prospect of spending the night in the house with Luc, she had the urge to find the priest and do whatever she had to do to rid herself of the demon's influence once and for all. But the danger from Cain loomed over her, somehow worse than Luc. She wasn't convinced Father Jeffries could protect her from the greater evil.

9

The front porch light was on when Anna returned, still arguing with herself for allowing the burning from the bond to drag her back.

She had a death grip on her house key when the door swung open. Luc *had* to start with the special effects. He couldn't stay out of her way and let her come inside on her own. Instead of going in, she sat in one of the rocking chairs, pulled a book from her purse, and pretended to read while the door stood open and ignored.

At least her hand wasn't burning now. Maybe she could sleep on the porch. Best of both worlds.

Fifteen minutes passed before she steeled herself enough to look up. Luc scowled at her through the window. She turned back to the book, willing her heartbeat to steady, breathing slowly in and out.

Moments later, he was looming in the doorway. If not for the barrier, he could have reached out and pulled her inside. She had to keep up a running stream of commentary in her head to reassure herself that was the case. That she was safe out here. When he finally spoke, she jumped anyway.

"Anna, get your ass in the house right now!"

She pretended to focus on her book. She'd managed to read one paragraph. About four hundred times.

"Stop bullying me," she said between clenched teeth, her eyes still on the page.

"I am quickly losing patience," he snarled.

"Yes, and what are you going to do about it?" She dropped the book and came to stand mere inches from the threshold. She didn't know what it was about him that made her throw her self-preservation instincts out the window, but he pissed her the hell off. After going to see Marshal and getting some of her fire back, she wasn't coming home to take shit from another bully. Her heart was in her throat as she watched his face darken.

"I told you I could have you brought to me." His voice was calm.

The calm scared her more than the snarling. "Cain said he wasn't coming back for awhile. For all we know, he's never coming back." She knew even as she said it, that it wasn't true.

"Get in the house. Now."

Anna was tempted to taunt him with a *make me* but his comment earlier about her being a child still stung. Not that he acted that much more mature for his age. The several hundred years age difference wasn't all that noticeable if you asked her.

"Not until you calm down. Luc, please, you're scaring me. I saw Marshal, and I can't come into the house if I think you might . . ."

"I wouldn't." The angry mask was gone as quickly as it had surfaced. "I don't beat on women. That bastard had that coming."

She bit her lip and looked away. "I know."

His voice softened, and he moved away from the door. "Please come inside."

She waited a few more minutes until she finally gained the nerve to step over the threshold. He wasn't in the entryway or living room, unless he was pulling the disappearing act. But she didn't think he was doing that either because she couldn't *feel* him. Ever since the bond, she could sense his presence when he was near. It was something she'd put in a file folder of things she wasn't thinking about.

She weaved her way through the house until she found him in the library with a book in his hand. He tensed when she walked in and sat in the chair opposite from him.

"You read?"

He snorted. "Of course I read. What else is there to do besides watch television and feed?"

She didn't know how it happened. One moment they were both sitting awkwardly in opposite chairs, the next he'd taken her hand in his, turning her palm up to inspect it. He stared for a moment as if he couldn't quite believe his mark was still there, then he released her and sank back into his chair in obvious relief.

"You *are* threatened by that priest. You know he can free me from you."

"I just wanted to make sure I didn't need to redo it. I was worried when you were gone so long. Cain has no conscience. The *creepy blood ritual*, as you call it, is the only thing protecting you from him when I'm not with you. I don't know if that priest of yours could undo it. He shouldn't have even been able to sense it."

They sat in silence awhile longer, then Luc spoke again. "I have to feed." The timbre of his voice sent goosebumps running down Anna's arm.

A small part of her thrilled at the idea of him feeding from her, but another part still recoiled in anxiety. Her breathing was shallow when he pulled her into his lap.

"I'm not going to hurt you. Relax." His voice was so seductive, and for a moment she thought he might be using whatever demon magic he had to lower her resistance.

Her head fell back as he ran his fingers through her hair and over her neck. It was so much easier to let him do whatever it was he was doing. She was already bonded to him. How much worse could it get?

"Luc, stop," she said with a half-hearted sigh.

"You want it. Just let yourself feel."

The words so similar to her dream seemed to smack her across the face. Anna scrambled out of his lap. "I can't do this with you."

"Why the hell not? You know I'm not going to hurt you."

She *hoped* he wouldn't hurt her. A part of her believed he wouldn't. He'd gone to a lot of trouble so far to keep her alive. But there were no guarantees. She might not be a religious person, but that didn't mean years of childhood indoctrination hadn't made their mark. Demon equaled bad. She was fairly certain even nonspiritual people could agree on that point.

"It's not just that," she hedged.

"Then what is it?"

"I don't do casual sex, okay? I can't sleep with someone I don't love. I'm not wired that way. I know you probably think that's foolish and naïve and old-fashioned, that I'm some kind of prude . . . "

He laughed, interrupting her speech. "I don't think you're a prude."

The soft way he was looking at her almost had her running back into his arms, but the consequences of a little pleasure with him were too serious.

"I can't get involved with you because I wouldn't be able to share you. You have to feed every day, but you couldn't feed from *me* every day. That equals sharing, and I can't do that."

He sighed. "As much as I can appreciate your feelings on this matter, my ability to behave in a somewhat civilized manner hinges on my getting fed regularly. If I don't feed I could lose control later. I don't want to do that. Cain means it. He won't come back until I've fed."

"He wants you to use the mind powers on me," she said, realization dawning.

"Yes. It would appear I've been in the presence of humans too long. According to him, I'm too empathetic now. He wants me to be the demon he knew before all this."

"Why me?"

"Because you're different. I can't just seduce you the way I can others without the mind tricks. You're stubborn and not exactly what one would call a slut. He knows you wouldn't give in before I lost control and enthralled you. And by that time I wouldn't be able to stop."

She felt trapped and resentful for the trapping. One way or the other it seemed some demon would have her. She thought about staying in her father's big empty house for awhile, but she was afraid Cain would find her and that the bond might not be strong enough to stop him. Besides, the scar would scream at her and never let her sleep if she and Luc weren't under the same roof.

"Luc, I can't let you ... "

His eyes were pleading. "Please don't do this, Anna. I really don't want to hurt you. Just give in."

The next words left her mouth before she could stop them. "I'll bring your meals until Cain comes back."

Now she knew how to shut Luc up. Just say something completely ridiculous. He didn't speak for a full minute, making her offer sound more insane and just plain sinister the longer it sat there without a response.

"I'm sorry, what? I must not have heard you right."

"I said I'll bring you women." That really *did* sound bad when she said it out loud ... yet again.

"Why?" He hadn't moved from the chair since Anna had jumped off his lap.

She paced. Now that she'd said it—twice—it sounded even worse. "Well, what are my options here? You've tied me to you. I could try to get it undone, but then I'm bait for Cain and his groupies of doom. I could just stay away from you, but we both know Cain will return, and he'll bring me right back because you're feeling all possessive. Especially if you're starved by then. Even if I wanted to, I can't sleep with you because I told you I can't share. It would hurt too much."

"You could just burn the house down."

Anna gave him a withering look. "And then you're free to feed anyway. At least this way I know you aren't killing them."

He threw his arms in the air. "Go ahead and justify it. I've never seen someone so selfish. You're willing to give women to me to fuck so you don't have to burn your precious house to the ground, and you're going to have to anyway."

"This is temporary. Cain will be back, and I'll find another way to get you out of here."

He laughed. "You're every demon's dream, little girl. I don't even have to be evil to get you to bring me innocent young souls."

Luc didn't try to stop her when she left. Why would he? She was bringing him take-out.

He should disgust her. She was disturbed by exactly how much he didn't. He couldn't help what he was. It was herself she was disgusted with. She should just leave him and not come back, get Father Jeffries to remove the mark, and get the hell out of dodge as far from Golatha Falls as possible.

But she couldn't bring herself to do it. She couldn't stand the idea of Luc starving, wasting away in that house waiting on Cain to come back and feed him again. What if he never came back?

Despite the circumstances, Anna couldn't just start delivering college co-eds, drunk and slutty or not. She changed her direction and headed for the interstate.

It was after midnight when she finally returned from Atlanta with a car crammed with five prostitutes. It was a decision she could live with. One she could justify. She didn't want to think too hard about the fact that she'd just created a harem for the man whose bed she wanted to be in.

They had sex for money and probably never got any pleasure from it. If she knew anything about the moans she'd heard in the house, she knew Luc never left a woman unsatisfied. Plus they had a place to live that didn't involve some smarmy pimp that would only beat them and take their money.

The front door opened as soon as her hand touched the knob. Luc looked disheveled and sexier than he had a right to. The second he saw her, the anger drained from his face.

"My God, Anna, I thought something had happened to you, or that you changed your mind and weren't coming back. You didn't do it, did you? I knew you couldn't."

She could see the way he fought the lust, and what her failure to bring him dinner meant.

"No, I did. I just couldn't keep bringing you different people. It just felt wrong, so . . . I um . . . " She mumbled the last part.

"You what?"

"I sort of got you a harem of prostitutes."

She could tell he was trying not to grin at her.

"They know," she said.

His features darkened. "They know *what* exactly?"

"They know what you are. One of them is part Romani. She sensed something was off. I wanted them to know what they were getting themselves into. They had the right to know and make a choice about it."

He sighed. "Bring them in."

"Stop scowling. You'll freak them out."

Anna motioned out to the car for the girls. When they were all inside, she got the introductions out of the way. "This is Renee, Olivia, Karen, Susan, and Maria."

The first four were bottle blonds with miniskirts and makeup too dark for their complexions. Maria stood out from the rest. She was dark-complected with long raven hair.

The brunette extended a hand to Luc. She was the only one of the group not intimidated by him. "Ironic," she said, her lips twisting in a cruel grin.

"What is?" he asked with some trepidation.

"A whore fucking whores." She didn't cringe from him when he growled. She only laughed, a light tinkling sound in the stillness of the room.

"Okaaay," Anna said, moving to stand between Luc and Maria. "I'm going to show you girls your rooms, then I'm going to bed."

"We each get our own rooms? In *this* house?" Renee squealed.

Anna smiled. She hated this plan, but it had its good sides. She got the girls settled in their rooms, then retreated to her own, Scarlett and Rhett sticking close to her heels. The cats seemed as uncomfortable with her house guests as she was.

She swiped at the tear tracking down her cheek. It was important to remember what Luc was, that he couldn't change, and she could never really have him. It was best not to start with him.

Beatrice's behavior was understandable. It had been wrong and stupid and suicidal, but Anna understood. It was hard to dislike Luc. She couldn't imagine how hard it was once a physical relationship started.

She took a hot bath and put earplugs in before climbing into bed.

. . . DEATH. DESTRUCTION. MAYHEM. ANNA FOUND HERSELF somewhere in the distant past on a cobblestone street lit by torches. The smell of sex was thick on the air.

She could see it as if she were him. She looked out from his eyes, could feel his thoughts, his emotions as he fucked and killed. He hunted for rapists and killers, attacking them, spilling their guts on the street with sharp claws. The grateful victim fell into the arms of her savior, not knowing the angel who'd just rescued her was the angel of death.

He didn't have to kill them. He did it because it was easier, and he had no conscience to make him stop. He reveled in it, making them want him, pleasing them, then taking their lives for their foolishness.

Anna tensed when she heard Cain approaching, still aware of the part of her that was Anna and not Luc, and desperately hoping he didn't somehow know she was there.

"You never get tired of this do you, Lucien? It's refreshing. You inspire me." Cain held a struggling brunette in his arms.

Luc dropped the beauty he'd just drained to the ground and turned to the other demon. "Why do you do that? You know you can't feed that way." To feed they had to have their victim's pleasure.

It made sense in a twisted sort of way. If they fed from sexual energy, it couldn't be their own. Where would it come from if the woman wasn't aroused? If she didn't climax?

Cain shrugged. "I'll enthrall her later, when I get tired of this. You know, fear is its own kind of food. You should broaden your horizons. We *are* demons after all."

Luc shook his head. "I think I prefer my way. It's sweeter when they come to me willingly. I'm going to call it a night. You have fun." He leaned in and kissed the girl on the mouth, smiling at the flush that tinted her cheeks. Then he turned and walked away.

The scene changed. Anna stood in her own back garden, still in the past, but not quite so distant. Cain perched on the edge of a fountain. "I don't understand why you didn't kill her."

"I just didn't want to think about her being gone forever. I wanted to have her again." Luc fought with the odd new feelings swirling through him. Why hadn't he wanted to kill her? *What's wrong with me?*

"Be careful with that," Cain said. "There's nothing good there."

Luc nodded, but he still felt compelled to ask. It was only trivia after all. He wouldn't actually do it. "But we can . . . if they say yes. I could have her forever if she was willing. Right?"

Cain laughed and shook his head. "You should stay out of the libraries. That was a long time ago. Our kind doesn't take mates anymore. If I didn't know better I'd think you didn't just want someone's soul; you want someone to love. It's a bad idea. The way the world is now? Face it, no one gives a demon anything willingly."

Cain looked off into the distance for a minute before turning back to Luc. "I take it you aren't coming with me to Europe?"

Luc shook his head. "I want to see what happens."

"I never thought I'd see the day you'd want to be domesticated."

Luc growled. He knew he shouldn't have tried to have a heart-to-heart with Cain about anything. He should have just kept his mouth shut. "I'm not saying I want to settle down. I just want to see what it would be like to be in the same woman's bed on a semi-regular basis. I want to know if there's something else besides this."

Anna felt herself ripped from the scene, and suddenly things were very familiar. She wasn't Luc anymore, because Luc was with her. His warm breath was on her neck as his hands roamed sensuously over her body.

"Anna . . . " he whispered in her ear.

She writhed beneath him. "Please, Luc . . . "

"What? Tell me what you need. Just say yes. I promise you won't regret it."

Her mind screamed, *Wake up! Wake up! Wake up!* a mantra in her head, even as her body arched toward his. Suddenly his lips were brushing against hers. She'd never been kissed like this. Possessive and sweet as honey at once. His tongue swept into her mouth and she could feel herself losing her tenuous grip on control.

"That's it. Let me in," he murmured against her mouth.

Her fingers twisted in the sheets as his head went down between her legs. His tongue flicked out to tease her, then he looked up. She was falling into his hypnotic, feral gaze. His eyes glowed bright green, and she snapped out of whatever possession had taken hold of her.

She focused harder on waking up. When it didn't work, she kicked him off her. He sailed across the room like he weighed nothing. She hadn't expected that. But then, why not? In dreams anything was possible. When she tried to wake herself again, she succeeded . . .

ANNA WAS PANTING, WEARING THE T-SHIRT AND PAJAMA PANTS SHE'D gone to bed in. He hadn't undressed her. Well, there was that. Small consolation.

"Luc?" she said. The room was shrouded in inky darkness, and she considered the wisdom of sleeping with the lights on in the future.

"Yes?" His voice came from the direction of the chair.

"Can you see me in the dark?"

"I can."

"Well, turn the light on, jackass." The lamp flicked on. "I hate you."

He winked at her. "Oh come now, Anna, you can't blame an incubus for trying." He looked quite smug and pleased with himself. "You'll break. It's only a matter of time."

"I said not to touch me. What? Five prostitutes aren't enough for you? Maybe I should have gone for an even half dozen. Stay the hell away from me!"

He flinched but recovered quickly. "I don't want to."

"Why not?"

He stood and moved closer to her. "You know it could be so good. You have to feel this thing between us. Those other girls, they're just food. It doesn't mean anything. You're the one I want."

She rolled her eyes and chucked a pillow at him. "Yes, the male argument from time immemorial. *They don't mean anything. It's just sex.* Bullshit. I told you I cannot and will not share."

"There is a way . . . "

"No!" If he thought she'd fall for the *if you'll just give me your soul* line, he was crazy.

"Fine!" He snarled and turned toward the door.

"Stay out of my dreams. I know what you are now."

He spun toward her, his voice becoming dangerously low. "What do you mean, you know what I am now?"

"I saw it. I watched you lie to women, tell them what they wanted to hear. I saw you lead them to your bed and kill them. I saw it. You're no better than Cain."

Anna didn't tell him she'd also seen him later, saw the change that had started. She was too angry. She understood why he'd try to show her the second part of the dream, to weaken her resolve against him. But she couldn't begin to guess why he'd shown her the first part. She knew he'd killed, but to see it was something quite different. Her sympathy for the demon in her bedroom was coming to an end.

"What do you mean you saw it?"

"In my dream, the one you were in. I was inside your skin. I saw everything."

She didn't think a demon could faint, but Luc might be the first. He looked awfully pale. "I was only in your dream when I was trying to seduce you just now."

Anna wanted to call him a liar, but his face revealed genuine shock and . . . shame? She felt the tingling start in her hand. The bond was infecting her dreams now.

10

*A*nna wasn't looking forward to breakfast. In the light of day, the harem seemed even more vulgar than it had the night before. But the kitchen was empty aside from Luc, who was flipping pancakes and drinking coffee.

"If I see Vince, he's dead," Luc said.

"What?" Of all the things he could have told her first thing in the morning, a mention of her ex-boyfriend in Atlanta hadn't made the top hundred.

"You're not the only one getting dreams. That shithead better hope he never comes back to Golatha Falls after the way he treated you."

She wasn't sure how to respond. Part of her was all melty that he'd kick Vince's ass for her, though another part was a little worried, considering her visit to the hospital the previous night. Also, a casual death threat from Luc was more than creative hyperbole.

So instead, she just lamely said, "Do we have orange juice?"

He gestured with his spatula. "In the fridge."

They were in the middle of suffering through a quiet and awkward breakfast when the doorbell rang.

"Oh shit!" Anna shoved the last bit of pancakes into her mouth and tossed the plate into the sink. "That's Tam. I forgot about her. You have to go."

Luc looked amused. "Go where?"

"Be invisible. You can't let her see you."

"But I like being visible." He waggled his eyebrows at her, and an image of them naked together on the kitchen island flew through her brain. She looked at him suspiciously, wondering if he'd put the visual there. He just smiled.

Yep. He'd put the visual there.

The doorbell kept ringing. "Just a second, Tam!" She turned to Luc. "You can't be serious. Do the poof disappear-y thing."

"No."

"Why are you tormenting me?"

"I will change into something less . . . conspicuous."

Before Anna could ask for clarification, there was a fluffy, white Persian cat sitting on the kitchen table.

"You've got to be kidding me. She's gonna think I'm becoming a crazy cat lady. Every time she sees me, I have a new cat."

"Mrarrr," Luc said, sauntering off ahead of her into the living room.

Anna was well on her way to gray hair. The doorbell rang again. "Dammit!"

Tam had her wonderful qualities, but patience was not among them. She was like a female Luc, minus the demon part and the great abs. She tried to stop thinking about the abs and focus on the demon part as she opened the door.

"Is it okay that I'm here?" Tam asked.

"Of course it is," Anna said, her voice going up a register. "Why wouldn't it be okay? I said ten o'clock didn't I?" She was wearing a smile on her face that would put any Vaseline-toothed beauty queen to shame.

Tam peered into the house and screamed. Anna turned to see what had caused the panic attack.

Luc had decided he wasn't really into looking like a Persian cat after all. He must have needed something roomier, because sprawled across her entryway floor was a giant lion with a look in his eyes that was way too self-aware for her taste. He let out a little roar for good measure, looking like the MGM lion and causing Tam to jump back. He slunk over to Anna and nudged her hand like a kitten that wanted to be petted.

"This isn't amusing, Luc." Anna tried to sound stern, but her lips kept twitching into a smile. She was coming to feel almost safe with the weird little annoying things he did. It was better than the angst and brooding, anyway.

"Bitsy and Mimi are gonna be by for their morning walk any minute. I don't want them to think I've got a circus in my house." She thought she saw him lift one shoulder in a shrug as he turned and went to the other side of the room.

"*That's* the incubus?" Tam looked disturbed.

"He normally looks human," Anna said, as he changed back into his human form. She was mildly surprised to see him wearing a black silk shirt and matching slacks. Demons could shift outfits, too? They were quite the magical multi-talents. She'd have to ask him about that later.

Tam leaned in and whispered, "Hot damn! *This* is what's living in your house? I thought you were crazy for wanting to come back yesterday, but now I can see why. I'd risk my life for some of that, too."

Anna could tell he was pretending not to hear, though he couldn't seem to help preening at the attention.

"Yeah, well, usually it's even worse. Most of the time he's shirtless, looking like he's about to pose for a *Harlequin* cover. Let me just get the kitchen straightened up, and we can get started."

She tossed the dishes into the washer and wiped down the counters, hoping none of the harem came downstairs before she had a chance to explain things to Tam. That was not a conversation she was looking forward to having. Explaining that she was now the madam of an incubus whorehouse sounded less than fun at the moment.

When Anna returned, Tam was cozied up on the couch with the incubus. She cleared her throat, and the two of them looked up guiltily. Of course they were guilty. They looked far too snuggly together on the couch, talking like old lovers sharing inside jokes. If he thought he could sleep with her friends, he was insane. Feeding him did not include giving him access to every female she knew.

"Stay away from her." She wasn't sure if her voice shook from anger or fear.

He looked up, his expression mild. "Why? Are you jealous?"

"Oh yes, I'm jealous that you might suck the life right out of her. Pick me, please pick me."

"Really, nothing was going on," Tam said, stars still in her eyes.

Anna ignored her. She wasn't angry with her friend. Who could resist Luc? He had that nefarious thrall thing going on that he was probably using to make Anna jealous. Which wasn't working, by the way.

She grabbed Tam by the arm and had to practically drag her into the kitchen.

"He's so . . . wow," Tam said. Her voice was dreamy and breathless, like a *Stepford Wife*. That bastard *had* hypnotized her. Anna was going to find a way to rip his appendages from his body, starting with the one he needed most for survival.

"Yes, I have eyes. I can see him. But I'm not going to think about having sex with him because I have this thing called a survival instinct."

Tam's eyes lit up like she thought she was in on a secret. "You *like* him."

"I do not!"

"But there was banter. I saw it."

"We don't banter. We snark, and that's a completely different vibe," Anna said.

"He likes you. Didn't you see the way he looks at you?"

"You mean like a fancy restaurant he can't get a reservation at?"

Tam was drooling a little bit. "But just look at him . . . My God, the muscles he must have hidden under that shirt."

Anna rolled her eyes. "He's trying to seduce you."

Luc walked in then, a mask of mock indignation on his face. "I am doing no such thing."

"Think about this for a second, Tam. Incubi are shapeshifters. They're obviously going to pick a form that's sexually appealing."

Luc poured himself a glass of juice. "I'll have you know, this has been my human form for going on more than five hundred years now. Also, I'm standing right here."

"Then leave."

"I told you, I can't leave the house."

"The house is big. Go to the far end of it." She turned her attention back to Tam. "As I was saying, that's an illusion he creates to lure women into his bed. His real form is probably very scary, like *put you in an institution* scary." Her eyes widened as soon as the words were out of her mouth.

"What?" Luc said.

"Sara Johnson." She backed away, remembering Caroline's daughter in the psych ward. "That's why . . . "

"Let me explain." His palms were up in a placating gesture as he inched closer to her.

Anna stared at him and shook her head, backing up even further until she reached the door. She fumbled behind her for the knob that released her into the garden, not taking her eyes from him as she stumbled down the steps.

When she was far enough away, she finally turned her back to him. The garden was devoid of life, the plants having dried up long ago from lack of care. Even the fountain had been drained. A dark green algae was forming in the bottom.

She felt a hand on her shoulder and jumped before she remembered Luc was trapped inside.

"Are you okay?" Tam asked.

"No. Even with the dreams, sometimes it's easy to forget what he is."

"Dreams?" Tam looked intrigued. Probably professional witchy curiosity.

Anna sighed and recounted the previous night's nocturnal adventures. Like a good friend, Tam shivered at all the appropriate parts.

"I would have lost my shit. Are you sure Cain couldn't see you in there?"

"Pretty sure." If he could have, he surely would have addressed her or tried the sexual mind control on her. Or, maybe not while she was in Luc's body.

Tam glanced back at the house. "You care about him."

Anna swiped at a tear that had slipped out. "I can't care about him. He's a demon. It's not safe. Besides, it's too soon. I don't fall for men this quickly. I want him. But then I figure: he's hot, I haven't had a real date in awhile, he's evil so maybe he's influencing me."

She traced her finger over the scar. It was burning again. She scrubbed her palm against her jeans trying to rub away the pain and looked up to find Luc watching her from the kitchen window.

"I can't get a moment's peace!" She picked up a smooth rock from the bottom of the fountain and chucked it at the window, but he didn't move away. The rock bounced harmlessly off and landed in the grass.

"We don't have to think about the business today. Let's just take a mental health day." Tam helped Anna to her feet and led her to the green Mitsubishi parked in the driveway.

Anna laughed hysterically. Tam didn't realize mental health was definitely something she was in danger of losing.

"Is there any place in particular you want to go?" Tam was still talking in the soothing tone as if Anna were a little rabbit that might get spooked and go hopping away.

"The Golatha Falls Sanitarium."

Tam quirked a brow.

"There's someone I have to see." Anna was going to remind herself once and for all what Luc was. She was going to get herself back on track with her plan and forget the lies he'd carefully constructed to seduce her.

Anna hadn't been gone thirty minutes when Olivia stumbled into the living room, pale and shaking. Her body weaved like she might pass out. Then she started pacing, a look of panic on her face.

Before Luc could say or do anything, Karen came into the room. "Sit down and calm down, Olivia."

The bottle blonde shook her head furiously and kept pacing, growing more agitated.

"What's wrong with her?" Luc was standing back, unsure what was going on or if he should intervene.

"Withdrawal," Karen said. "Most of us are clean, but her pimp kept her so coked out she barely knew her name half the time. I'm surprised your girl didn't notice last night."

He hadn't noticed last night, and he'd had her in his bed. Then again, Luc had been pretty hungry. Looking for symptoms of drug addiction hadn't been on his to-do list at the moment.

"Olivia," he said.

Her head jerked up. Her eyes were wild.

"Come here." He stared deeply into her eyes and put a heavy

dose of hypnotic suggestion in his voice. She stood in front of him, putty in his hands, waiting for his next command.

He should have sensed this last night. She was so pliable. She'd been pliable the night before, too. Drug addicts were always easier to control.

He put his hands gently on either side of her face, needing a physical connection to control her mind more strongly.

"What are you doing? Anna said you couldn't . . . not twice in a row."

The fear in Karen's voice was palpable and distracting.

"I'm not feeding. I'm going to help her."

"How?"

He growled in frustration at the twenty questions routine and Karen took a step back. "I have no intention of harming anyone in this house. Sit down, and let me concentrate."

She sat in a nearby chair and didn't say another word, her eyes riveted to him and what he was doing with her friend.

Olivia was shaking against him. "I have to go back . . . I need . . . "

"Shhh. You don't need anything. Listen to me, Olivia. You don't need the drugs. You are not a drug addict. You don't do cocaine. You will have no pain, no withdrawal symptoms, no bad dreams. Do you understand me?"

"Yes," she said a little breathlessly.

When he took his hands off her face, Olivia looked around, seemingly embarrassed and confused as to why she was in the living room. The shaking and restlessness had stopped.

"Is there anything to eat?"

"I'll make you some pancakes if you go into the kitchen," Luc said.

She blushed as she seemed to come back to herself and remember their activities the night before, but just nodded.

He smirked. A prostitute blushing. It was adorable.

Karen watched him, slack-jawed. "What did you just do?" she asked when the other girl was out of earshot.

"Gave her a strong suggestion. It'll keep her from experiencing the symptoms while she's going through withdrawal. I'll need to use a new suggestion every day until she's in the clear."

Luc sank into a chair. It would have been nice if Anna hadn't run off terrified of him. She would have witnessed him playing the hero; he could have used the brownie points.

11

"*I*'m here to visit Sara Johnson."

The receptionist looked up. Thick, dark-rimmed glasses perched on a beakish nose. Anna couldn't decide if the woman was going for *chic librarian* or *school marm*. A silver nameplate read, *Becky*.

Becky's eyes swept clinically over her. "Are you family?"

"I'm her cousin, Anna."

She held her breath hoping there wasn't a roster with a list of relatives. Or if there was one, that by coincidence there was an Anna in the family. She had to see with her own eyes what Luc had done to this girl. Her resolve where he was concerned was already starting to crumble.

"Anna Worthington?" Becky asked, checking a little box beside her name. "I'll need you to sign your check-in time right here. And then sign out when you leave." She indicated a line with an X beside it.

Anna signed the paper and logged her time, trying to shake the startled look from her face. Caroline must have called ahead on the chance she'd think to visit.

"Your friend will stay out here," Becky said curtly, indicating Tam.

Anna nodded and followed the tall woman down the hall to 212. It was a private room with a single window that seemed set apart from the rest of the world. A clean, protective bubble upon which reality couldn't intrude.

Sara had long, chestnut hair, much like her mother's. It stood out starkly against the colorless cell. She sat on the floor in a white gown with fuzzy, pink socks on her feet. Sara looked up briefly, a vacant stare on her face, then back down at the little white table she was sitting at, stacking small blocks on top of each other.

She built for a few seconds until they fell over, then she gave a cry of dismay before starting the repetitive action again.

Becky shook her head. "I'm afraid she isn't going to be much of a talker. Her lucid moments are rare. She's probably had less than ten since she's been with us. She should be okay for a short visit. Just don't expect much." The woman closed the door quietly on her way out.

Not knowing what else to do, Anna sat on the edge of the bed, her hands folded in her lap. "I bought your house a couple of weeks ago, and I know what's in it."

Silence.

What had she been hoping to find or learn? This girl was clearly beyond communication. All it took was one look to learn all she needed to know about Luc. She stood to leave, feeling foolish for coming.

Sara turned sharply, her eyes meeting Anna's, the blank stare suddenly gone. There was a person in there, and she was awake.

Anna stared at the girl for a moment. "You're not crazy are you?" She blushed at her rudeness. The girl had caught her so off guard she hadn't been able to think of a more polite way to phrase it.

Sara shook her head, but remained at the table with her blocks. "Not for a long time. I guess you came to find out what happened?"

Anna glanced about, wishing there was anything for her eyes to settle on, something to distract her from the suddenly uncomfortable moment she'd found herself in. Whatever had happened to Sara wasn't really her business.

"It's okay," Sara said. "I don't mind sharing. I have the *lucid moments* sometimes just so I can have conversation. It's mind-numbingly boring pretending to be a lunatic all the time." She continued stacking the blocks and letting them fall, either to stay in practice, or for fear someone might come in the room.

"I know it's personal, but if you don't mind sharing, I'd be grateful to hear it." Anna sat back down while Sara took a deep breath and started her story.

"I was crazy at first. Then one day I just woke up, I guess. They took me to a doctor here in the hospital and ran a bunch of tests and asked me all these questions I couldn't answer. Then they talked about how many sessions I might need before I could go home.

"That scared me. I managed to find out I'd been in whatever state I'd been in for a few months, and Luc hadn't come after me. I was safe here, so I just started acting crazy and spaced out. Whatever I did, it worked because they stopped talking about releasing me. I've been pretending since then." The blocks clattered on the table again.

Anna started to open her mouth to speak, but Sara wasn't finished.

"Sometimes I talk to the catatonics when no one else is around, so I know I haven't forgotten how to speak." She got up from the table and plopped down on the floor, her long legs stretching out in front of her. "My dad used to touch me."

Anna's face must have shown shock because Sara laughed a little. "Yeah, not the story you were looking for, huh? I'm not looking for sympathy. It's important. We moved into the house, and my dad didn't seem as interested. I don't know what he'd gotten involved with to distract him, but I was glad for it. Then I started to feel this presence in my room. Eventually, Luc introduced himself. That's his name, right?"

Anna nodded, not sure if she wanted to hear more but unable to ask her to stop.

"Good. I would hate if everything had been a lie. We talked. About me mostly. He listened a lot. Then we started sleeping together. A couple of times a week after my parents went to bed, he would come to me. He told me what he was. I didn't know anything really about incubi until I looked them up on the Internet in the school library.

"I found out they often killed their victims, not that I'd felt like a victim up until that point with Luc. I tried to tell myself, maybe he wasn't all bad. I liked him. He made me feel good, like maybe he could erase the stuff my dad had done, you know? Then one night when we were together I looked up, and he didn't look like Luc anymore. He looked like every stereotype of a demon you could think of. Sometimes I still have nightmares."

She paused and sat silently for a few minutes as if doing this much talking at once was too much for her. Anna stayed quiet, afraid if she interrupted she'd break the spell.

"I knew I was about to die. I guess with everything that had happened it was all just too much. I must have just snapped or something. The next thing I remember, I was here and had doctors telling me I'd been out of it." She shrugged.

Anna felt the need to put Sara's mind at ease. "He's trapped in the house. It's a curse. He can't get out." She was beginning to think Luc being trapped was a good thing. Maybe she should move into her father's estate and keep the house on Cranberry Lane empty. Assuming she could withstand the burning from the scar at that distance. Knowing what went bump in the night, she was too scared to get the mark removed.

Sara's eyes shot up to hers. "No. I didn't know. He never said anything like that. I thought he just came to visit me sometimes."

"If I have anything to do with it, he'll be trapped forever. You should try to get out of here. Start your life. If you need some help financially, just call me."

Sara looked uncomfortable. "Oh, no. I couldn't take your money."

"You may have saved my life. You can't put a price tag on that. I need to ask one more thing. Did he ever try to bind you to him in any way? Like with a blood ritual?" Anna held out her hand, revealing the scar.

Sara shook her head, her eyes widening. "No. He never did anything like that." Her voice lowered to a whisper. "Get out of that house."

ANNA SPENT THE NIGHT AT TAM'S AGAIN, REFUSING TO ANSWER questions about what had happened at the sanitarium. She was coming down the stairs from her shower when she heard her friend speaking in hushed tones on the phone.

"I thought you'd want to know where she was . . . Yeah, she's fine. She wouldn't tell me what happened . . . Okay . . . Okay . . . Yes . . . Okay . . . Well, I just didn't want you to worry . . . Yes, Goodnight."

"Hey," Anna said, still wringing water from her hair.

Tam jumped, a guilty expression painting her face. "Hey! You ready to watch the movie?"

Anna crossed her arms over her chest. "Who were you on the phone with?"

"Anna . . . "

The look on Tam's face confirmed her suspicions. Luc. "I think I'm suddenly out of the mood for a girl's night. I'm going to bed."

"Anna, wait!"

She marched up the stairs without waiting for Tam's explanation and slammed the bathroom door behind her. The noise of the hair dryer on full blast drowned out her friend's voice on the other side.

What had Luc done? Put Tam under some kind of thrall? Turned her into his spider-eating zombie? Great amount of willpower she had. Apparently love and true friendship could overcome any obstacle but an incubus. When her hair was dry, she stepped into the bedroom, unsurprised to find Tam sitting on the edge of the guest bed.

"I thought he'd be worried. He cares about you and deserved to know where you were."

"No he doesn't *deserve* anything. He's a demon. He's evil. If you'd heard Sara's story, you'd know that, and you wouldn't be going behind my back betraying me."

"Well you wouldn't tell me what happened!"

Anna furiously pulled the brush through her hair. "Because it's private. I'm not going to betray her confidence. Believe me when I tell you, Luc is a bad guy. I don't need you going *Renfield* on me and reporting back to your master."

"Oh my God. You've completely gone over the edge. Yes, I felt loopy around him at first, and I don't doubt he was doing some kind of mind thing . . . but I felt it. This is not that.

"You might want to ignore the witch thing," she continued, her voice rising, "but I *am* a witch, and I don't get the same vibe off him that I do off other demons. I'm sorry about the way you feel, but I'm not sorry I didn't let the poor man worry all night."

"Are you finished?" Anna asked.

"Yes."

"Then I'm going to sleep."

. . .

. . . Anna felt Luc's anger as a man moved toward one of the upstairs bedrooms of her house. The stranger fell hard on the floor and looked around, startled. Luc had gone invisible as he looked down at the waste of flesh lying, trembling, in the middle of the hallway.

"Harold, honey, come to bed."

Caroline Johnson poked her head out of a bedroom, wearing a diaphanous white nightgown. Luc felt a pang of hunger shoot through him and licked his lips, tempted to take a ride on the asshole's woman.

Harold grumbled, but got up and went toward the other bedroom. He looked back once more in Luc's direction, his eyes searching the hall for evidence of the thing that had blocked his path. Luc growled under his breath just loud enough for the man to hear and quicken his retreat.

When Harold disappeared behind the bedroom door, Luc slipped into the room he'd been guarding.

"Dad?" the girl asked.

"No." Luc sat in the chair next to the bed. He'd been doing this for awhile, usually going through the wall to watch her. He couldn't stand her not knowing she was safe from that bastard. But she was starting to sense his presence, and he didn't want her to be afraid of him, too. He switched the lamp on and materialized.

She tilted her head to the side, no fear evident on her features. "Are you an angel?"

He chuckled. "I've told that lie before, but something tells me you're too old and too smart to fall for it." He brushed her hair out of her face, wanting so badly to taste her. No. Cain brought dinner. This wasn't dinner. She was under his protection.

The scene kept changing, almost too fast for Anna to track. Each scene showed Harold trying to get to his daughter and Luc stopping him. Both men were like determined terriers pissing over territory. Slowly, Sara became too much of a temptation for the demon.

The scene shifted again. Luc kissed the side of Sara's throat as they made love. He took gentle tugs of her energy, feeding, being careful not to take too much. This one mattered to him.

He'd told himself over and over she was too young, but she was the age of consent, and hadn't he fucked much younger back when times were different? Her soft sighs and whimpers were driving him over the edge. Waiting for it to be safe to feed from her again was becoming more maddening each time, but he'd do whatever he had to, to keep her safe.

His heightened sense of hearing picked up the dull, flat throb of footsteps coming down the hall. The bastard just would not give up. Well, neither would Luc. The door opened and the light flicked on.

The incubus whirled in anger, a searing heat flowing through him as his true form came forward, sending Harold fleeing down the hallway in hysterics. Luc turned, unable to pull his demonic visage back. Sara looked into his eyes, a mask of terror frozen on her face. And then he couldn't reach her.

Anna was ripped away to another, more recent scene. Luc's rage boiled as the change rippled over his skin. He used every ounce of control to remain invisible.

Anna's cries had pulled him out of his self-indulgent stupor. He'd made it to the landing when he saw her being dragged by her ankle down into the living room. She couldn't have known safety was upstairs, but for a moment he imagined she'd been running to him for his protection.

Protection he sure as fuck planned to deliver on, whether she was aware of its existence or not. A growl slipped from his throat as he tore down the stairs and ripped the motherfucker off her.

He wanted to verbally threaten him, needed to, wanted to ask him what right he had to come into his house and terrorize her. But he couldn't think straight enough for language. All he could manage was a litany of snarls and growls as he sliced the man up.

Luc had the presence of mind to stop before he killed him. He couldn't leave a body for her to have to dispose of or explain away. He had to leave the fucker breathing. For now.

The scene shifted again. Luc sat at the kitchen table, the rage still simmering, the heat still prickling along his skin. He was still too angry to change back. Luc hated scaring her, but he couldn't let her see him. He watched as she huddled in the corner with the candlestick in her hand.

---

12

*B*y the following morning, Anna and Tam had come to an uneasy truce. When they walked into the house on Cranberry Lane, Anna blinked, sure she was hallucinating.

The kitchen island held a large buffet spread. Croissant sandwiches, pancakes, eggs, fruit, English muffins, biscuits, and gravy. Suddenly she was very hungry. All Tam had at her house, besides popcorn, was coffee.

The harem sat around the table chattering and eating. Anna felt left out in her own home. It wasn't like it was easy to strike up conversation with the women who were sleeping with her man.

Strike that. Not her man. Never her man. Not a man, period. Demon. He was Luc, and he wasn't quite the level of evil she'd thought he was, but he couldn't be hers. They could be friends, that was all. Yes, he was hot, and they had banter or whatever. But it ended there. The alternatives of sharing him or losing her soul weren't options she was prepared to entertain. Ever.

"You ladies look hungry." Luc untied his apron and laid it across the counter. "The girls slept in, and I thought brunch would be nice."

It was easy to forget blood rituals, growling, and shapeshifting when he was doing his master chef routine.

"Oh," Anna said, forgetting her manners. "Tam, this is the harem."

"Anna! Don't call them that!" Tam said, looking horrified.

"It's okay. It's true, we *are* the harem," Karen said with a shrug.

"Yeah, I like the word. It makes me think of sultans and all those gauzy veils and stuff," Renee said, adding her two cents. The other girls giggled and went back to trying to decipher their crossword puzzle.

"We should have gotten the word circle thing. I hate these. They always use weird words no one knows," Olivia said. Susan and Maria both grunted noncommittally, engrossed in painting their nails a color that should have been called *hooker red*. Endorsed by prostitutes everywhere.

Luc handed Anna a glass of orange juice, avoiding eye contact. If that was because of the whole, *hey, I'm sleeping with the whole world* thing, Anna was over it. Really. He couldn't change what he was. And if she wasn't going to sleep with him, it wasn't her business. He was just her roommate. She had no claim on him.

"What did you do?" Anna asked when the guilt didn't leave his face. It couldn't be too bad. He hadn't killed anyone. There were still five hookers sitting in her kitchen having breakfast.

Luc busied himself fixing plates for Tam and Anna. "Um . . . well, you see . . . I'm trapped in the house, and incubi as I'm sure you're aware, have little need for money . . . There are five ladies here. And there was no food except for leftover Chinese which I believe is growing a fur coat, and some cookies and ice cream and I . . . stoleyourcreditcard."

"You what?"

He sighed and finally looked into her eyes, a sheepish expression on his face. "I sent Susan and Maria to the store with your card to buy food. It was a bit extravagant, I admit, but I'm cooking now. See?" He held out the plates like a peace offering. "You'll eat much better than you ever have before." He smiled a little too brightly as he waited for them to take the offered food.

Anna snorted. She couldn't help it. That smile looked severely weird on Luc. He should stick to the smirking bad boy thing he had going on. Not that he could simultaneously maintain *bad boy* and *master chef*, but everybody needed something to aspire to. She couldn't deal with *petty breakfast theft* Luc. He was too surreal.

"Of course I don't mind. Thank you for doing it." She surprised herself by kissing him on the cheek.

His mouth hung open. "Anna?"

"I had another dream. I was wrong about you. I'm sorry."

"Yes, well, don't get too comfortable. I'm sure you'll have another nightmare and be back to the hysterics in no time." He set to work scrubbing a pot so hard, she was sure he'd take the Teflon coating right off it.

Anna lowered her voice so the others couldn't overhear. "I said I was sorry. I know there's more to you than I thought there was. Okay? Can't you just accept that at face value?"

He stood stiffly, working to maintain his ire as he continued to take his aggression out on the cookware. Finally, his shoulders relaxed, and he nodded. "What did you see?"

Anna recounted the dream.

His eyes rose quickly to meet hers. "Did you see me?"

She knew he was asking if she'd seen his demon form. "It doesn't work that way. I can't actually *see* you. I see through your eyes, feel your thoughts and emotions. Thank God I don't physically feel everything you do, because gotta say, I don't swing that way. I've seen more naked females than I ever cared to. That's plenty up close and personal for me."

He smirked, the relief evident on his face. *How bad can his true form be?* Obviously bad if a bright and together girl like Sara had ended up in the looney bin, and Luc had decided it was preferable to let Anna cower in a corner rather than allow her to see him. She shivered as her eyes drifted to the corner in question.

Then she noticed how quiet the room had gotten. "Something wrong?"

"You ask them," Karen said, nudging Olivia.

"We thought, I mean, we understand why you brought us here, and it was really nice of you and all ... "

"You're kidding, right?" She didn't consider bringing women to her house to service Luc to be a *nice* thing to do. "This is horribly ... I have no words for it. I've tried to justify it a thousand times in my head, but all I can think is that I'm doing something wrong and dirty. At the same time I can't bring myself to let him starve, either. I'm going to Hell." She sank into one of the chairs and put her head in her hands.

"No!" They all began protesting at once.

"Are you kidding me?" Maria asked. "This is the first time I've felt safe in a long time. And you're putting us up here, and feeding us. And it's not like sleeping with Luc is a trial."

Anna blushed and looked around for the demon's reaction, but he'd slipped out of the room. Karen cleared her throat and kicked Maria hard under the table.

"What? Ow! Anyway," she said, glaring at the blonde, "we asked Luc what he thought we could do to pay you back for all your kindness."

Olivia picked it back up. "Yes, we were wondering if we could help with the candle stuff. We could make a lot more, all of us together. And you'd have plenty to sell by the weekend."

Tam shrugged. "I don't see why not."

Anna wasn't sure she was comfortable turning them into her indentured servants, but she wasn't taking a cut of the profits. Maybe Tam could pay them. They were only trying to help after all.

"This is going to be so fun!" Susan said.

Anna had her doubts about that. She avoided the knowing look in Karen's eyes. Was it that obvious? Did Anna have a sign on her head that said, *Here, sleep with Luc. I wish it was me, but I'm too damn uptight?*

Tam steamrolled over the tension by getting straight to business. "Since we've got so much help, we're going to need more supplies. I'll stay here with Maria and Susan to clean up. You can walk with the others to the craft shop." She pulled a slim notebook from her purse, jotted down a quick list, and handed it to Anna.

"I don't know what half of this stuff is," Anna groused. "Wouldn't it make more sense if I cleaned my own kitchen and you went to the store?"

Tam smiled sweetly. "If we're going to work together, we both need to be comfortable. I need to be comfortable with the kitchen, and you need to be comfortable with the supply list. Get the store clerk to help you."

Anna was about to protest further, but Tam had already started straightening the kitchen. She sighed and followed the girls out the back door.

Once outside, she felt like the odd woman out at a Barbie doll convention, with her long dark hair, flanked by perky bottle blondes. And they *were* perky.

She wasn't sure if it was being in Luc's presence or leaving their old lives behind them, but they'd quickly come alive, and Anna was starting to feel something like jealousy. Why couldn't she be like them and share him? Wasn't a small bit of Luc better than no Luc? Judging from the extra bounce in their steps, she was pretty sure it was.

Anna stiffened as Bitsy and Mimi and their yappy dog approached. They were running behind schedule on their daily walk.

"Well, hello dear. And who are these young ladies?" Mimi asked.

Her voice was all politeness and drippy syrup, but Anna could see the disapproval in her shrewd eyes.

The girls tensed beside her, as if they thought she'd introduce them as a harem or hookers. It was one thing in the house, but she would never . . . Then again, maybe they were reacting to the predatory looks on the sisters' faces.

The lie tripped off her tongue easily. "These are my sorority sisters from college. They're staying with me for a while. This is Karen, Olivia, and Renee."

She was painfully aware of how out of place they must look, walking down the street together. Anna in her usual jeans and t-shirt, her long, wavy hair hanging loose down her back, surrounded by three girls with too-blonde hair and mini skirts.

Thankfully, they'd left the fishnets at home. Despite their attempts to clean it up, miniskirts just didn't fly in Golatha Falls. Hell, skirts two inches above the knee didn't pass inspection. Anna had a flashback to Catholic school and the dollar bill test, the excruciating and demeaning ritual meant to determine they hadn't rolled their skirts up at the waist.

"Don't you think you're wearing just a touch too much makeup for the morning hours, dear?" Bitsy said, deciding to pick on Renee first.

"And those skirts . . . honestly. I know college can be wild, but you're grown women now. You shouldn't be walking around looking like streetwalkers," Mimi said.

Renee drew herself up to her full imposing height and stared Mimi down. "Maybe we *are* streetwalkers. Do you have a problem with that?"

The sisters were too shocked to speak. The dog barked hysterically at the blonde interlopers, sensing imminent danger.

"Yes," Karen said, "or maybe we come from a big city where dress codes are more relaxed than stuck up little towns."

Olivia put the icing on. "Puce is not your very best color. You should get one of those color tests done. They do them free at the mall now. And matching outfits for twins? Even a streetwalker knows *that* look is over."

"Well, I never . . . " Bitsy said, clutching her sister as if the girls posed a germ threat, and they just needed to get to the safety of a pay phone to call in the CDC.

"Yes, and you never will," Karen said, leading Renee and Olivia around the two old women.

Bitsy and Mimi stood there, their poodle weaving in and out of their legs.

"Anna, really. Those girls are just . . . surely you must have better company to spend your time with than that . . . trash."

"Actually, I enjoy the company just fine," Anna said. "Have a nice day ladies." She brushed past them, and glanced back over her shoulder. "And Olivia was right about the suits."

She knew she was going to pay for that little scene later when the mob came to her house with the torches and pitchforks. Maybe the harem wasn't so bad. She could be friends with these girls.

"Why aren't you sleeping with Luc?" Olivia blurted when she'd caught up to them.

Or maybe not. Anna flushed bright red. "Because. I don't want to," she said lamely.

"Why not?" Renee pressed, as if it was the weirdest thing Anna could possibly think to say. "I mean, I haven't yet, but Olivia has, and she said . . . "

Karen, seeming to be the only one of the girls with any tact at all, stepped in. "Renee! She doesn't want to talk about it. I'm so sorry about that, Anna."

Renee was unperturbed. "But why wouldn't you want to? I mean, look at him. He's so . . . and he cooks. And he's sweet. And he likes you. He can't help what he is." Her eyes narrowed with suspicion. "You think you're better than him, don't you? Because of what he does."

Anna shifted, suddenly uncomfortable. This was getting into personal territory for them. They felt a kinship toward Luc, and if she wasn't careful she'd have to fight off his crazed protectors. "It's not like that. I just don't see him that way." *Good, Anna. Say the lie out loud enough times, and it'll start feeling true. Any second now.*

"Bullshit," Olivia said. "You're just scared to get your heart broken. He wouldn't just be a good lay to you. He'd be more. And he is . . . a good lay," she clarified, as if clarification was necessary.

"Stop talking about him like he's a piece of meat!" Anna said, falling over the sanity ledge. She was going to have a breakdown if they didn't stop treating him like their paid escort.

"So you *do* care." A satisfied smile spread across Olivia's lips as if it had all been a plan to bait Anna into some honesty.

"Oh look, we're here!" Anna said. She'd never been so happy to see a craft store.

Luc leaned against the door frame watching Anna's friend fluttering about the kitchen. She looked like a little pixie with her delicate elfin features and glitter-filled hair. Susan and Maria were standing back as well, no doubt trying to stay out of her way.

He cleared his throat, causing all three of the women to jump. "I don't think so," he said.

Tam's hand froze. She'd been laying craft supplies out on the kitchen table. "Excuse me?" she said, off-balance.

"You heard me. Do you understand that every piece of furniture in this house is a priceless antique? This particular table, for example, is over a hundred years old and hand-carved."

She stood there gaping at him like a fish. Finally, she came up with something intelligent to say. "This is Anna's house."

He allowed the glow to come to his eyes, and she took a step back. "No, this is *my* house. Anna is just the one with the paperwork. But I'm the only one who can't be removed, forcibly or otherwise. That makes it mine."

Tam moved behind the table, putting one of his priceless antiques between them, betting he wouldn't go after the furniture to get to her. Smart girl. Susan and Maria seemed to be practicing the forgotten art of pretending to be wallpaper.

The level of fear in the room was prodding at his darker urges like a little fork. He let out a low growl for effect and chuckled when all three of them jumped again. Susan and Maria's wallpaper act needed work.

"I'm feeling very cranky," he said. "And when I get cranky, I get hungry. Who wants to volunteer?"

The little witch seemed to snap out of her panic. "I called you last night because I felt sympathy for you. Now you're being a gigantic ass. Do you know how much groveling it took this morning to get my friendship with Anna back on track?"

Mentioning Anna caused him to regain focus. *What the hell am I doing?* He wasn't used to so many attractive females in such a closed-in space. It was like a starving person suddenly being transplanted to the middle of a buffet. It was fucking with his head. And he couldn't get out of the house to escape them and all their girlie smells and hormones and arousal.

Just being an incubus, even without actively using the mind tricks, females seemed to just melt in his presence. It was hard to remember he had to be civilized and couldn't act on every base urge that flitted through his head anymore.

Anna wouldn't like it. He'd never gain her trust if he couldn't maintain self-control. "I apologize. But you can't put that wax and stuff on the table. You'll destroy it."

Before Tam could protest further, he disappeared into the guest bathroom down the hall and returned, his arms full of bath towels.

Tam held up a hand. "Oh, no. You think you're crazy about your furniture, Anna will freak if we hurt her fluffy towels."

He arched a brow. "And which one of us is scarier?"

13

*A*nna glared at Tam as she dropped her bags on the kitchen table. "You and I will have words later," she hissed.

"Why? What happened?"

Anna was momentarily distracted by Luc. The kitchen table had been pushed against one wall, and he was dragging the dining room table in to join it. The effort seemed to be causing him physical pain.

"Luc?" Surely a table wasn't too heavy for a demon to lift, even one as large and ornate as this one.

He glowered. "Tam said she needed more space to work on. But you listen to me . . . we are covering the surface with your bath towels. I don't want to hear one word about it. This table should not be used to make handicrafts on."

Anna glanced away to hide her smile. She'd thought it would be hard to look him in the eyes after spending the morning shopping with the harem, but he had that funny way of disarming her.

"So help me, Anna, if you laugh I will blister your ass."

She lost the smile. He hadn't just said that. And no, she was *not* going to fantasize about what he hadn't just said. *Bad, Anna.*

"I wasn't going to laugh." *Plan B. Ignore all innuendo. Do not respond. Do not engage. Check.*

"Then what was the smile about?"

"You. With the cleaning up Chinese food and wiping off the mirror. I thought you were just being creepy and ghostly, but you're an antiques fiend. You couldn't stand anything getting messed up."

Instead of denying the accusation, he shrugged. "So?"

"I don't know why you're protecting it. If I burn the house down it's all going to be ashes anyway."

He cringed, no doubt imagining all the beautiful antiques going up in flames along with that gorgeous banister.

"WHAT?" the girls shrieked. They stopped what they were doing and gawked at the couple.

"Luc wants me to burn down the house, to break the curse that has him trapped."

"But you can't! You can't even be thinking about it!" Renee was near panic.

"I wouldn't turn you out on the streets," Anna said, assuming that was the reason for the freak-out. She'd taken them in; she wasn't heartless enough to just throw them back to their pimps. That would be worse than bringing them there in the first place. The current set-up was starting to feel less sleazy and more *Pretty Woman*, but with an ensemble cast.

"No, that's not it," Susan said. "We'd be okay, but please tell me you aren't thinking of burning this house down."

"I'm not. We'll find another way."

"Then what happens? When we get him out?" Karen asked.

"I don't know." Anna hadn't thought that far ahead.

For the briefest of moments, she entertained the idea of never letting him leave. *Stop being crazy. You can't even bring yourself to sleep with him.* But the thought of the big, beautiful house with no Luc inside made her feel cold. Could she bring herself to stay without him there?

"I hate to say it," Tam said, "but freeing Luc is going to be like getting a middle-aged man out of his mother's basement. Do you even know where to start?"

"I thought about calling the archbishop, seeing if they could bring someone higher up in. Maybe that would make a difference. And I made an appointment with some paranormal investigators I saw on TV. They'll be here tomorrow"

"I could just call the coven," Tam said.

"No!" Both Luc and Anna shouted at once.

"I'm just saying. A witch started this mess. Maybe other witches can undo it."

"Thank you, Tam, but no," Anna said.

Tam had been claiming to be a witch since high school. Anna had thought it was a phase. When her friend didn't grow out of it, she decided it would be the thing no one acknowledged, like the uncle who farts when company comes over.

With evidence right in front of her of not only demons but witches, well, she liked to keep pretending she had a normal life. If Tam started breaking out the pointy hats, she didn't know how long she could maintain that fantasy.

Maria cleared her throat. "No one is talking about it . . . but I *do* have gypsy blood. And I have relatives who are full Romani. I haven't spoken to that side of the family in awhile, but I'm sure that . . ."

Anna looked at Luc and shrugged. "Gypsies aren't witches."

"Yes, but Gypsies aren't traditionally good news for my kind either."

"What do you have against witches?" Tam said. "It's not like I hex people."

Anna turned back to Luc. He was making her brain fuzzy. The scar on her hand tingled pleasantly, as if happy to be so close to him.

"We really have to try something. If we aren't going with the coven, we should at least try the gypsies," Anna said.

"Fine," he grumbled. "But I'm putting your fluffy bath towels on the dining room table." The look in his eyes dared her to challenge him.

"Luc!"

"It's fluffy bath towels or no gypsies. You keep them in the guest bath anyway."

"So?"

An arched eyebrow.

"Fine. Take my fluffy towels." She thought she might cry.

. . . LUC SAT IN THE MIDDLE OF THE LIVING ROOM FLOOR STARING OFF into space. The house was deathly still except for a constant, irritating drip from a leaky faucet in the kitchen. He made no move to shut it off.

He hadn't fed in weeks. All he could think was that she was gone, and it was his fault. He heard the back door fly open. It wasn't a woman. He would have known instantly if it were a woman. If it wasn't food, there was no point wasting any more strength. Without food or means of escape, immortality became a true curse for the first time.

Footsteps stopped in front of him.

"Luc, my God. What's happened to you?" Cain said.

"I killed her. She was right there for two whole days." Tears streamed down his cheeks as he pointed to an empty spot on the couch.

Cain's eyes were wide, his face filled with horror and disgust. "Why on earth are you crying?"

As if Cain had the right to be disgusted. He had no soul, not the slightest bit of empathy. "Why wouldn't I cry? I killed her. I loved her, and I killed her."

The other demon's jaw clenched. "Why haven't you left this place?"

"I can't leave." Luc didn't have the energy yet to explain about the magic. He couldn't rid himself of the image of Beatrice's lifeless eyes staring up at him. *All my fault. All my fucking fault.* "They finally found her and took her out. She was still pretty."

Cain ran a hand through his hair and took a deep breath as if trying to gather a tsunami of patience. "Why can't you leave?"

"Trapped. She didn't want me to leave her . . . trapped me."

Cain grabbed an unresponsive Luc by the arm and dragged him to the door. He tried pushing him out, but the magic smacked against Luc, sending a shock of pain through his body.

The other incubus took Luc's face in his hands and stared hard into his eyes. "Snap out of it! She was a witch. Goddammit! I knew something was wrong with you. I should never have left you here."

Luc jerked out of his grasp and started to pace. Anna stared out from inside him, wanting to back away from Cain.

Luckily, Luc needed to rest against the wall, and moved, getting both of them out of the other demon's immediate sphere. The only thing keeping her from screaming to wake up was the reassurance that Cain couldn't hurt her.

"Luc, you have to listen to me. She's using the same mind tricks our kind have used for thousands of years. She made you want her, made you care for her. It's *not* real. None of this is real!" Cain swiped his hand over the mantel, breaking half a dozen knick knacks. Luc didn't even twitch.

"Doesn't matter. I feel it. It doesn't matter what she did. It's done now. I can't stop seeing her face."

Cain growled in frustration. "You need to feed. I'll be back. We'll find a way to get you out of here."

Anna wanted to leave. She wanted the scene to shift like it always did. She wanted to wake up. Anything to no longer be swamped by Luc's anguish.

Why wouldn't the scene change? She was gripped with panic that she'd be trapped forever in this time and place with him. She couldn't stand it. Anna never thought she'd be so happy to see Cain return.

"Here, this one's already under." Cain shoved a very willing female at Luc. He ravaged her mindlessly as she moaned and writhed beneath him.

"Yes, oh yes," she cried.

He felt the life slipping from her, and his mind screamed at him. *No No. You have to stop. Stop right now. Stop.* But he was too hungry. Her little pants of *yes* kept goading him on.

Cain had two other girls, holding them each by one wrist, his grip punishing as they struggled.

Luc flung the girl away, his self-disgust raging through him at having taken another life. He didn't want to kill anyone now. The witch had unlocked his long-forgotten human emotion, and now that the floodgates had been opened they could never be resealed.

Cain stepped forward with the second girl. She was under his thrall now and clawed at him, begging him to satisfy her needs.

"Come on, now. You want to please me don't you?" Cain said, his voice a seductive purr.

"Yes, please," she whimpered, trying to unbutton his shirt.

"Then go to my friend. He's very lonely."

The girl detached herself from Cain and stalked Luc as if she were the predator instead of the prey, and Luc went through the motions. The edges of his hunger slowly abated, but he couldn't stop in time as the life left the second girl.

Cain was about to put the last one under.

"Don't," Luc said. "No more."

Cain sighed and shook his head. "One more, Luc. I'm sorry for what's been done to you. You shouldn't feel bad killing them, but we'll fix it. Until we do, the more you feed the less likely you are to kill."

Cain was right. Of course he was right.

"Don't put her under. Let me." Luc hated the way his brother turned them into zombies and had never done it himself. He'd have to now. You couldn't seduce a woman who'd just watched you kill her friends. He closed his eyes and breathed slowly, focusing on what he needed to do.

When his eyes opened and settled on the target, he allowed his mind to touch the edges of hers, enough that her body relaxed. But there was still awareness in her eyes.

Cain released his grip, and she slunk toward Luc. She was trembling and trying not to go to him.

"Don't play with your food," Cain said.

Luc growled. "I'm not playing. I need to talk to her first."

"Please don't kill me," she whispered, her eyes brimming with tears.

"I'll try my very best not to. I have to put you under. If I can't stop, know that I'm sorry, and it won't hurt." Then her eyes glazed over, and she was willing in his arms.

He fucked and fed, feeling more in control this time. He was fully alert when he pulled away. She blinked as she came out of it, surprised to be alive.

"Sleep," he said. Luc stood and passed her unconscious form to Cain. "Take her home."

"As much as I am trying to appreciate how you feel, this is a lost cause. Even if she remembers tonight as a dream, when her friends turn up missing she's going to know. She won't make it through this. It would be a mercy to kill her. I'll do it if you don't want to."

"No. She's strong. She'll make it."

Cain shrugged. "Whatever you say. I'll take her back and clean up here." He indicated the two bodies on the floor. "Then I'm going to bring you a couple more."

"No more. I'm done."

"Just to be sure. I'm trying to support this new feeding pattern. If you don't get enough, tomorrow you'll just kill someone else."

Luc nodded and slid down the wall until he was sitting on the floor again. The sea of conflicted emotions overwhelmed Anna. Then the blackness engulfed her.

*a*nna sipped her coffee while a leftover biscuit and some gravy heated in the microwave. Her foot tapped nervously on the kitchen tile as she read the same paragraph of the paper for the third time. When she managed to stop her foot, her hand started shaking. She needed a steady hand to drink coffee, so the tapping would have to be coped with. The microwave dinged and she jumped, almost spilling the hot beverage.

Luc appeared then. "Are you all right?" He propped himself against the counter and observed her. How long had he been there?

"Fine," she lied. But the tapping wouldn't stop. It had been a nervous tick since childhood. She poured the gravy over her biscuit and started cutting it into little triangles.

She chanced a glance to see a troubled expression knitting Luc's brow as he tried to decipher what she was thinking.

"Anna, please. What is going on?"

"You could just read my mind if you wanted to know so badly."

"No, I can't."

"But you have the thrall thing."

"I can touch emotions and send thoughts and images. That's different. I'm getting fear from you, but I don't know why."

He crossed the kitchen to sit in the chair beside her and placed a hand on her knee. "Anna, stop. Tell me what's wrong."

"I just need to know, okay? I won't be mad."

"Know what?"

"I had another dream last night, and it made me think about the first night with Cain here. Those times when you were in my dreams, were they really dreams or do I just remember them that way? Did you really . . . ?"

"No, I didn't touch you. Why would you think that?" He seemed hurt by the suggestion.

She moved his hand from her knee and backed her chair away. Being too close to him made it hard to think, and she wondered if he was using the thrall just a little bit to make her more pliant. After all, it didn't always have to be as strong as what Cain used. She knew that now.

"I just . . . you do it with other people and don't seem to have a problem with it."

"I don't do mind thrall. That's Cain's thing. Even when I was more evil, I didn't do it. It's like cheating. I prefer to hunt, to seduce a meal fair and square."

She still wasn't ready to let it drop. The issue was too important. "You did it once. And you do it after you feed."

His eyes lit with recognition as it occurred to him what exactly she'd dreamed about. "I had to that time. I was starving. And yes, I do the tricks afterward, but only as a security measure. What's to stop someone else from finding another way to hex me? I'm a sitting duck while I'm here. I have to protect who and what I am. With you, it's different. I need you to know about me to break the curse. There's no need to use those tricks on you."

He traced his index finger down her cheek, and something in

him seemed to shift. "Do you know how hard it is? To not take what's mine?"

Anna wanted to deny she was his. She wasn't. He didn't have her heart. But cracks were forming in the walls she'd built around herself. At some point, tears started flowing down her cheeks.

Luc edged his chair closer to hers. His hand stroked soothingly through her hair as he murmured reassuring words in her ear. Anna's arms looped around his neck, and she laid her head against his chest. She couldn't stop the dam now that it had broken.

She was overwhelmed with the memories from the dream, the things he'd had to endure all because of a curse placed on him by a spoiled, selfish witch.

Luc's head was bent against hers as he spoke. "I know you loved Vince. I'm sorry he couldn't commit to you. But I'm not him. Just because things look similar on the surface, doesn't mean . . . "

She raised her mouth to his and kissed him. She had to, to shut him up. She didn't want to think about Luc being inside her dreams the way she was in his, knowing things about her previous relationships. Despite her best intentions, they were becoming more tightly entwined. She didn't want to think about any of it, and if he kept talking, she would.

"Anna," he murmured against her mouth.

She could feel herself falling farther into a pit she wouldn't be able to claw her way out of. The only thing she'd end up with was a broken heart. If she managed to survive him at all. She couldn't share him with the harem but she couldn't seem to stop kissing him either. She wanted this to be real.

The doorbell rang, and she pulled away, thankful for the interruption. Anything to stop her before clothes started hitting the floor.

Luc kissed her palm, and she pulled it away to go answer the door. Her hand tingled where his lips had brushed over the scar.

A sound like loud music blared out as she reached the front door. "What the hell is that?" Luc asked, just behind her.

Anna pulled back the curtain to reveal a white van with a cartoon haunted house on the side. *Haunt Enders* was painted in bright red lettering beside it along with a phone number and a slogan that was too far away to read.

The sound in question happened again. Anna looked more closely at the driver's side. Someone was laying on the steering wheel.

"That's the car horn." Anna smacked a hand over her forehead. The sound they'd just heard was part of the *Ghostbusters* theme.

"This is gonna be fun," she said with an eye roll as she opened the door

"We're here about the haunting."

The guy standing on the porch couldn't have been more than twenty. He was short with thick glasses, unruly dirty blond hair, and a pocket protector. Forces of darkness beware. He looked like he'd decided D&D was so much fun he wanted to live out his gaming exploits for real.

Anna stepped aside. "Come on in." Luc stood beside her but had made himself invisible, at least to anyone who wasn't her. He was also non-corporeal since the guy walked right through him, then shivered.

"Ah . . . there's a cold spot right here," he said, already pleased with his findings. "My assistants will be here in a minute. They had to get supplies out of the van. I'm Dale, by the way. We spoke on the phone." He extended a hand to Anna.

"Nice to meet you." She was already having doubts. A man thrilled by slight temperature variations didn't seem promising. She'd already told him the house was haunted and she needed help getting the ghost out. She wasn't trying to assemble a case for Luc's existence to present in court.

Moments later the other two joined him. Frank was tall and

lanky, with adult acne, black hair, and navy blue eyes. Lonna was an attractive, leggy, redheaded woman in a short skirt. Frank and Dale seemed unfazed by her charms.

Luc showed no apparent interest in Lonna, either. Something which relieved Anna. She didn't know why it mattered, but it would have bothered her if he wanted every female who crossed the threshold. Maybe he just wasn't hungry.

As if on cue, Susan glided into the room, a pleasantly sated look on her face. She wore a pink terrycloth bathrobe, her hair was wild and mussed, and the look on her face said, *I had amazing sex last night. Don't you wish you did?* She collapsed onto the couch and part of the robe slid back to reveal a long expanse of thigh.

"These the ghost people?" she asked.

Frank and Dale, who must have been vaccinated against Lonna, were gawking at Susan like she was a Christmas present all wrapped up for them. Anna looked to Luc again. She was irritated with her sudden need to watch his reaction for everything, but he was as unaffected by Susan as Susan probably was by most of the men she'd slept with for money.

She gave Anna a meaningful look, then excused herself to get dressed. Anna didn't want to be unkind, but she couldn't help feeling the production had been set up for her as part of the harem's new mission to get her in bed with Luc.

Frank and Dale snapped out of it and started setting up a bunch of machines. One of the items looked suspiciously like the ghost trapper contraptions from the movie they seemed desperate to emulate. If they thought they were putting Luc in a little steel box, this would not go well.

Lonna flitted around the room, taking temperature readings with a digital room thermometer. "Where all has the apparition been?"

Why did everyone keep asking that? What did it matter? Luc was in the house. He needed to be out of the house. Anna's life would be much less complicated once that happened. How did cataloging his favorite rooms help?

"Everywhere. He's been trapped for fifty years by a spell."

Lonna wandered out of the room with the thermometer.

Frank laughed. "You expect us to believe in witches?"

"You believe in ghosts, don't you?"

He shifted uncomfortably. "We just went on TV that one time for publicity. We aren't sure we're full-fledged believers yet. We investigate. We take a scientific approach and do not pass judgment on the phenomena we encounter."

Anna was pretty sure if there was a brochure, he'd just quoted the ad copy. Luc let loose with what Anna was sure was his calculated, evil laugh. She almost burst out laughing herself when Frank and Dale nearly jumped out of their skin. They might not be able to see him, but they could hear him. Anna turned to Luc, who just winked at her.

"Do you believe now?" she asked, crossing her arms over her chest.

Dale shifted gears. All at once he was pure professionalism. "Maybe you could tell us a bit about what's been happening here." He pulled a notepad from the black fanny pack around his waist, a pen from his pocket protector, and clicked on a recorder.

Anna took a deep breath. This was a waste of time. What were paranormal investigators going to do besides say, *Yes ma'am we believe there is activity of a potentially supernatural nature occurring in your house?*

"Well," she said, "it started small. Things being cleaned up behind me. Writing on the bathroom mirror. Then he beat a guy up in front of me and threw him out of the house."

"He?"

"Yes, he."

"How do you know it's a male?"

"I've seen him. And also, he's a demon, not a ghost." She'd

skipped that part on the phone, just wanting to get them to the house.

Dale visibly paled and turned the recorder off. He managed to collect himself. "So you just want us to try to get him out, right? Not prove he's here?"

"Right." Give that man a stuffed bear.

"Okay, well, I suppose we could summon him and talk to him."

As if on cue, Frank pulled a Ouija board out of his duffel bag. Luc made it across the floor in two strides, grabbed the box, and flung it out the door.

"Was that really necessary?" Anna asked.

"Yes. They were amusing for about five minutes, but they toy with things they know nothing about. You might as well put a large neon sign on the top of the house that says, *all evil beings camp out here.* I don't want that thing in here."

Anna shrugged and turned back to the investigators. "When a demon thinks it's a bad idea . . . "

Frank and Dale seemed ready for retirement. Lonna returned with a little notebook indicating her temperature readings.

"We just wanted to talk to him, try to reason with him to leave," Frank said.

"He's already right here. No summoning is required," Anna said. "And I told you, just asking him to leave won't work. He's been hexed by a witch."

"What did you expect us to be able to do?" Lonna asked, confused. "We don't know anything about spells."

"I don't know. I saw your ad, thought it was worth a try. But I see I was mistaken. Luc, thrall them."

The demon's eyes widened comically. "Come again?"

"You heard me. I mean, come on. A priest we can trust. These jokers? They don't even know what they're doing. They're just publicity hounds. You don't want this on the news, do you?"

He shrugged. "Very well. If you say so."

Luc appeared before them. Frank and Dale fainted. Lonna looked like she wanted to go to bed with him.

"Hey, ghostbuster, back off." Anna would be packing Lonna in a little steel box if the redheaded bimbo took one more step toward Luc.

When all three had been taken care of, Anna and the girls carried them out to the van. She leaned over the horn accidentally, causing a second recording to play through the loudspeaker. "Who ya gonna call?"

"Someone else," Anna muttered. She'd just wasted an entire morning.

Half an hour later the doorbell rang, as she'd known it would. It was Dale.

"We're here about the haunting."

Anna smiled brightly. "We managed to get him to leave on our own. Sorry to have brought you all the way out here."

An odd expression came over his face, then he shrugged and turned to go back to the van. Anna shut the door and sagged against it. Luc gave her an *I told you so* look.

"Don't say it," she said. "The gypsies are coming tomorrow. It can't be more lame than this attempt."

"This doesn't even count as an attempt," Luc countered. "And the priest was a lot more fun. These guys didn't give me very much to work with."

His eyes glowed as he stalked her, clearly intent on picking up where they'd left off in the kitchen.

"I need to get out of the house for awhile. Stuff to do," she mumbled, before slipping out the door and out of his reach. He let her go, but the look in his eyes said he wouldn't indulge her running from him for much longer.

15

*A*nna reached the coffee shop before she spotted Bitsy and Mimi. The two women turned away like they hadn't seen her. If she'd known that was all it would take to get rid of the Baker sisters, she would have gotten herself a gaggle of live-in hookers from the start.

As she continued down the sidewalk, a few people looked at her, then away, while others smiled and nodded, some of them giving her a thumbs up. Apparently the sisters had been hard at work making the rounds, and now the town was divided into two factions: those who supported the wearing of matching puce suits, and those who did not. Maybe it would make the paper.

She looked up to see Father Jeffries blazing a rapid trail in her direction, not paying attention to where he was going. She side-stepped quickly, managing to get out of his path just in time. He stopped on a dime and turned back to face her.

"Anna, I'm sorry, I was on my way to your house."

Frazzled didn't begin to describe the priest. His previously well-groomed hair shot out in all directions. The robes he wore had deep creases as if he'd slept in them.

"Come with me. I need to speak with you. It's of a most urgent nature." His eyes darted from side to side.

When Anna just stood there, he grabbed her by the arm and manhandled her back to the church. Every time she tried to speak, he shushed her. Whatever he had to say was either so sacred or so terrifying that it couldn't be spoken out in the open.

"Have a seat, please," he said when they finally reached his office. He shuffled through a pile of books on the desk until he found what he was looking for.

The book was thick with yellowed, uneven pages and bound in dark brown leather with gold leaf detailing on the edges. It looked ominous. Maybe it had come straight from the Vatican. Anna tried to picture Father Jeffries somehow getting the Pope to part with a secret volume they'd held hostage for centuries.

He opened the book to the proper page, and Anna was surprised to find it was painstakingly handwritten in English.

"I've been searching for something to help you since I left your house the other day. I happened across this book."

"How does one *happen* across a book like this?" Anna asked skeptically.

A sheepish look crossed his face. "Since you know about demons, you may as well know about the rest. It's not official ortho-doxy, though the clergy know. We've been sworn to secrecy, but your soul is a trifle more important than my oath."

Anna braced herself in her seat. She felt like Alice falling down the rabbit hole. This was a whole different Father Jeffries. This was a whole different world. She kept waiting to wake up. Two weeks ago she hadn't believed in anything. Now there were demons and witches, and priests with weird, magical-looking books.

Father Jeffries sighed. "There is more than one dimension."

Well, that was anticlimactic. "I thought the church was pretty clear on that already. There's supposed to be Heaven, Hell, Purga-tory, Limbo, and here."

The priest shook his head. "No. Purgatory and Limbo we made up. Well, not really. Purgatory and Hell are the same, but they aren't what you think. *This* is Hell. Where we are right now. There's here, Heaven, and then several other dimensions with different rules and regulations. This realm was once all there was. There were many gods, and they fought. The Hebrew god won and took over. The other gods created other dimensions that live alongside this one."

Anna was still too stuck on the *this is Hell* concept to bother with any of the rest. "Huh?"

"Many demon breeds have their own dimensions as well. This book wasn't available here. I got it from a contact in a neighboring dimension."

"Why is it in English, then?" Anna started looking around for pill bottles. She decided it was either a side effect from a prescription or 'shrooms. Maybe Father Jeffries did 'shrooms. Or there could be a bong involved.

"Magic. Certain books translate themselves into the native tongue of the portal point when they jump dimensions. It's as if they are, in a sense, alive. We don't have those books here. Information originating in this dimension is quite limited." He glanced furtively around the room as if he expected God to strike him down for revealing secrets.

"And we needed this book because ... ?" She really needed him to get all the insane commentary out of the way before she had some kind of fit. She was starting to long for the days of Bitsy and Mimi stalking her. Back when life was simple.

"Because it speaks of the incubus."

Anna's eyes narrowed. "How did you know he was an incubus? I only told you he was a demon." She never would have told him it was an incubus. That was a conversation she didn't want to have with a priest. Demon was bad enough. Sex demon was just out of the question.

"The mark on your hand, child. That mark is specific to that *breed*, for lack of a better term." He indicated a picture in the book. "And the mark is why we're here."

Anna felt the mark in question tingle to life as if it knew it was being talked about. "What about it?" She ran her fingertips over the scar. She didn't like the priest knowing about it, nor did she like what she thought he might suggest next.

"We have to undo it. You don't know what this demon could do to you now that you've allowed him to mark you."

"Excuse me? I didn't *allow* anything. He just came at me with a knife all snarly and was like *here, this will protect you*. I didn't have a choice in the matter. It wasn't like I said, *hey, let's be blood brothers*."

Father Jeffries looked a little flustered. "I apologize. I shouldn't have assumed. But the fact remains that he can make you feel sympathy for him through dreams. Anytime doubt sets up in your mind, you have the dreams, don't you? It makes you more vulnerable to him. He doesn't just want your body, Anna. He wants your soul."

"It's not like that." But wasn't it? Hadn't he already tried to take Beatrice's soul? "He's not like that."

"Think about this for a moment. How do you know anything you think or feel about him is real? Break the bond and you can know for certain. You can separate your own feelings and thoughts from his."

"I . . . " It wasn't like the priest wasn't making sense. "He said he did it to protect me from the others. If you think Luc is bad, Cain is worse. The bond protects me from Cain."

"Who will protect you from Luc?"

Hadn't she asked herself the same question? Hadn't she seen the mask slip with Luc? This was her life, her soul on the line. Would she feel for him if not for the dreams?

The priest picked up a second book and thumbed through it. "There is a ritual here. It won't take long. Stay and we'll perform it.

The church has many resources. We can protect you. You don't have to make a devil's bargain to stay safe."

The door opened then, and a brunette slipped in. Her gold wedding ring glinted off the light. "Father Jeffries?"

Anna watched the brief, unspoken sexual exchange between them, and it reminded her of what Luc had told her. Father Jeffries wasn't a righteous man. But Luc had killed thousands of women. He wasn't exactly all bright and shiny either.

"Anna?" the priest said, catching her gaze. His voice was level when he spoke. "My sins may be great, but his are far greater. Think about that."

"I'll think about it."

WHEN ANNA GOT HOME, THE SOUNDS OF LUC AND THE HAREM talking and laughing drifted out from the kitchen. He poked his head into the foyer. "Would you like some dinner?"

"I'm really tired. I think I'm going up to bed."

He looked like he might try to stop her, but instead nodded and went back to the kitchen. She suspected he thought she was having issues with the earlier kissing episode. She wished that was all she was having issues with. Had he been manipulating her and trying to play on her emotions? Just because there was a book about it didn't mean the book was true.

. . . A BOY WAS CRYING IN THE NEXT ROOM.

"But there's monsters in the closet!"

"There are no monsters in the closet. We've been through this a hundred times," an elderly man said. "Now, go to sleep. I'll leave the door open."

The man left, and Luc stepped out of the shadows. His jaw tightened as he warred with himself. It was one thing to care about killing, it was another to care if some stupid kid cried himself to sleep. Luc rationalized he'd never get to go downstairs and feed if the adults of the house were awake.

Who was he kidding? He felt bad for the kid. The boy had just lost his parents and was in a new house. His grandparents didn't know how to deal with him and were treating him like a miniature adult. Something about the child pulled on a part of Luc he'd long ago tried to bury, memories from when he was human and innocent himself, as fleeting as those moments had been.

Finally, he materialized. "Don't worry about the monsters, kid. I'll keep them away." His voice was more gruff than he'd intended. He was such a pathetic excuse for a demon.

The boy swiped at his eyes and settled down. "Are you an angel?"

"Yeah," he said, chuckling, "an angel . . .

ANNA SAT UP IN BED. SHE'D THOUGHT LUC HAD ALWAYS BEEN A demon, assuming he'd been created with leftover evil floating on the ether. Had he lost his soul? Been bad as a human? She wanted to go back to sleep and find out, but her body rebelled against not being fed.

She got up and crept down the stairs. To get to the kitchen, she had to pass Luc's room. He'd chosen to take up residence in what was once probably servants' quarters. A room under the stairs, next to an alcove. She heard a moan through the cracked door and cringed.

"Shhh. Hush now," Luc said.

"I'm trying to be quiet," a female voice responded. It was Renee. She let out a soft sigh, and Anna heard the bed creak.

"Bite a pillow if you have to."

"Why? What does it matter if I'm loud?"

"I don't want to rub it in her face."

"You care for her, don't you?"

Anna waited, holding her breath, wanting to hear him say yes, but unsure she'd believe it, even if she overheard it. Her earlier visit with the priest still had her shaken.

There was no answer. He'd never specifically said it to her, but Anna suspected if he could sleep with only her, he might do it. He didn't seem to get the same kind of thrill out of his nature that Cain did.

It was wrong to keep punishing him for something he couldn't help. What did she expect? He was giving everything he had to give. Just the fact that he wasn't using thrall on her and taking what he wanted anyway should mean something.

It should mean everything.

"Why can't she just sleep with you, too?" Renee said. "It's not like we won't share." So he *had* answered? Maybe just with a look or a nod.

"She can't share," he said.

"Well, that's silly."

Anna barely heard his quiet reply.

"No, it isn't."

She slipped past the door, to the kitchen. He'd left a plate for her in the fridge. These weren't the actions of an evil demon. Whatever Beatrice had done had changed him. Anna trusted him. If she didn't, she wouldn't still be in the house.

It didn't matter what the priest said. She didn't want the bond broken. Somehow the thought of losing that connection with Luc scared her more than anything else.

16

*L*uc stood next to the stove, trying to stay out of the cat fight. The girls were gathered behind Maria who was facing off with Tam. They'd been arguing loudly for the past thirty minutes, enough that it woke Anna. When she entered the fray, Tam whirled on her.

"Gypsies? The fucking gypsies are coming today?"

The girls, who had been hiding behind Maria, used the distraction as an opportunity to leave.

"I'm not sure. Why?" Anna said. She looked to Maria, who nodded. "I guess they're coming today. Is that a problem?"

Anna's hair was a messy mane of curls Luc wanted to thread his fingers through. He had to fight to keep from kicking every female but Anna out of the house so he could get some alone time with her, but Tam looked even more irritated than before.

"Look, I know we got a lot done the other day, but I agreed not to come by yesterday because the weirdo ghost people were coming. How did that go, by the way?"

Luc and Anna both avoided her eyes.

"I see," Tam said. "Now we have to give up another day to the gypsies. And really, you can have gypsies but not witches? You know me. Am I in any way creepy or evil?"

"No ... but ... "

"But nothing. I can't believe you'll go to complete strangers and use gypsy magic but you won't use witch magic. How many options do you have left here?"

She looked from Anna to Luc as if he'd give her support. It wasn't a misplaced appeal. He wanted the spell broken, and the sooner Anna could run through her list of pointless attempts, the sooner he could convince her to just burn the damn thing down.

Karen rushed back into the room. "They're here! And they look just like real gypsies. I'm so excited!"

Maria scowled. "They *are* real gypsies."

"I know," Karen said, "but I thought they'd be wearing jeans, not cool skirts and jewelry. It's like they just stepped off a caravan."

Maria rolled her eyes. "That's because they work as fortune tellers with a traveling carnival. I cannot believe they're wearing that. It's just reinforcing stereotypes. I hope they're wearing shoes."

"I like the outfits," Karen said defensively.

Maria turned to Tam. "What if your coven showed up wearing long black dresses and pointy hats? Wouldn't you be appalled?"

"Oh my God, yes."

Luc gawked at both of them, unable to believe they were bonding now after they'd spent the past half hour at each other's throats. He stole a glance at Anna and was surprised to find her looking at him. She seemed to have abandoned the drama around her once Karen had returned. There was a heated expression on her face that said there might be a chance. For what, he didn't know.

He reached out to her, unsure of the plan past feeling her skin against his, when the door opened and in glided three gypsies. They each had long black hair and kohl lining their eyes. Their lips were a deep ruby red that would have made other women look like harlots.

True to Karen's description, they looked like real gypsies in brightly colored skirts and layers of jingling coin scarves that made a *cachink cachink* sound when they moved.

"Maria! Darling. Why are you living in this house of sin?" one of the gypsies asked with a thick accent.

"I am a *hooker* or had you forgotten?"

"We were hoping you would stop that and come work with us," a second woman said.

"I don't think so." Maria looked down her nose at the women. Luc raised a brow at the interplay. There must be some serious family drama if she preferred the life she had to the one they offered.

She turned to the rest of the group. "These are my aunts on my mother's side, Lenora, Merripen, and Zenda. They are sure to lie to you about their exploits, but the magic is real, and that's what matters."

"Maria, really," Merripen said. "We aren't that bad."

Lenora was the oldest, sixty at least, though her hair was black through the miracle of hair color. She turned her hawkish gaze on Luc.

"This is the demon, then?" Her eyes glittered dangerously as she pointed a long, manicured fingernail at him. Her head whipped around to Anna suddenly as if she were receiving some sort of vision. "And you. You've been tainted with him."

She grabbed Anna's hand, an act that was starting to wear on Luc's nerves. Did no one from this century have manners or a sense of personal boundaries? Although it did lend credence to them being the real deal if they could sense the blood magic on her, unlike the ghost hunters of the day before. Either way, he was tired of it. Luc growled before stepping forward and physically moving Anna behind him.

He felt his eyes burn with the light that was brought on by

strong emotions for his kind. "Don't touch her. You are here to break a curse, nothing more."

"Oh, this is interesting." Lenora moved closer to him without a trace of fear. If Anna weren't there to witness it, he could have broken through that wall of bravado quickly enough. But behaving like an animal would get him nowhere in gaining Anna's trust.

The gypsy gave him a once-over and laughed. "A demon with feelings. It's been a long time since I've crossed paths with one of those." She looked back to Anna, assessing. "You haven't slept with him. And yet you are the one that he wants. Very strange."

Luc growled again. He wasn't sure if the gypsy had intended to be more insulting to him or Anna. Either way felt like a good reason to be pissed.

She held her hands up in surrender. "Calm yourself. I'm not going to touch your girl again." Then to Anna, "Where would be the best place to do the ritual, dear?"

He could feel Anna was shaken. Besides the slight tremor of her body when they'd briefly touched, emotions were pouring out of her so strongly he could feel them without effort.

She led the three women to the living room. "Here is fine."

"No, it's no good," Zenda said, her eyes glazed over. "Magic has already been worked here. Catholic magic. We will have to cleanse the space."

When they started working, Anna excused herself to look for Tam. Luc didn't attempt to follow, more concerned with babysitting the gypsies to make sure they didn't try anything funny.

ANNA FOUND HER BESIDE THE FOUNTAIN IN THE GARDEN, STARING down at the green algae and smoking a cigarette.

"Want one?" Tam asked. She seemed ready to forgive Anna's witch-prejudice as if no ill words had been exchanged in the kitchen. But that was how their friendship was. Little spats, a little crisis, then all's forgiven. Like sisters.

"You know I don't smoke anymore."

"Yes, but now seems like a good time to start again. It's very tense in there," she observed, gesturing toward the house.

Anna shrugged. "What the hell. Yes, I would love to take up smoking again."

Tam smirked but passed her a cigarette. "You remember when we were in high school and we used to pretend to smoke just to upset our parents?"

Anna laughed and took the offered lighter. She was already making promises to herself, planning to quit again when Luc was free. She was aware of Tam's eyes on her, gauging markers only longtime friends even knew to look for.

"So you wanna tell me what's wrong?" Tam said, finally.

Anna spent the next twenty minutes describing her run-in with Father Jeffries and the choice in front of her.

"Yeah, I knew about all that."

"You *what*?"

"Well, not about the bond and stuff, but I knew about the other dimensions. I mean, hello? My gods don't live here."

"Why didn't you tell me?"

"Oh, I don't know. I think your exact words were: 'Tam, whatever you do, just don't tell me about it.' I took you at face value. Sue me."

Anna was still having a bit of trouble with the witch thing. For years they'd been out of touch, and before that, her friend had mostly kept it hidden. Now that the world had turned out to be so magic, Tam wasn't bothering as much with discretion. Anna couldn't really blame her.

Merripen poked her head out the door. "We're ready to start."

Anna nodded her acknowledgment, and the gypsy went back inside.

"I really think Luc's okay," Tam said as if reading Anna's fears right off her face. "I know you don't like the witch stuff. But I've been using magic for a long time now. And I told you, I don't get the same vibe off him as I do other demons."

"But you were under thrall the first time you met him."

"I took care of that problem."

Tam didn't elaborate, and she didn't push. Whatever rituals were being done behind closed doors were none of Anna's business. "You coming in?"

Tam laughed. "And have a freak-out about conflicting magical techniques? Or have them sniff the unclean non-gypsy magic on me? No, thank you. I'm going down to Sally's to see how much we can reasonably fit on the shelves. I'll call you later."

When Anna returned to the foyer, candles and incense were already lit. Odd items lay scattered in a strange pattern on the floor.

"Oh, good, you're here. Anna, dear, come. I need you for the ritual." Lenora motioned for her to step into the circle. Scarlett and Rhett sat just outside the ritual space, wary but curious.

Luc watched the proceedings from the corner. "Why do you need her?"

Lenora met his eyes and something passed between them. When she spoke, it seemed more for the benefit of Anna than Luc. "I need her blood. You know blood is the only thing strong enough, and she owns the house now."

His jaw clenched. "It's up to her. I'm not going to make her do this."

"Anna?" The gypsy woman asked.

Anna looked uncertainly from Lenora to Luc. "Will it hurt him?"

Lenora's eyes widened. "Even more interesting. You care for your demon as much as he cares for you. I had thought it was one-sided."

"He's not my demon," she said. *Denial*, a traitorous voice in her mind whispered.

The woman looked deeply into her eyes, then nodded, satisfied when she found what she was looking for. "Take it from an old gypsy fortune teller. He will be." She held Anna's hand in hers, and looked at her palm. "Ah, just what I suspected. You have a very long life line. Shall we?"

Everything the gypsy said or did was cryptic and seemed like an inside joke. It made Anna uncomfortable, but she stepped into the circle anyway because Luc was counting on her.

Lenora withdrew a gilded knife with tiny rubies set in the handle. The knife vibrated with a power that was palpable even to someone like Anna who, until recently, had been unused to magic. Lenora cut a thin line down the center of Anna's unmarked palm, causing her to hiss with pain. A low growl came from Luc, but he didn't move to intercede.

"I will heal it before we begin," Lenora said. The growling stopped. Merripen and Zenda sat on the floor just outside the circle mixing herbs and chanting. After Lenora had gotten several drops of Anna's blood into a saucer, she held out her hand expectantly.

Like doctor's assistants, Merripen and Zenda gave her damp muslin they'd soaked in water and then dipped in the herbs. Lenora wrapped Anna's left hand while chanting quietly. A gentle breeze picked up, then the burning sensation from the cut was gone. Lenora unwrapped her hand, and it was healed.

Anna moved to Luc as the three sisters sat together drawing symbols onto the hardwood floor with her blood. She couldn't help thinking she'd have to deal with *neurotic-Luc* if this didn't work and bloodstains were left on the floor. Maybe they could get an oriental rug to cover it.

After a few moments, the gypsies joined hands and started to chant in their native tongue as they swayed slowly back and forth. A wind picked up, causing the candle flames to flicker in and out. As their voices grew louder, the wind turned to a full-on gust, zipping around the room. Luc wasn't responsible for it this time.

The candles puffed out from the force of the wind, leaving the mid-afternoon sun filtering through the windows as the only remaining light. An invisible energy flung the door open, and Luc was pulled toward it. He bounced hard off the barrier.

The chanting continued. It happened again, causing Luc to slide against the floor and land in a heap. The barrier wasn't going anywhere.

"Stop it!" Anna shouted. She rushed over and crouched next to him as the chanting died down, her hands skimming over his arms in search of injury. "Are you okay?"

"I'm fine," he growled. "The only thing hurt is my pride. That wasn't incredibly manly." He clasped her hand in his, holding her gaze. "But it's nice that you care."

Anna, looking for a distraction from the intimate moment, pulled her hand away, and turned to the gypsies. "I'm sorry, but I couldn't let you keep flinging him against the barrier like that."

"It's all right," Lenora said. "Unfortunately, we cannot undo the curse. Was there a clause to break it?"

Anna stared at an interesting spot on the floor. "Yes, but we were hoping not to have to do it."

"You will probably have to. We felt the anger. And pain. There was too much fueling the spell. Our magic may be strong, but vengeance is stronger."

"You could see the original spell?" Anna asked.

"We could sense it, yes."

The gypsies turned then as one organized unit and started packing bags. They seemed to consider their business done. No small talk or chit chat or staying for lunch. Anna almost had whiplash as she watched them file out the door.

She was quickly running out of options. Maybe she should take pictures of the house before she burned it down. Then she could move all the furniture into storage, so she wouldn't lose that, at least.

The harem stood over in the corner whispering amongst themselves. Maria had gone outside to see her aunts off, and no doubt to get a lecture about her choice to remain under the same roof as a demon.

"We're never getting that blood out of the floor," Luc grumbled, interrupting her thoughts.

"Oh, here we go. I knew it was just a matter of time before you started in on that. I'm going to burn down the house just so I don't have to hear about the antiques and the walls and floor anymore. Do you know your demon status is the only thing keeping you intimidating? All the cooking and the obsession with antiques . . . "

He growled. "Don't push me, Anna. I don't care if there are witnesses."

A shiver––though not from fear––ran down her spine.

Karen came over then. "We're going to Mama Bella's for lunch. Want to come?"

Anna glanced over to Luc. The look in his eyes was so possessive she wanted to flee to the safety of the restaurant with the others, but the excited twinge in her stomach wouldn't let her.

"No, that's okay," she heard herself say.

Karen shrugged and rejoined the group. Anna practically ran to the kitchen. What was she doing letting herself be alone with him, without the harem as a buffer? She ran hot water in the sink and started putting the breakfast dishes in.

"We have a dishwasher," he commented.

"I like to do them by hand." *I like to keep my hands busy so I won't put them on you. I like to distract myself from temptation.*

She felt the demon behind her, pressing himself firmly against her back. He pulled her hair away from her neck, kissed the side of it, and whispered in her ear.

"Gypsies are rarely wrong about the future, you know."

"Luc . . . " She was holding onto the *rarely* part of that sentence.

His hand slipped underneath her shirt to caress her lower back. "I don't know why you fight it. You are mine. There's nothing you can do about that."

She bristled. It was one thing to voluntarily go to him, it was quite another for him to act as if he had some kind of special claim over her that she was powerless to fight. She could fight it. She was pretty confident Father Jeffries could undo the bond.

"Stop saying that! If you think it helps your cause, it doesn't. You know you can take what you want. I know you can take what you want. You can use the hypno mind thrall thing or whatever if you want. If you're going to do it, do it. But stop hanging it over my head. I don't like being messed with like that."

Luc didn't say anything more. He just kept rubbing her back in small, soothing circles. And like an idiot, she kept leaning into it so he didn't stop.

"I start to see you as something other than a demon, and you keep reminding me."

He stopped touching her and stepped back. "I don't want you to forget it."

She turned to face him, wiping her sudsy hands on her jeans. "Why the hell not?"

"Because I'm not human. I don't want you to be disappointed by that. If you decide to be with me, I don't want you to pretend I'm just another guy you're dating. I need you to be aware."

She threw her hands in the air. "I'm aware! I'm so aware, there's no more aware I could be. Unless you start stomping around the house in demon form."

He cringed.

"See? Double standard. You say you don't want me to forget what you are, but you've yet to show me. Show me, and maybe I won't be so forgetful." She knew she was baiting him, and she didn't care. She was tired of the hypocrisy. It wasn't her fault she forgot he was a demon when he acted so much like a person half the time.

"You never have to see that." He reached out to touch her, but she sidestepped his hand.

"Whatever."

He moved to sit in one of the kitchen chairs. "Anna, why must we always fight? Why is it so hard with you?"

"It's four o'clock."

"So?"

"Last Saturday the Townsends invited me to dinner. It's today." She draped a hand towel over the draining dishes.

"You're being avoidant."

"Yes, but I'm not lying. The issues we have can't be worked out in twenty minutes. I promise we'll talk when I get back."

The frown lines around his mouth showed his disapproval, but he let her go.

17

*C*ecelia Townsend had gunmetal gray hair, which she held forever captive in a loose bun. She was pushing in on seventy—if she wasn't already there—and though her face was lined with wrinkles, she gave off the kind of youthful glow most young people couldn't successfully pull off.

Everyone in town wanted to know her secret, as if she'd somehow found the fountain of youth. Her fountain of youth was living. She did it very well.

"Get on in here," Cecelia said, pulling Anna into a hug as she crossed the threshold. The older woman's grip was still strong as ever.

When they reached the dining room, Charles was already seated at the table.

"I thought we were going to have drinks first," Cece said when she saw him. It was clear she'd wanted everything to be perfect.

Charles just grunted. Anna couldn't determine exactly what the grunt was meant to convey, but she kind of wanted to smack him for messing up an evening Cece had taken so much time to put together.

She had never disliked Charles, but she'd never much cared for him either. He was the most monosyllabic man she knew. Maybe it was asking too much, but she preferred a man who could string together full sentences.

"Cece, I used to spit out the raisins from the cookies you made onto the back table when I was a kid. No need for formality on my account."

Cecelia just laughed at that, the darkness lifting from her expression. "And then when I told you to eat them, you slipped them to the dog. That mutt would eat anything."

The cook came in then. "I apologize, Mrs. Townsend. I should have waited until Ms. Worthington arrived to announce dinner."

"It's no problem, Hannah," Cece said. "I wasn't very clear. Since we're here, we may as well sit." She shot Charles a glare, but he didn't seem to notice or else had become impervious to her disapproval after so many years.

The rest of dinner went without incident with the best pot roast and vegetables Anna had ever consumed. She didn't remember Cece's last cook being this good.

They went through the obligatory *how have you been since your father passed* questions, as well as the polite platitudes about what a good man he was. Anna regretted how she and her father had parted and was glad when that portion of the conversation was over.

Inevitably the discussion turned to Anna's new house.

"I can't believe you forgot about the ghost stories," Cece said, leaning forward in her seat.

Anna shrugged. "I think I was practicing selective memory techniques since I wanted the house so much. You know how much I loved it."

The old woman chuckled. "Indeed. I wasn't surprised when you bought it. I was just thinking the other day about a dream I had about that house when I was in college. You'll never believe what a party girl I was."

Anna somehow doubted Cecelia Townsend had ever partied a day in her life. Seeing her expression of doubt, the woman became more animated.

"No, I was! There was this one time I remember. I was a senior, and I met these two girls at a bar. They were seniors too, except in high school. They'd snuck in and had been getting older men to buy them drinks. We got hammered and danced on a couple of tables." She blushed and let out a girlish giggle at Anna's expression.

"I must have passed out because when I woke up, I was in my dorm, and the girls I met were gone. I was just thinking about that because I still remember this odd dream I had. A lot of it's fuzzy, like it started out a nightmare . . . I think . . . The girls were in it and they died or something. But then there was this gorgeous man and . . . "

Charles cleared his throat, and she blushed again. "Well, that's not really the point. What I was going to say was . . . the dream was inside your house. Or well, you know Beatrice's house back then. And ever since then I've always wanted to know if the house looks the same on the inside as it did in my dream. I mean I know it's a silly thing to wonder, but we used to talk about going in there and checking it out when you were little.

"I should have gone by and looked at it myself one of those times it was up for sale, but I never did work up the nerve. It was hard back then with Bea gone. Anyway, curiosity has finally won out, and I'm rudely inviting myself over to get a look at your house."

Anna had dropped her fork the second the older woman mentioned dreaming. Once she was sure Cecelia was talking about what she thought she was talking about, she almost choked on her roast.

"Are you all right?"

Anna coughed before finally swallowing enough sweet tea to cause the food to go down. "Fine. It just went down wrong."

"Luc!" Anna bellowed, as soon as she got through the door. "Luc!"

Karen was curled up on the couch watching TV. "He's in the library," she said, not taking her eyes from the screen. "He's been holed up in there ever since you left."

Anna ran down the hall, not slowing as she slammed into the library. "The dreams have to stop." Her eyes narrowed when she saw him working his way through a bottle of brandy. Something on the grocery list he hadn't mentioned?

He put the alcohol down on the side table and closed his book. "What happened?"

"Cecelia Townsend happened. You know the dream I had the other night?"

He didn't have to be told which dream she was talking about. He took another drink.

"Well, take a wild guess at who you managed not to kill."

His eyes lit up. "Cecelia? Really?" He let the name roll over his tongue as if testing it. "So she's okay, then? Alive and not crazy?" His voice was so hopeful, for a moment Anna forgot about being mad.

"Are you kidding me? She's a bastion of mental health. This is the best, kindest, most together woman I've ever known and I've seen her twenty-year-old self naked. Cece has been like a mentor to me. Like a second mother or grandmother or whatever . . . and now I've seen her naked! The dreams have to stop."

She knew the naked part was the wrong part to focus on, but she couldn't bring herself to think about the fact that Luc had put Cece under a thrall, had sex with her, and nearly killed her. Suddenly the things the demon had done were coming into sharper focus. They weren't abstract notions and random women she didn't know anymore. They were friends.

"I knew she was strong," Luc mused. "Cain didn't kill her. I'd always wondered but was afraid to ask."

"Can we please focus on *my* problem here? I can't deal with this anymore." Anna didn't say that what she couldn't deal with was the fact that everywhere she went, Luc was there in one form or another. Infecting her dreams, seeping into her fantasies. She needed a break from him. She felt smothered.

"How did you come to discover this?"

"She remembered part of the *dream*," Anna said, making air quotes with her fingers. "She was curious about the house, which she recognized, by the way. And she wants to come over and see it."

Luc visibly paled. "Surely you told her that was impossible."

At least his thoughts on the matter meshed with her own. "I sort of choked on my pot roast. After that I changed the subject. So I'm safe for a while. But we need to figure out how to make the dreams stop."

"I've been looking into that."

She hadn't expected him to actually be searching for something to help her.

Luc led her to the large oak table on which he'd laid out several books that looked eerily similar to the volume Father Jeffries had shown her. She wasn't surprised they were all in English.

"It might be hard for you to accept this but these books come from . . . "

"Other dimensions," she finished for him, not sure she could handle a re-run. She'd been fighting back the nervous breakdown the first time she'd had it all explained to her.

Luc looked at her oddly.

"What? I know stuff. Tam's a witch." No sense mentioning how she'd really learned about it.

"That makes this easier to explain, then. Cain used to bring me copies of the books from the libraries where most of the information about our kind is housed. I found a footnote mentioning the bond a few days ago but I didn't have enough information to bother you. While you were out, I found more in another book."

Why did she feel like he was stalling? "How do we make the dreams stop?"

He hesitated as if judging whether he should tell her anything at all. "This is the part you aren't going to like. I promise when I did it, I didn't realize. It wasn't as if I had an ulterior motive. I just wanted to protect you from Cain and knew a simple mixing of blood would do that, would temporarily mark you as mine and protect you."

He was pacing now. The act made the hairs on the back of Anna's neck and arms stand up in agitation.

"Well?" she said.

"The mark. It connects us, gives you dreams about me, makes you more sympathetic to me. Although, it's very uncommon for an incubus to start having dreams about someone he's marked," Luc said thoughtfully.

"Maybe we're soul mates," Anna quipped. She didn't like the soft look Luc got when she said it. Like he wished it could be true.

At least he wasn't lying to her about the purpose of the dreams. If he had, she might have had to bludgeon him to death with one of the musty old books.

"It makes you more likely to want to complete our mating ritual . . . the soul transfer."

"No! Absolutely not. Undo it. Make the dreams stop." Her voice was shaking with rage and a bit of fear. She didn't like what this was doing to her. Father Jeffries had been right.

"The dreams will stop if you give me your soul." At her stormy look, he rushed to continue, "Or . . . it'll just wear off. If the ritual isn't completed it will wear off. The scar will eventually fade and the dreams will cease."

"How long?"

He looked away.

She moved in front of him, forcing him to meet her eyes. "How long, Luc?"

He sighed. "Five or ten years. There isn't an exact time given, but that's the average."

"Are you kidding me? I'll be tied to you and these psychotic mind-fucked dreams, possibly for the next decade?"

"Or there is the other option . . . "

"I'm not giving you my soul." She held her hands out like scales. "Hmmm, five to ten years or eternity. Which sentence is less? Math was my worst subject, but even this isn't hard for me. I'll take the five to ten, thanks."

A tiny voice in her mind reminded her of the third option Father Jeffries had presented. Luc didn't have that book, but there was a ritual that could end it, and she wouldn't have to be stuck with him for another confusing several years. She pushed down the flutter in her stomach at the idea of being with Luc forever. That could never happen. She couldn't give him her soul.

Her hand started itching. She scratched furiously around the scar. "And what is up with this? The scar tingles, it burns, it itches . . . "

"It is dependent on your feelings."

"So my hand is a mood ring now? Unbelievable."

Luc moved to her, taking her hand in his. The itching stopped. She looked into his eyes, fathomless pools of bright green. No man had eyes like that. She could feel herself falling into them.

She looked up helplessly at him. "What are you doing to me?"

"Nothing. You want me. But you fight it, and I don't understand why. Why is giving your soul to me so frightening? You know me. You've seen who I am––more than anyone else has. You know I would never harm you."

She pulled her hand away and tried to look bored, something

difficult to accomplish with his primal maleness hovering right over her, smelling dark and delicious.

"Try to get over yourself. Have you ever stopped to consider that I'm just not ready for that type of a commitment? I mean, come on. I'm young. A lot of women my age aren't even ready for marriage. I've known you a week, we haven't even slept together, and you're talking eternity." It had to be the bond making them both feel this way.

His face fell, but he shook it off quickly. "No," he said, his eyes so assessing and intense she almost lost her breath. "It's something else. I don't know what, though. And I'm not sure you do either."

"Luc, put yourself in my position. Your kind is known for deceiving women, telling them what they want to hear and then killing them. I'm supposed to believe that a demon wouldn't turn on me once he had my soul?"

"No, but *I* wouldn't. And you know that."

"Do I?"

She pulled a pack of cigarettes and lighter from her pocket. Her hands were shaking. She hated that. She didn't want him to see how nervous he made her.

"I wish you wouldn't do that," he said.

"Are you my mother now?" She cringed at how she was snapping at him, unable to stop the bitch train once it pulled out of the station. She tried unsuccessfully to flick the lighter, but her hands were shaking too badly.

Luc took it from her, and Anna leaned in, thinking he was going to light the cigarette like some gentleman in an old Humphrey Bogart film.

"Take it outside if you must smoke it. Not in the house with the antiques."

She wanted to argue. It was her house, no matter who had been there the longest. But she gave in because being in his presence another second was likely to end with her flat on her back, feeding him.

She grabbed a pack of matches from the kitchen junk drawer on her way outside. Somehow developing a chain smoking habit seemed like the least dangerous thing she could do right now.

Anna savored the nicotine as it curled into her lungs, and the artificial calm washed over her. She wanted to push the rewind button on her life and redo it all. This house was going to be the death of her. She just knew it.

The sound of boots crunching over gravel jolted her out of her self-pity. She looked up, startled to find five smarmy-looking men standing in front of her. She wasn't big on profiling, but you knew these were thugs from two hundred yards away. The ringleader stood out in front, pointing a gun at her.

"Where are our girls, bitch?"

Anna let out a hysterical peal of laughter. She was snapping. She could feel the little places in her brain that held her sanity together bending and buckling under the strain of the past week.

"Are you laughing at me?" the ringleader asked. "We're here for our girls. You took them. We're here to take them back where they belong."

"Yeah, sure thing," Anna said. The pimps couldn't have picked a better time to arrive.

he ringleader wrapped a meaty hand around Anna's throat. "Move, bitch!"

"Luc!"

"Shut up. One man can't help you."

The harem stood behind the cooking island, a frozen tableau of horror. They'd been gabbing and eating chips and salsa when Anna and the pimps busted through the back door.

"Luc!" she shouted again.

"I said shut up. Maria, get your shit. We're leaving."

Maria nodded, eyes wide, and scampered from the room. The other pimps just looked at their girls, sending them scurrying. Then it was just Anna alone in the kitchen with five nasty guys in desperate need of a shower and shave.

"You know," one of them said idly, touching the side of Anna's face, "We could bring you back with us. Put you to work." The leer he gave her caused bile to rise in the back of her throat.

"That one is mine."

Luc leaned in the doorway, a disturbingly calm look on his face. Anna breathed a sigh of relief. She knew that tone. That tone meant death. It sounded pleasant enough, but that was only until you were getting your guts ripped out. He strode purposefully into the room while the girls fanned out behind him.

"Maria came for me. I'm sorry I didn't hear you. I was in the wine cellar."

"We have a wine cellar?" Why hadn't that been on the tour?

"Trap door in the library under the rug. I didn't want you drinking my wine." He turned his attention back to the thugs who had formed what they probably thought was an intimidating semi-circle around Anna. It only seemed to further piss him off.

The ringleader held out the gun in warning. "Don't come any closer. She's ours now. There are five of us and one of you."

Luc stopped a few feet short of the man wielding the gun and smirked at the barrel pointed at his chest. "I don't think you boys know how to count. I see six girls and me. So that's seven against five."

"The girls don't count." The pimp pulled the hammer back.

"Hmmm," Luc said. "I've lived a very long time, and I can tell you, girls will surprise you sometimes."

The ringleader seemed tired of idle chit chat, ready to take the harem back along with the newly-acquired bounty. If Anna hadn't been so confident of her safety now that Luc was here, she'd be more upset.

He pulled the trigger, then gasped when the bullet went straight through the demon and hit the back wall. Luc turned toward the bullet hole.

The thug's eyes widened as he looked as his gun then at the incubus. "Wh . . . what are you?"

Luc whirled to face the gunman, the mask of calm long forgotten by his face. "Someone very pissed off that you just put a hole in my wall."

"Oh, gee thanks. I'm feeling the love," Anna said. He could be calm about the smarmy cretin touching her, but put a hole in his wall, and it was all over except for the screaming and dying.

"Sorry dear, but it goes without saying I'm pissed these criminals threatened you."

Anna tried not to let the way he casually called her *dear* get to her. She failed. Of all the times to have warm, fuzzy butterfly feelings in her stomach, this was the worst. Luc knocked the gun out of the man's hand and grabbed him by the lapels, moving him away from Anna.

He could kill a man easily, but like a cat, Luc preferred to play with his prey, holding back his strength, letting them believe they had a chance. While he pounded on the gunman, Anna ran across the kitchen and took a cast iron skillet from a rack hanging over the island. She hauled back and hit one of the pimps square on the jaw, forcing him to stumble back.

The rest of the harem, shaken out of their complacency, seized pots and pans of their own in a re-enactment of every cartoon featuring wives chasing deadbeat husbands around.

Anna was only partly focused on the fight; the other half of her attention stayed on Luc. It wasn't that they didn't deserve death, but she wasn't sure how she felt about him killing willy nilly right in front of her. She wasn't going to try to stop him from beating them to a pulp, but she kept watching to make sure that was all he was doing.

When he got bored with his prey, he locked eyes with him and spoke. "When you wake up, you will forget why you came here. You will never seek out Maria or any of the other girls again. You've never even met them. Do you understand me?"

The man's eyes were unfocused and glassy. "Yes."

"Sleep."

Luc caught the man when he fell and went to the front door to toss him out onto the lawn.

"Who's next?" he said, when he returned, rubbing his hands together in boyish glee.

The harem was doing a commendable job themselves. Anger, confidence, and cookware made for an intimidating combo. Maria's pimp had been the only one with the foresight to bring a weapon. They must have thought it would be easy.

Luc grabbed a second thug and repeated the process while the harem got their kicks out on the remaining three. Anna moved out of the way to watch. Aside from her initial shot with the skillet, she let the girls get their rage out at the men who had tried to keep them helpless and dependent.

The second man was put under and sent on his merry way flying out the front door. Anna sincerely hoped they woke up quickly and got out of her yard. The last thing she needed was to give Bitsy and Mimi another reason to harass her. Five smelly guys on the lawn was just the kind of thing that would make the front page of the *Golatha Falls Gazette*.

Luc took out his aggression on the third guy, while the harem beat up on the other two. It would be overkill for him to kick the shit out of them, too. They were already looking pretty pathetic. One of them managed to crawl away from the enraged harem and closed his hand around the gun.

It happened before Anna could react. White hot burning. A crunch. The world blurred and flashed white, then snapped back into focus. She was on the ground, confused as she felt wetness pooling around her shoulder.

There was a flurry of activity around her, but the cold tile against her skull was all she could feel. And her ears ringing. And the dull, throbbing pain.

"Stay with me, Anna."

He'd moved so fast. Luc held her while she struggled to maintain consciousness. "Flesh wound. Won't kill . . . Mr. Psychotic," she managed weakly. That wasn't exactly the way that sentence was supposed to come out.

She felt Luc touch her mind and wanted to hate him for using thrall on her, but the pain had faded to nothing. It was an illusion but one she would take as gladly as a morphine drip.

"Relax," he soothed. "It just missed the artery, so I'm going to take the bullet out first. Close your eyes." It wasn't a request, and she didn't have the power to resist it.

Her eyes fluttered shut. Then the air charged around her, causing a moment's panic when she realized he was shifting partially into the demon form. She was struck with a sudden clarity that he was using his claws to remove the bullet, though she could barely feel what he was doing.

Several minutes later he said, "Okay. Open your eyes."

She looked up and tensed when she saw the knife in his hand.

His smile was kind. "This isn't for you. Why would I make you bleed more when I'm trying to make it stop? That seems counter-intuitive at best."

"Big word. You really *can* read," Anna said, but it came out a faint whisper.

He chuckled. "Save your strength. You can be sarcastic and annoying later." Luc sliced his hand, reopening his bonding scar, and let the blood flow into the gunshot wound.

Anna looked away. If she never had to witness or participate in another creepy blood ritual again, it would be too soon. A few moments passed before the wound was sealed, and only a scar remained.

Luc was clearly rattled as if just realizing how fragile humans could be. He helped her sit up. She wrapped her arms around him and sobbed against his neck.

"Shhh. Anna, really. You're fine now. You were bleeding out on the kitchen floor trying to be quippy, and now you're fine. There's no need to cry about it." But his voice cracked when he said it, and she could have sworn she felt something like moisture as he pressed his own face into her neck.

The pimp Luc had left on the floor to attend to Anna stirred.

Luc searched her eyes, then seeing whatever it was he was looking for, he kissed her quickly and pulled away as the man against the wall struggled to stand.

He put the third man under and threw him out the front door. When he returned, Anna was leaning against the counter taking slow breaths.

His hand was suddenly around her waist, supporting her weight. "You're sure you're okay?"

"Fine. Stop hovering. You're worse than a mother hen. See? No bleeding. No wound. All magically healed up."

Her hands itched to pull his mouth back to hers, but the two remaining pimps were tied to chairs and gawking. The harem must have tied them up during her near death experience. She didn't like an audience on her best day, especially not this audience.

"Anna, you might wish to leave the room," Luc said, his fingertips grazing her cheek.

"No." She had a feeling she knew where this was headed.

"I could make you."

"And lose the momentum you're gaining in the strapping hero department?"

He growled.

"Luc, I'm serious. I don't want you to torture him."

"I'm just going to snap his neck."

It unnerved her they were having a casual conversation about killing a man in her kitchen. It unnerved her more that she got a small thrill of satisfaction from the slimy pimp begging and struggling in his bonds.

She was going to Hell. Then again, if the priest was right, she was already technically *in* Hell. But she was coming back in her next life as something unpleasant.

When Luc continued to stare at her she said, "I'm staying. Look, you were all big with the *I don't want you to forget I'm a demon* stuff. Now you think I can't take a little neck snapping? I've had dreams of worse. This isn't an innocent. Get to it." She gave him a shooing motion.

"I have to kill him," he said as if he were talking to someone lacking basic comprehension skills.

She was trying hard to be casual about it, but she was tired of the bullshit. If he was going to do something semi-evil, he wasn't going to hide it from her. She was a big girl. She'd seen him kill lots of people. Hell, she'd been inside him while he'd done a lot of it. After seeing one of her dearest friends naked, this wasn't even rating on the disturb-o-meter anymore.

"Anna, I can't just let this go. He shot you."

"Yes, and he'll hurt other people. I'm totally on board with this. I'm just not slinking out of the room while you do it." Whatever weird reason Luc had for not wanting to kill someone in front of her who very much deserved it, it was causing him some distress.

"Anna . . . "

She could almost see the cogs turning in his brain. "You put me under another thrall, and I'll never forgive you. I don't want you protecting me from everything."

The man awaiting his sentence chose stupidly to speak then. "This is touching." He pinned Anna with a glare. "I guess you just aren't worth killing for, bitch."

That was all the impetus Luc needed. He spun, moving across the floor faster than the pimp could process, and snapped his neck. The other guy started screaming.

"Oh shit! Oh shit! Oh shit!"

Luc put him under, cutting off his shit litany. He ordered the man to carry his friend and never return to the house.

"I'm sorry," Anna finally said when they were alone in the kitchen.

"For what?"

"For making you do that. If you wanted me to leave the room I should have left. I just wanted you to know I wasn't going to judge you for it."

He collapsed in a kitchen chair, his head falling into his hands. "I'm such a pathetic excuse for a demon."

Anna grinned. "Yes, I believe I've heard that before."

He looked up. "Where?"

"In dreams. A guardian angel dream in particular," she said, giggling. She felt high. The adrenaline rush from the events of the evening had finally become too much.

His mouth twisted in disgust. "Let's never talk about that."

"Face it, you're not that evil anymore." She sat in his lap straddling him and took his face in her hands to brush her lips across his. The kiss lingered longer than she'd intended as she greedily sucked on his lower lip.

She could feel his hard length pressing against her. Was she really doing this? She tried to remind herself of all the reasons she should get off him.

Making out with Luc like some horny teenager was probably a bad idea. That was when unwanted images flitted through her mind. She just had to think the words *horny teenager*.

All of a sudden she couldn't stop the memories of the two high school seniors. He'd killed countless women, but she couldn't stop thinking of the two who'd died in Luc's arms not a hundred feet from where they were.

She didn't blame him, exactly. He hadn't wanted to kill them, hadn't meant to. Still. She pulled away. "Luc?"

His green eyes burned with desire. "Hmmm?"

"We have to stop."

"Anna, I have to feed."

"I know, but . . . I can't . . . yet. I just need some time. I have a lot to process." Seeing the hurt look on his face had her wanting to backtrack over her words, but she really couldn't shake the images.

"Is it because of what I just did?"

"No," She answered truthfully. "It isn't. Just give me time."

"I don't want to feed from someone else tonight." It was a plea.

"I know." She felt like an evil bitch, but she had to get away from him. She needed time to sort through the pro/con list in her head before she threw caution and her clothing to the wind with him.

The harem stood clustered in the foyer. How much had they witnessed? As she brushed past them, she looked back to see Luc leading Karen rather reluctantly to his room, his eyes not leaving Anna's.

*a*nna attempted sleep, but she couldn't wipe from her mind the fact that Luc and Karen were downstairs in his room. And it was her fault. He could have been with Anna. But then what? He couldn't be with her the following night. Or the night after that.

She was supposed to sleep with him in shifts? Like the favored number-one wife? It was already practically killing her to know he was touching someone else, whispering sweet words in her ear, kissing her. Like he'd kissed Anna.

The alternative if she wanted to be with him was out of the question. Couples who got married after just a week or so weren't notoriously known for their happily ever afters, and handing over your soul was a bit more than just marriage. As far as she knew there was no equivalent divorce.

Independence was important to her, possibly more important than anything else. When she was twenty-one, she'd taken her college degree, flipped her father off like a child, and ridden off to Atlanta on the back of Vince's Harley.

Quinton's response had been to cut her off, at least for awhile. She'd gotten a crappy job and a shitty apartment and joined the real world. A world without debutante balls and charity luncheons. It had been wonderful because she'd been free.

Luc was asking her to give him the one thing she'd fought too hard to acquire. But she couldn't deny that her body cried out for his, and her heart and mind were well on their way to agreement.

The best and simplest solution would be to stay the hell away from him. Let him have the harem until she could get him out of the house and they could part ways.

If he would even let her go. The bond seemed to mean something almost sacred to him now, assuming demons held anything sacred at all.

If she hadn't had the morbid reminder of the last two girls he'd killed, she'd likely be romping it up in his bed this very minute. Anna shuddered. She could still feel his hands on her body, his mouth on hers, coaxing her to dance with him. She was never getting to sleep.

She'd just slipped her hand between her legs for the drug-free version of an Ambien, when the door opened. Her ghostly voyeur was back. Of course he was. He wouldn't miss a show like this. He probably had a mystical demon-cam on her that went off anytime she moved to do anything even the slightest bit sexual.

Her movements stilled.

"Don't stop."

Anna's heart rate jumped. "You just fed." Her cheeks were hot at being caught.

He moved to the bed with that beautiful grace only Luc seemed capable of. Her breath caught as he settled on the edge. The light from the hallway filtered into the room, highlighting the muscles of his chest. She licked her lips.

"Yes. I did." He eased the covers back, revealing the pale pink satin gown. He growled low in his throat, approving the choice. "Did you wear this because I like it so much?" He traced his hand lightly over the material.

An involuntary shiver.

"N . . . no. It's the middle of the summer. This is the only thing cool enough to sleep in."

He let the lie slide.

"Touch yourself. I want to watch."

From any other man, the request would have seemed crass, but Luc made it sound like ice cream on a hot day. Tempting, but innocent.

"I can't."

"I'm not asking to sleep with you, I just want a little . . . taste."

"I've never . . . "

"You've never done this for anyone before? No man has ever asked to watch you?" He seemed to weigh the honesty of her words.

She shook her head, wishing she was lying.

"Please?" he said.

She wasn't an exhibitionist. Hell, she was a *lights off* kind of girl if she wanted to get baldly honest about it. No kinks, nothing fancy. But the *please* was her undoing.

Anna started to wriggle out of her panties. "Close the door." She couldn't believe she was doing this.

"But it would be dark," he said reasonably, a hint of teasing in his tone.

"And you can see me just fine."

"But I want you to see me. I could turn the light on?"

She shook her head again. The light from the hallway was quite enough, thank you. She moved her hand to cover her mound, her fingers teasing the edges of her clit.

"Lift the gown." His voice was so low it was practically a growl. It crawled inside of her, awakening something wanton that had lain dormant for far too long. She pulled the soft satin up over her belly to expose her lower half.

His eyes glowed. "Spread your legs wider."

She didn't know what prompted her to do it, but she slipped two fingers inside herself and started pumping slowly in and out.

"Faster."

Every word he commanded, she obeyed. She had no idea what had gotten into her, but it wasn't letting go. Anna could feel the moisture slipping down her thigh. Her stomach tightened in the most pleasant way, and she wondered exactly how much she'd missed out on sexually. Not just with Luc, but with anyone.

The door standing open had bothered her at first, but now it excited her. She found her mind going down naughty little paths it never would have ventured toward before Luc.

Her fingers began working in tempo to the soft growls the demon emitted. She couldn't stop the moan that escaped her throat.

"Look at me. Don't take your eyes off mine. I want you to watch me while you come."

She did as he asked, wondering if he could see the color flood her cheeks as she met his eyes. He moved his hand over her, not touching, just hovering over her flesh, running the contours of her body. When he moved his hand a little higher away from her skin, still tracing her curves, her body arched involuntarily closer to meet him.

"Do you feel it, Anna?"

She could barely find her voice to say, "Yes."

He was feeding. Small, gentle pulls of energy. A warmth spread through her, and she knew it wasn't just her approaching climax. It was Luc. She hadn't expected his feeding from her to be its own kind of orgasm.

"You like it?"

"Yes," she breathed.

"Come for me now."

Anna heard a keening sound and was shocked to realize it was coming out of her as she went into a free fall.

Then she lay there, panting and flushed, looking anywhere but at Luc. She moved to pull her nightgown down, but he stopped her with one hand, gripping both of her wrists together.

With his free hand, he ran a finger over her wetness and inside her. Then, without ever breaking eye contact, he slipped the digit into his mouth and sucked off her juices. He released her wrists, leaned over, and kissed her on the forehead.

"Goodnight, sweet Anna," he said, before withdrawing from the room.

. . . ANNA KNEW IMMEDIATELY WHERE SHE WAS. SHE WAS LOOKING INTO the eyes of Beatrice. She recognized her from her picture. This was where it had all started. She could feel Luc's growing impatience.

"I can't keep sharing you like this," Beatrice said. "I can't. It's killing me. I love you, and I can't stand it when you walk out that door to sleep with someone else."

Luc growled. He wanted to shake her. Why the fuck was she so stubborn? "I've told you how it has to be. I can give you what you want. It can just be us, but there's only one way it can happen. I've explained the ritual to you. You'd give me your soul, and I'd bring you over."

"You'd kill me, you mean," she said, as if catching him in a lie.

"You can't die. Your soul is immortal. But you can't sustain a permanent, exclusive relationship with me while trapped in a human body. You know that."

She looked away. He felt the sorrow pouring off her, and her fear. His voice softened. "Beatrice, I love you. I don't know what you're afraid of, but I'd never hurt you." He reached out to touch her, but she pulled away.

He'd spent weeks combing the libraries, reading everything he could about the mating ritual that could bring a human woman and an incubus together. He'd never had a hard time convincing any woman to do anything before. But Beatrice wouldn't be moved.

"I'm sorry, I can't do it. You must be insane if you think I would give my soul to a demon. I could never go to Heaven. I'd be tied to you forever in this . . . limbo." The last word came out with disgust.

A piece of him broke.

The scene shifted. Something different stirred the air as Luc entered the house, and Anna knew he'd just left his freedom behind. Beatrice stood with her arms crossed over her chest, satisfaction shining out from her eyes.

"You've just cheated on me for the last time," she said.

He growled in frustration. They were back to this again? "I told you, I'm not cheating on you. You knew what I was, what I have to do, and you keep punishing me for it."

"I won't share you anymore." Luc opened his mouth to speak, but she held up a hand. "And I won't do that, either."

"Why not? You love me. I love you. This isn't that difficult, Bea!" He was pacing now.

"You're a demon. And I'll never let myself forget that. Ever!"

Anna felt the pain lance through him at the easy way the woman he loved spoke so callously, and she hated Beatrice for it. If the woman hadn't already been dead, she might have killed her herself.

"Fine," he growled. "I love you, but I'm done. You spend all your time accusing me. You refuse to give even an inch. I will be leaving now." There was a finality in his tone, and Anna wished things were different, that he'd made the choice just one day sooner, before Beatrice had the chance to wrap the house in magic.

He slammed the door against the wall and tried to go through it but bounced off the barrier. The shock and betrayal overwhelmed him as he turned toward her.

"What. Did. You. Do?" Luc felt the glow start in his eyes as the heat rose within him. He had to fight back the change, though at the moment, it was tempting to let her see just what she'd locked herself up with.

He stalked toward her until she had nowhere to run, slamming one hand against the wall on either side of her face, blocking her in.

She laughed at him. It wasn't a laugh of victory, but of sadness and resignation. "I can't live without you, Luc."

"You don't have to."

"I know."

Panic coursed through him. Oh no, that wasn't her plan. It couldn't be. "Beatrice, I have to get out. I have to feed. I was just with you last night. You don't know what you're doing."

Her sad eyes met his, the tears sliding down her cheeks. "I know what I'm doing," she whispered.

The scene shifted. Anna felt the beast barely restrained in his cage as Luc paced, and Beatrice waited. She seemed calm, accepting. Her long, silk nightgown was transparent, and it was driving Luc crazy.

He hadn't fed in five days. Maybe if he'd taken a small amount at a time, he could have been careful. But he was afraid he'd hurt her. He snarled and shoved her against the wall, sniffing her like she was the best meal he'd ever had. And she was because he loved her.

Now that he'd had her, he didn't want anyone else. He had to do whatever was necessary to scare her into reversing the spell. "Bea undo it NOW! Undo it or so help me, I will slowly torture the life from you." His words came out hard and guttural, barely human anymore.

"Will you?" she asked smoothly, meeting his eyes in challenge. He couldn't smell a drop of fear on her.

Luc slammed his fist into the wall next to her face. "You bitch! What have I ever done to you?"

"It's not what you've done to me. It's what you've done to every other woman you've been with. How many before me did you let live?"

He looked away, ashamed. She was the first one, and she knew it.

When he turned back to her, the expression on her face was smug. "That's what I thought. And you can't imagine why I can't trust you with my immortal soul?"

"We've been together for months . . . "

"Months too long. I'm lost to you now. I know it. I wish I was strong enough to leave or let you leave me, but I can't."

"I'll kill you. I don't want to, but I will. Please Bea, let me out. Let me go."

"No." She let the straps of the gown slip from her shoulders. The fabric fell in a whisper to the floor. "Take it," she said simply.

The hunger tore through him as he moved forward, unable to stop himself. He felt as if he hovered outside his body as he grabbed hold of her.

Luc took her there on the couch, listening to her soft cries and moans of pleasure until they died away, leaving nothing behind but her memory. She went slack in his arms, and for the first time in almost five hundred years, he cried.

20

*L*uc was looking at the television, but not really watching, when Anna came downstairs. He sat in the big chair and continued to pretend to be engrossed in the cooking program while he listened to her heartbeat.

"The girls are at Sally's setting up the candles. Tam wanted to wake you, but I thought you needed rest," he said, breaking the silence.

She sat across from him on the couch and pulled her feet up with her. He noticed with disappointment that she'd changed out of the pink gown. He grimaced at the pajama pants with cartoon candy. Oh, she still looked beautiful, but the wardrobe change seemed to indicate she was pulling away from him again.

Anna raised her hand to finger-comb her hair, and his eyes zeroed in on the scar. He couldn't seem to shut off the relentless chanting in his brain. *Mine. Mine. Mine.* The entire Playboy mansion could take up residence here, and he'd only have eyes for her. He wasn't sure anymore if it was the bond or something more.

Luc flicked the television off and turned to her. "More dreams?"

"I saw her."

He didn't have to ask who *her* was. The look in Anna's eyes told him it was Beatrice. Had she seen him kill her? *Fuck.* She must have.

"I see." Luc's first instinct was to stay where he was and give her space. After all, she probably wasn't feeling so attracted to him at the moment. Not with the Bea dream still spinning through her head.

But she looked so lost and forlorn that he couldn't stop himself from joining her on the couch and pulling her against his side, even if he'd somehow put that look on her face to begin with. He wrapped an arm loosely around her and kissed the top of her head.

She tensed. "Luc, even if I wanted to, I thought you said you can't feed two days in a row from the same..."

"Shhhh," he said. "I'm not feeding. I'm just holding. And what we did last night, it was just a taste. It wouldn't hurt you if we decided to..."

"Good to know," she said cutting him off with a nervous twitter as she tried to subtly wrench herself free from his grasp.

He held on, not willing to let her escape. "Anna..."

"Can you have sex without feeding? I mean could you with ... whoever, and then..."

"No. I can't."

She pulled out of his embrace, and he let her this time. He didn't attempt to touch her again for several minutes, and she didn't pull farther away. If she was asking these types of questions, she was still considering things. Even after the dream. Luc moved closer again, letting his warm breath feather over the back of her neck. He could feel her anxiety warring with lust.

"I'm sorry," he said. "I know what you can give and what you cannot, and yet I pursue you. I shouldn't. But I feel calm when you're near me. I haven't had nightmares since you moved into the house."

Anna spun around suddenly, her wide eyes meeting his. It was almost comical. He knew she saw him as some larger-than-life demon without any frailties or fears because it was the image he wanted her to see. The idea that he could have a nightmare, that he could have a heart in there, was probably more than she was prepared to deal with right now.

Tough.

She must have guessed what the bad dreams were about, because the next words out of her mouth were, "Are you sorry for all those people you killed?"

"Yes and no." He weighed the words carefully. "It's hard to be sorry for what you are. Are you sorry you had a cheeseburger last night?"

"No, but I can't have a cheeseburger without a cow somewhere dying first. You can feed without . . . "

He shook his head. Best to get this nonsense out of her head right now. "I can, but it's not easy. I've gained self-control but only because I had to. It hurts more to kill than it does to stop now. If I don't kill, I have to feed every night. When I killed, I could go much longer periods without feeding. I'm a demon. I told you I didn't want you to forget that. I can't live up to your standards of morality. The man I killed last night . . . I'm sorry you *saw* it. I'm only truly sorry for three lives I've taken, and you've seen those."

"Oh." She was quiet for a long time. "You said you had nightmares?"

"About Bea and the two girls after her. I would have nightmares about more, but I vowed never to kill another innocent, and I've kept that vow."

"You're being punished?" She'd moved back into the circle of his arms, letting him hold her and stroke her hair through the Q&A session.

"Yes. By God."

"What for?"

"When I was human, my mother said that a part of the devil lived inside me and that I'd return to him someday. She was right."

"You actually met the devil?"

He laughed. "Not literally, no. The jury is still out on that one, I'm afraid. When I died I was told I showed no remorse for my sins. I'd had my last chance and would never gain entrance into Heaven. Then they turned me into a demon.

"After that, the only time I felt anything was when I was feeding and killing. Until Beatrice. She put a spell on me that made me love her. It made me feel human again. And now I'm *this*. I still can't go to Heaven, but I can't enjoy being a demon anymore."

Her nose wrinkled as she looked up at him. "Um . . . sorry? I don't know what else to say. I don't think Hallmark makes a card for that."

Luc laughed, the warmth for her bubbling out of him. "I love you."

Anna jumped from his arms and this time moved back to the chair she'd started in.

He moved to get up, his hands held out in a *be reasonable* gesture. "Anna, I didn't mean . . . " But he had. He'd just stupidly blurted it out, and the look of fear in her eyes told him he'd pushed too far.

"Yes. You did. Don't come any closer."

He nodded and sat back down. What else could he do? Arguing the issue was pointless.

"Have you had more dreams about me?" she asked.

"I have only had a couple. My dreams haven't been as forthcoming as yours. I suspect your mind is more naturally closed. You suppress things and won't let them come out. How can I have dreams about what you avoid thinking about?"

"I need space. I need you to back off. Let me come to you. I feel like all my options are being cut off, and it makes me feel backed into a corner. I don't like that."

He didn't blame her. It wasn't as if she'd volunteered to have a demon for a roommate. A demon who had been slobbering all over her almost from the moment she'd arrived. She hadn't asked for any of this. Anna seemed ready to bolt when he stood up again.

"I want all of you, but I'll take whatever you have to give. I'd rather have small stolen moments with you than nothing at all." It was as good of an exit line as he was getting, and he used it to excuse himself from the room. He needed to find Olivia and help her through her withdrawals again anyway.

ANNA SAT FOR A FEW MINUTES, STUNNED. SHE WANTED TO RUN AFTER him, but she couldn't. He was giving her everything and she was giving nothing. What was her problem? It wasn't like the women he'd killed hadn't died happy.

Did I really just think that? This was exactly why they couldn't be together. She was going to lose her soul anyway if she found a way to rationalize things. He'd been bad as a human and had been given the freedom to be that forever. Until Beatrice had leashed him and taken it all away.

She showered and grabbed a Pop-tart. It was no longer her breakfast of choice, but Luc wasn't her cabana boy. She couldn't just snap her fingers and expect him to make her meals.

When she arrived at Sally's, the harem had just finished setting up the candles.

"You're a convenient riser," Maria said.

Anna started to bitch back, then realized there was no venom in the taunt. Whatever she decided to do, she couldn't blame the girls. She'd chosen them for Luc, and if she didn't like him sleeping with them, she had only herself to blame.

"Anna! Just the woman I wanted to see." A heavy brunette, wearing a bright red top and jeans, stepped out from behind a beaded curtain.

"Hi, Sally."

"I can't believe you haven't been by to see me before now." She held her arms out, and Anna stepped into the hug.

"Oh, well, you know . . . I've been battling demons and dealing with gypsies and priests and alternate dimensions and evil curses. It's hard to find the time sometimes."

Sally laughed. "You always were a very witty girl. Listen, I was just speaking with Tam. The flower shop next door is closing. I own the building, so I thought if your candles do well here, maybe you'd like to open your own shop."

"I told you not to ask her. She's done enough," Tam said.

"I'll think about it." It was a good idea. Anna wasn't taking profits off the business; she was just doing it for something to do. This was nickel and dime stuff. But it could really help Tam. And with a bigger store, the girls would be able to make some money.

Being away from Atlanta had caused them all to gain a lot of confidence. And pride. They were going to start getting upset about being *kept women*, especially kept by Anna. The whole thing was just too sordid. Once they got Luc out of the house they'd be going their separate ways, and Anna would feel a lot better if their separate ways didn't end them back up on street corners.

"I'm going to grab a bite to eat from the coffee shop. Tam? Wanna come with?" Anna said. The breakfast pastry didn't have staying power. Her body had started getting too used to being fed real food.

They left the girls with Sally and crossed the street to the coffee shop.

"I'm sorry about putting you on the spot there. I don't think you exist to finance my business," Tam said after they'd ordered.

Anna rolled her eyes. "Oh, please. Like I even care about that. I'm completely rolling in it. I could buy the whole town if I wanted to. That's not why I brought you over here."

"Oh?"

Anna just smiled and raised and lowered her eyebrows a few times.

"OH!" Tam said. "With Luc? How was it? Was it hot?" She leaned across the table, her hands clasped under her chin.

"We didn't actually sleep together, but it was . . . yeah."

After she filled Tam in, she waited for judgment to fall, but it didn't.

"So what's the problem?" Tam asked.

"You're kidding, right?"

"Nope," she said, finishing her chicken salad.

"He. Is. A. Demon," Anna hissed. A few patrons turned to stare at them.

She didn't bother including the part about the Beatrice dream. From her vantage point inside his head, Anna knew how much it had cost him to kill her. And in a way the bitch had had it coming. She'd set the trap. It had been suicide by demon. He'd been the victim in that one. No, the issue was his previous crimes, not the ones he hadn't been able to help.

"He's reformed." Tam waved a hand as if turning from your ways erased centuries of murder and mayhem.

Anna felt something prickle over her skin and looked up. Standing across the coffee shop was one of the most attractive men besides Luc or Cain she'd ever seen. She didn't know if she was developing demon radar, but she knew the man staring at her was another incubus.

21

*D*amn. How had she just sailed through life and not ever noticed there were demons floating around masquerading as humans? There couldn't be that many incubi in the world without huge unexplained death tolls, unless most of them didn't kill their prey. But Cain did. And Luc had.

The incubus across the room was trying to use the mind tricks on her. It caused the scar on her hand to flare to life. She mentally pushed. The demon took a step back, a look of surprise on his face, but he didn't leave the coffee shop.

"Tam, incubus at nine o'clock," Anna said.

"My nine o'clock or yours?"

Anna rolled her eyes. "Just look."

Tam turned around. "Dear Jesus, he's hot."

"Yes, and a killer. Let's try to focus and remember that part."

"Right." Tam turned away from the temptation, a look of resolve on her face.

Anna doubted the demon would try to hurt anyone in broad daylight. It seemed unlikely their kind had lived below the radar for thousands of years being careless. And he didn't look hungry. Not that he wasn't looking at her with that special brand of predatory that said he wouldn't refuse a snack, but he seemed in control of himself.

A preppy t-shirt clung too tightly to his body, outlining lean, sinewy muscles. Not too beefcake. He was definitely working the Abercrombie look. Anna was sure, anytime before all this, she would have thought he was a regular human college boy with more magnetism than most.

She turned to speak to Tam again, but the seat across from her was empty. She wasn't sure where her friend had gone, but suddenly she was worrying about just how long she'd been staring at the demon, oblivious to her surroundings. She'd thought it had only been a minute or two.

Anna took a deep breath; she wasn't going to sit there all after-noon playing chicken with a demon. Her heart was in her throat as she approached him, and she had to physically fight her reaction.

His eyes hardened in frustration. He was *really* trying. It was clear he wasn't used to receiving anything less than complete acqui-escence from the women he stalked.

Electricity curled the air as he tried and failed to touch her, bouncing back as if a force field had wrapped itself around her. At that moment, Anna felt very much like a superhero. *He can't touch me. Why not taunt him a little?*

"Hi there," she said, smiling.

The demon rubbed his hand on his jeans as if it had been burned, and eyed her warily. "I can't believe it. You've been marked."

"I bet it's really killing you to find out you aren't all that. You probably existed for centuries under the delusion you were just so hot no sane woman could resist you. Nice updated look, by the way. It's very J. Crew."

He stared at her a long time, cocking his head to the side. "Bizarre."

"Well, if you'll excuse me . . . " Anna started around him, but he blocked her path. She shrugged. He couldn't hurt her, but she'd already hurt him. She shoved him out of the way, and again the barrier forced him to back up to let her pass.

Moments later, the demon was outside, matching her stride.

Anna sighed. "You can't touch me, I don't know why you're following me," she said, feigning boredom.

He couldn't touch her against her will, but she wondered if he could if she let him. He was still trying to hypnotize her, and she was still pushing him away. She worried what would happen if he broke through her mental defenses.

Then again, she couldn't lie; she was feeling pretty kickass right about now. She was going to have to buy some black leather pants. You couldn't be kickass without black leather pants.

"I have my orders," he said.

In the bright afternoon sun, red scorch marks glared against his skin from where she'd touched him. Anna couldn't help smirking. She'd spent over a week alternately feeling safe and terrified, and now she was at least safe from everyone but Luc, who didn't seem interested in hurting her. *That's right incubi of the world. Watch out.*

The temptation to abuse her new power a little more was too great. She turned and leaped at him, holding her hands out like claws. "Boo!"

He jumped back, an annoyed look on his face. "I might not be able to touch you, but I have to follow you. Those are my orders. I'm Jackson, by the way." He offered a hand as if to shake, then, remembering his new crispy critter look, pulled it back hurriedly.

"You guys are all so very polite until you're sucking the life out of some poor, starry-eyed girl. I don't care what your name is. Who told you to follow me?" If it was Luc, she was going to be pissed. She didn't need or want a bodyguard.

"Cain."

Luc had mentioned Cain had minions. It was just that normally when one heard the word *minion* one thought of gross, sewer-dwelling creatures. Not potential underwear models.

He was still eyeing her as if she were a sideshow freak. "I haven't seen a woman marked by my kind in a long time. We don't do it. Fucks with your mind. No one wants to fall for their food around here." He shook his head. "I can't believe Luc did it."

"He did it to protect me from Cain. And *his minions*." She gave him a once-over. "How many of you are here?"

"Just me and Cain. The rest are in our dimension. We don't need an army for this."

Army for what? The word *army* put a damper on her superpower excitement, but she kept moving.

"Where are we going?"

"I'm going to church. I don't know where you're going," Anna said.

He visibly flinched at that. *Interesting.* Holy items had no effect, but the church itself might be a different story.

When they arrived, Jackson didn't follow her inside. "Allergic?" she asked.

His eyes glowed in irritation. "Churches are consecrated ground. A sanctuary. It's like a mirror of Heaven, a place we cannot enter."

"Okay, well bye now." She smiled brightly at him and disappeared inside the building before he could regale her with more fascinating demon history.

Within moments of shutting the door, her mood shifted. The church was too quiet. It was only a few hours before Friday night mass; someone must be there.

"Father Jeffries?" She hurried down the empty hall, trying not to be spooked by the sound of her shoes echoing in the silence. Shadows danced along the walls in flickering candlelight. The demon was outside, so why was she so uncomfortable being inside?

"Hello?"

She found him in his office and mentally berated herself for not checking there first.

He looked up from a disorganized pile of papers on his desk and removed a pair of reading glasses. "Anna. Have you decided?"

"I'm not here about the scar."

The priest looked troubled but nodded for her to go on.

"I was just wondering how you kill a demon."

"You can't."

"What do you mean you can't? There has to be a way. Nothing's immortal."

"Everything's immortal," he said. "Your soul. Mine. We aren't immortal in our current forms, but we are immortal. A demon has been cast out of Heaven. He's at the end of the line so to speak. And we *are* in Hell, Anna. This is their domain, their playground, even if they have other dimensions to go to."

"But . . . "

"This isn't a movie. They can't be killed. Sometimes immortal really does mean immortal. You're in danger. You know it or you wouldn't have come back here. We must do the ritual immediately to keep you safe." He scooted his chair back and started toward her.

"No. I didn't come here for that."

Father Jeffries pursued her as she backed herself against his office door; his pale blue eyes seemed to look into her. "I spoke with a seer. The demon will have your soul if you don't do the ritual. I know you don't want that. You have to know what's between you isn't real."

"Stop it!" She was falling for Luc. She'd tried to keep her distance, but it didn't matter. She wanted him to love her.

She fumbled for the doorknob. When it turned, Anna almost fell out into the hallway, then took off in a dead run. The irony of running from a priest and toward a demon was not lost on her. She'd wanted to know how to kill the others in case they started trying to hurt her friends, not how to break the bond with Luc.

The priest gave chase. For an old guy he could book it, and she wondered if he was endowed with superpowers of his own. On an ordinary day she would have checked herself in to the nearest mental health facility for even thinking something so odd, but she couldn't unsee the things she'd seen.

When she reached the awning outside the church she leaned forward, her hands braced against her knees. Father Jeffries spotted Jackson standing there growling, and backed into the shadows of the church.

Anna took a few deep lungfuls of precious oxygen. When she'd gotten her breath back, she started the trek home, knowing the priest wouldn't follow with a demon there.

Jackson kept pace beside her. What was it with demons? They were the most tenacious . . .

"Are we going back to your house now?"

"What are you? My pedestrian chauffeur? Shut up."

It was bad enough he was following her around. She didn't need streaming commentary the whole way. Jackson shrugged but shut up.

She should have known Cain would be inside the house with Luc, yet seeing him caused a chill to go through her.

"You're right to be afraid of me," Cain said, his eyes raising to hers.

He was perched in a chair by the fireplace looking about as regal as an evil being could. It was clear from their body language that she'd interrupted some kind of argument between the two demons. Maybe she was paranoid, but she felt like they'd been fighting about her.

"Anna, come here." Luc held a hand out to her. Jackson was forgotten at her back as she went to him. He took her scarred hand in his, and for once she was glad he was doing some weird possessive demon-y thing. She could feel him sending her power through the bond, as if she were a battery being charged up.

Cain laughed and shook his head. "I can't believe you think you can protect her from me. Someone like Jackson, perhaps, but not me. I'm older and stronger than you."

Luc growled and held onto Anna's hand tighter. She was relieved the harem wasn't home. The last thing they needed was other people in the mix who could be used as pawns.

Cain chuckled. "You'll come back to the fold one way or another. Once you're out of this house, things will be different. You'll remember who and what you are."

"No," Luc said.

Cain's eyes danced with amusement as he turned his attention to Anna. "Come here."

His mind pressed in on hers, and she felt the insane, maddening lust he'd created in her the first night in the kitchen. She wanted to go to him. She wanted to shake Luc's hand off and follow the seductive voice whispering inside her head. Wicked thoughts of all the wonderful things he could do to her flitted through her mind, and a slutty little moan passed through her lips.

Luc growled beside her, gripping her hand so tightly she thought he might break it. "Fight him."

She pushed back, like she had with Jackson, only much harder. The pressure eased off her mind, and the lust she'd felt only seconds before was replaced with her usual disgust with regards to the other demon.

His head whipped back from her effort, and he laughed. "Impressive. I can see why you marked her. I may not be able to make her come to me, but I can go to her."

Anna felt Luc's muscles tense in response, ready to pounce. Cain crossed the floor in three easy strides and reached out, touching her arm. No barrier locked him out.

His hand began sizzling as he fought to keep a grip on her, and her courage returned when she realized she still had a defense arsenal.

She smiled. "Get your dirty hands off me, Cain."

He snarled, still holding on while the smoke rose off his flesh. "I can take it." He gritted his teeth, unwilling to let a human woman best him.

"Sure you can," Anna taunted.

"Leave," Luc said. "I don't need you or the clan anymore."

Cain looked almost hurt, then his face hardened. "Fine!" He withdrew his hand from Anna's arm and stood. "But when she leaves and you lose your mind from marking her, know that we are your family. We're all you've got."

The front door opened and in walked Tam and the harem. She couldn't have picked a worse time to show up. Cain's eyes lit with malice as he saw the scales tip in his favor.

"Tam, get out of here!" Anna said.

Cain smiled. "This one means something to you? Come to me." He extended a hand toward Tam, arrogantly waiting for her to obey and fall into his arms like a cheesy romance heroine.

"Um . . . no," Tam said.

"What?" He shook his arm like it was an electrical instrument that had a short in it. "Come here!" he demanded again.

"I said *no!*" She crossed her arms over her chest, smirking at him.

"Tam?" Anna said. "Luc thralled you. How . . . ?"

"Oh, please. Yeah, I admit my guard was down that day, but seriously, fool me once . . . Well, you know . . . blah blah blah. Point is, I've got really good shields up now. Thanks for that heads up, by the way, Luc."

"Not a problem," he said, grinning.

Cain shrugged. "It doesn't matter. I don't have to feed, I just want to hurt you." He rushed toward her.

Tam was eerily unconcerned. She hauled her hand back like she was going to throw a baseball, and then suddenly, she had something to throw. In her hand, she held what could only be described as a glowing purple ball of energy. She threw it and sent Cain flying across the room to land in a heap on the floor.

He glowered up at her, sweeping a clump of hair out of his eyes, and growled. Tam arched a brow in challenge. "Wanna look stupid in front of your immortal pals again?"

Cain got up and brushed himself off. He pushed past Tam and the harem, calling over his shoulder for Jackson to follow. Then to Luc, "Fuck it. I'm done. Don't expect my help again."

"Are you all right?" Luc asked when the door slammed behind them. He ran his fingers over Anna's hand gently, checking to see if he'd hurt her with his grip.

She nodded.

"So, yeah," Tam said, "I took the harem to my place for awhile, and we put up a barrier spell. No one that isn't invited can get in. I looked into doing the same thing here, but the original spell prevents a barrier from being put up. It's this whole *you can't have two spells of similar nature on the same object* thing. We'd have to break the spell currently on the house first."

After seeing Tam go super-witch on her, she had no other choice. They were going to have to put their witch issues aside for the greater good.

22

Something was different about Luc in this dream. It took a minute for Anna to notice the hunger was missing. In earlier dreams, it had blended so well into the background, she'd never paid it much attention. Now it was obvious by its absence.

He was human.

He crouched behind a cluster of bushes at the mouth of a dark forest. Rage and desperation curled inside him, waiting for the opportunity to be unleashed.

A carriage was on its way around a corner. The horses slowed, sensing danger, and Luc attacked. He held a knife in his hand as he ripped the carriage door off its hinges and peered inside. Two women, one older, one younger sat together, wedged against the back corner.

Pretty, he thought. He hadn't decided on a plan, but he could practically smell the wealth coming off these women, and it made him angry. How easy and pampered their lives were. The least he intended to do was relieve them of some of their money.

"Please, don't hurt us. We have money. Just take it and go," the younger one said, holding out a bundle of fabric that must contain coins.

Luc leaned into the carriage and brushed a hand against the young one's cheek. "I wager you wish you'd stayed home today, eh?"

The woman flinched, and he laughed. "Just take the money . . . please."

Anna wanted to shut her eyes. He was hungry and cold and tired and enjoying scaring someone of better means than himself. She wondered how far he'd take it before he stopped, and if she could ever forgive him for whatever he did.

Moments later, he flew backward and landed on his ass. The driver of the carriage was the last thing he saw as strong hands gripped his head and twisted.

The scene shifted, and Luc was in an ornate room made almost entirely of gold. A short, balding man in a nondescript cream-colored robe stood behind a gilded podium reading from a scroll.

All at once, Anna was ambushed by Luc's past memories. She struggled to hold herself together as image after image assaulted her, memories from other lives merging into one, blending and overlapping. Stealing. Murder. Betrayal. Over and over the patterns replayed showing her the kind of man Luc had been with alarming consistency.

A male voice rose suddenly above the din, as if he were repeating himself.

"Do you understand the charges against you, Lucien?"

She was torn between sympathy for Luc and anger at what he'd been. Had he really had a chance with the lives he'd lived? And yet all sorts of people were faced with all kinds of life challenges and didn't become monsters.

"Lucien!" the man shouted.

"Yes?" Luc was jolted from the memory dump as he looked up at the little man. Though his stature wasn't the least bit intimidating, the man seemed to hold the power of existence itself in his hands.

"Do you understand the charges?"

"Yes." He wasn't about to show this man fear.

"You've been given multiple chances to change your path, and yet you refuse. You are weak and inhuman. You feel no remorse for your crimes. You've behaved as an animal. From here on you will exist as one."

It wasn't true. Luc *did* have remorse. Anna could feel it. It was small, but it was there. Surely there was something in him worth saving. But he didn't speak to defend himself, and the self-important balding man seemed ill-prepared to listen to an alternate perspective.

"You'll spend the remainder of eternity back in Hell and whatever other dimensions you can manage to slither through. You'll have no further chances to get it right."

Then there was a flash of light, and he was on the ground in a town he didn't recognize, surrounded by people and noise.

The hunger gnawed at him, making his senses narrow to the desperate need to touch someone, to connect, to feed. He saw a beautiful woman and moved toward her. She screamed and ran when she saw him. He chased, tackling her to the ground. But he couldn't feed this way.

Realization dawned immediately, as if new instincts had been transplanted into his brain to match his new form. They had to want him or he couldn't satisfy the hunger.

He looked down. His skin was a brownish red and scaled, like the monsters people in small villages often spoke about. Where fingernails once grew, he had long, black talons. He could only imagine what the rest of him must look like.

For once he didn't care about image or if he appeared weak to someone. He was so tired of everything. Life, the never-ending struggle only to have more shit. He fell to the ground and sobbed, allowing the girl to run away in a hysterical fit.

"And they call *us* animals."

Anna recognized the voice right away. Cain. Luc looked up. For a moment she thought the demon had found her in the dream and was using the thrall. She was noticing how indescribably beautiful he was. Then she realized the feelings weren't sexual. They were Luc's thoughts when he'd seen the other incubus for the first time.

"I'm Cain," he said, extending a hand. "I'm what you are."

Luc looked at his claws and then at Cain, his brow knitting in confusion at their disparate appearance. He wondered if the man was only teasing him.

"We're shapeshifters," Cain said. "I'll teach you to find the form that will be most pleasing to help you catch prey, and I'll teach you how to hunt and feed. You're a demon now. You'll learn very soon how freeing it is to live without consequences. The old man at the gate did you a favor . . .

ANNA HATED THE IDEA OF WITCHES, PROBABLY BECAUSE IT WAS A witch that had created the Luc problem in the first place. She had a hard time understanding how not one witch, but several, were going to fix anything. But seeing Tam in action the previous night had left her no alternative.

"You look like hell," Tam said.

Four strange women were seated around the kitchen table. The harem was in the living room watching a horror movie marathon and squealing like teenagers.

"Thank you," Anna said.

Luc, as always, was right there, pressing a glass of juice into her hand and urging her to have some breakfast. "Are you all right after last night?" he asked.

Her eyes widened. Did he know what she'd dreamed about? She felt almost embarrassed at having witnessed such ugly and weak moments, knowing he'd never want her to see him like that.

Then she realized he wasn't talking about dreams but about Cain and his less-than-disgusting minion. She couldn't believe she'd forgotten.

"I'm fine," she said.

Luc stood behind her, trailing a hand over her back. She leaned into his touch. How could she want him after all she knew? She didn't have a comforting abstraction when dealing with his dark past. She had vivid, Technicolor dreams.

Anna didn't have to guess his thoughts or emotions. She'd soaked them into the deepest parts of her soul while she'd slept. She had so much in her head now that wasn't her, she felt she was losing herself in the deluge of Luc.

His hand continued to gently stroke up and down her back. She wanted to lash out at him. Hadn't she asked him yesterday to let her come to him and to stop pushing her? Stop trying to seduce her?

She glared at him over her shoulder but caught the guarded look on his face as he watched the witches. He didn't seem to know he was touching her. Was it for comfort? For himself? He felt tense, and he reached for her. She felt tense; she reached for him. She didn't want to think what that meant.

"This is my coven. Not huge, but enough to get the job done. This is Mel, Lisa, Ursula, and Wendi," Tam said, gesturing at each of them in turn.

The women sitting at the table looked normal enough. Maybe normal was an overstatement. They looked like hippies. Cute, clean hippies who didn't have an unnatural love of patchouli. Ursula and Mel had short, black hair and looked like they could be sisters.

Wendi had long, strawberry-blonde hair pulled into braids on either side of her face, while Lisa's was long, free-flowing light brown. They all wore natural fibers, and Anna was sure someone was going to light up a bong and start playing The Beatles any minute.

Anna drank the juice down greedily, her throat gone suddenly dry. The coven was making no secret of ogling Luc. She wanted to shout, *Hey! That's my demon!* but thought it would be a little too daytime television. Besides, she couldn't keep him.

A moment later, a plate was passed to her. Food. Good. Eating would keep her from wanting to claw out the coven's eyeballs, then having to worry about why she'd felt the need to do it. The harem ogled him all the time, and it didn't bother her. He wasn't even ogling back. Was he? She looked up, but his eyes hadn't strayed from her as she moved to the table with her breakfast.

Tam unfolded a large piece of coffee-stained parchment. "This is our moon phase chart. We've figured that tonight would be the best time to do the working."

Anna stopped chewing. "Why can't you just do it? The priest didn't need a special time . . . or the gypsies."

Wait. Did some of the witches just hiss at her? If the spell worked, she was bringing Father Jeffries back in to do some kind of cleansing. These chicks were freaking her out.

"Gypsies? You had filthy gypsies in this house, and you called on us second?" Lisa asked.

"Um . . . well . . . " Anna said.

Wendi stood then. "We should go."

"Wait!" Anna said. "Tam, talk to them."

Tam sighed. "Look, Anna is my friend. Despite her lack of wonderful judgment here, she needs us to help her get Luc out of the house."

"Thanks. I love you, too," Anna said.

"I don't know why she'd want to get rid of him," Lisa said. "If he was in my house, I'd never let him go." She made no secret of looking him slowly up and down as she licked her lips in invitation. "I mean, look at him. What a hottie."

Anna clenched her fists. She had the urge to swing first and worry about possible curses being cast on her later. "And that's just the kind of attitude that gets women killed."

She looked up, suddenly remembering Luc was standing right there. He had a pained expression in his eyes.

"Sorry," she mouthed, feeling about an inch tall. He nodded, but it didn't make her feel less guilty for the thoughtless remark. However true it may have once been.

"And besides," she added, "this isn't just about what I want. He wants out of the house, too. Right?"

"I do," he said. But the way he said it made her think he didn't intend to leave forever once he was free.

Wendi prowled around the demon. "I just want to lick him like a big lollipop." She ran a hand over his arm, which was a mistake.

Anna lurched out of her chair and flung the witch away. "Enough!" she said. She stood in front of Luc, her arms spread wide, as if she physically needed to protect him.

Wendi hissed. No, Anna hadn't imagined the hissing. Then the woman hauled back and formed a purple energy ball much like Tam had the night before. These women were completely out of control, like a bunch of middle-aged housewives at a Chippendales.

Tam's voice rang out. "Ladies, calm yourselves. We are here to reverse the barrier spell, and that is all. Luc belongs to Anna."

"What?" Anna spluttered. "He does *not* belong to me."

Tam arched a brow.

"He doesn't! He's not a pet. He's a person. Um kind of . . . but that's not the point. My God, are all witches like this?" She'd never seen women behave this way before.

"No," Tam said dryly, "just my coven. They're hornier than most. I blame the bonfires and late night nudity."

Anna didn't want to know.

"Fine," Wendi and Lisa said, both folding their arms over their chests in a display of unified disgust.

"What about you two?" Anna asked, glancing at Mel and Ursula.

The other two merely nodded that they were on board. Anna was betting those two were mute. She was beginning to feel claustrophobic surrounded by so many women who wanted to jump on Luc like he was a carnival ride.

Her eyes drifted to his bare chest as she tried not to think about riding him herself. "You can come back tonight. I've got to get some fresh air, and there's no way I'm leaving any of you alone with him."

"My heart flutters with how much you care," Luc said. His hand was on her back again doing that wonderful light rubbing with the pads of his fingertips.

She didn't have the energy to snark back. And if she did, he might stop touching her. Which would be bad. Finally, realizing the coven was looking at her with amused expressions, she stepped out of his reach.

"I'm going into town. I need shoes."

Before Anna could make any headway, Luc grabbed her arm. "No. You aren't going out."

"Uh, yeah I am. Let go of me."

"I said no. Cain and Jackson could be out there, and he may have brought others. I cannot risk that the bond won't hold up." He met her eyes, his gaze turning softer. "I can't risk you getting hurt out there."

If they'd been alone in the house, there was a real possibility she would have thrown caution to the wind and gone upstairs with him. But with so many eyes on her, she chose arguing, instead.

"What? So I'm under house arrest now? I don't think so."

Tam moved between them to diffuse the situation. "It's all right. I had Ursula and Mel do a spell this morning to see how much demonic activity we had going on in town. We needed to make sure no other energies would interfere with our magic. They've left. Luc is the only incubus in town at the moment."

His grip loosened, but he didn't release her. "They could return. They could have simply hopped dimensions for a few hours."

"What if she doesn't go alone?" Tam asked.

"I don't need bodyguards, especially these bodyguards."

"Think of it this way," Tam said diplomatically. "If they're out with you, they aren't here groping your man."

"Okay, girls," Anna said, "we're going shoe shopping now. Chop. Chop."

23

*A*nna wanted to scream. Tam had stayed behind, leaving her alone with the coven of horniness. Wendi popped her gum as they walked past the courthouse. If that bubble came out of the witch's mouth one more time, Anna was going to smack her in the face. Of course, there would be retaliation. She kind of doubted the mark on her hand protected her from pissed-off witches. It seemed to be species-specific magic.

Since she'd known Tam, Anna hadn't really thought there was *real* magic, not *energy ball throwing* magic. The kind you could see. This was the *gee whiz golly wow* stuff of Hollywood.

She shuddered. Demons and gods and magic. *What else is real? Werewolves? Vampires? Fairies?* She had the urge to loop arms with the witches and start skipping down the street singing, *Demons and gods and magic, oh my.*

"You're awfully quiet," Mel said.

"Says the mute girl."

"Quiet is my normal state. It helps keep my mind even. You notice I didn't jump your boy back there like those two." She pointed at Wendi and Lisa who looped arms and stuck their tongues out in response.

Mel's *quiet is my normal state* mantra seemed to be conditional on being in the presence of a sex demon because now that she'd started talking she wasn't shutting up.

"So," she said, her tone casual, "you going to mate with him?"

Mate? What was this? Animal Kingdom? Yes, I would like to mate now. Where is your cave located?

When Anna just stared at her, Mel said, "You know, the ritual. I used to think it was a myth. Guess not." She shrugged as if the details on mating with an incubus were common knowledge anyone with a local library card and an afternoon of free time could easily acquire. "He's already marked you as his. You really don't have a choice. It's going to happen."

"I have a choice," Anna said. She'd been refusing him just fine. She was brimming with free will.

Wendi and Lisa had skipped on ahead and were inside Sally's looking at the candle display.

Ursula moved to her other side. "No, you don't. There's no way a regular human can resist an incubus, especially not when she's been marked like you have. It's just a matter of time, girlfriend. You're inside his head. You feel for him even though you know you shouldn't. Even though you know all the bad shit he's done."

What Anna *felt* was herself seizing up in a panic.

"Oh come *on!*" Mel said. "You act like this is some horrible torment. I mean you have eyes, right? I wouldn't be kicking *that* out of bed for eternity."

"I . . . " Anna opened and closed her mouth a couple of times like a fish, then settled on keeping it closed. They were just trying to scare her.

"Just sleep with him and be done with it, at least," Ursula said. "The sexual tension humming over you two is insane. Wendi and Lisa probably should have shielded better, but they wouldn't have been so slutty if it hadn't been for the tension. You could always undo the bond and hop dimensions later."

Before Anna could reply, Cece approached them. At the same moment, Wendi and Lisa stepped out of the shop, their arms still looped together, each holding a brown paper bag.

"I got some candles we can use in the spell tonight," Wendi said.

Real subtle.

"Spell?" Cece said.

"I'm going to buy shoes," Anna blurted, sounding like a mental patient. She knew she came off like a demented crackpot but hoped Cecelia was as easy to distract as Bitsy and Mimi.

"I got some lovely sandals last week. They're having a fifty-percent-off sale, you know," Cece said.

No, Anna hadn't known. She'd been too busy dealing with the newly-discovered supernatural world to be bothered with such pedestrian things as shoe sales. Something she was about to remedy.

"You never did tell me when a good time would be to come by and get a tour of that lovely house you just bought," Cece said.

Anna searched frantically for something, anything, to get her off the house tour idea. She loved the woman, but Cece just would not let go.

The hardware store next door had a white sign painted with black letters that read, *Paint. Buy one can, get one free.*

"Paint!" Anna shrieked.

"Paint?" Cecelia asked, clearly baffled by all the strange subject changes.

"Paint fumes," Anna said. She looked around self-consciously, wondering how many denizens of Golatha Falls had just witnessed her spastic outburst. "We have them," she finished with more composure.

"Oh, dear. That is a problem because you know I'm allergic."

Anna nodded sympathetically, trying not to jump with glee and run in to kiss the person who'd decided to put the paint on sale.

"When do you think it'll be cleared out?"

Damn. She really wanted to see the house. Luc was right about the strength of her mind. It was so strong she was now desperate for the truth. Cece might not realize it consciously, but Anna was willing to bet some dark part of her knew what she believed to be a dream, hadn't been.

"It'll be weeks at least. I'm not too crazy about the fumes myself, and I'm repainting the entire house. It could take a while."

Surely she could get Luc out in that time and redecorate the area Cecelia had been in drastically enough that she wouldn't suspect anything. Anna didn't want to explain why the man she was seriously considering taking as a lover had slept with her friend and erased her memory.

Cece's face fell. "Oh. Well, some other time. It's not like the house won't be there."

ANNA WAS IN A STATE OF BLISS WHEN SHE ARRIVED BACK AT THE house. All thoughts of demons and spells and evil had been temporarily banished under the onslaught of shopping, foot massages, hot pink nail polish, and aromatherapy candles.

The peace lasted until she opened the door. Tam had gotten everything set up while they'd been out. Incense burned in several censers around the room. *Cleansing the space*, she'd said. What was it with everybody and cleaning space?

The harem sat bunched like sardines on the couch, eating popcorn, while Luc paced the floor.

"Oh good. You're back," he said.

He pulled Anna into the alcove under the staircase. It didn't escape her notice that he was running his fingertips over the scar.

The more often he did it, the more she saw it for what it was. Comfort, not possession. He was seeking to make the bond stronger, to connect with her in the only way he could until she finally let him into her bed.

Her irritation with him dissipated, leaching out through her skin as he caressed her and nuzzled his face into her neck. She intended to push him away, but she found her fingers threading through his hair, instead.

She never could have forgotten he'd spent centuries seducing women, finding the right buttons to push. Anna wasn't aware of any specific signals she'd given out, but he'd zeroed in on her neck as a major erogenous zone. Kissing and licking and sucking there . . .

Goosebumps popped out on her arms as he growled into her skin. Maybe after centuries he knew all the sexual statistics. The percentage of women who like this in bed or that as foreplay. Maybe he was just playing the odds.

A throat cleared. She spun to see Wendi smirking at her.

"We're ready."

Anna didn't let go of Luc's hand as they went out to the foyer. This could be it. He could be free. The witches might actually do it. And then what? Would he leave her?

It had been the plan all along to get him out of the house, not fall for the seduction. But she couldn't close her eyes now without seeing his. What if it worked and he left her?

Candles were lit as Tam walked around the circle spilling salt.

"It's just salt," Anna said when Luc grasped her hand tighter. Sure, they'd both pretend it was salt on the hardwood floor that upset him.

Luc and Anna stood in the center of the circle. Blood wasn't required this time, but they were. Anna, because she was the current owner of the house, and Luc because the spell had been cast against him. Even the harem had been asked to join in.

Scarlett and Rhett wove around legs, freely moving in and out of the circle. The harem and coven stood around them, hands linked, chanting in Latin.

For the first time, there was a physical manifestation besides the effects of wind. A pink circle of light suffused them all, then started to rise, binding tighter and tighter. Light wrapped around light as if forming a strong twine, then wrapped itself around Luc and Anna.

Each woman fell into a trance while the chanting rose higher. Anna held onto Luc as light pressed around them. The spell went on, causing tension to coil inside her. Her anxiety ratcheted higher and she wanted nothing more than to get out of the house.

Finally, the glowing band shattered into pieces, and small pinpoints of pink light fluttered to the floor like glitter. The candles snuffed out as the power ebbed from the circle, and they stood in darkness.

"Try the door now." Tam's voice sounded ethereal.

Luc attempted to leave and bounced off the barrier. A stream of curses flew from his mouth, and Tam flicked the light back on.

Anna stood in the circle, trembling. Now that it was over, the panic washed over her in a wave she couldn't stop. Luc snapped out of his own anger long enough to rush back to her.

"Witches," he spat with disgust. "Always causing trouble. What did you do to her?"

"Nothing," Tam said. "I love her like a sister. I'd never hurt her."

"Then why is she shaking like this?"

"It's just fear," Mel said. "I think she's scared of magic."

"She wasn't like this with the gypsies or the priest. I want to know exactly what was done," he said, not placated.

"We redid the original curse with a small change so we could more easily break it. Then we bound the two curses together so that when we broke ours, the old one would break too. It's worked on similar spells before. But only ours broke this time."

❄

THE COVEN PACKED THEIR MAGICAL KNICK KNACKS AND LEFT SOON after the failed ritual. Anna had never been so happy to see anyone go. Mel was right, the magic scared her.

She didn't know what made it different or scarier than the priest or gypsies, but it had caused a visceral reaction. After Luc kicked the coven out with a few choice words and the comment that they should all be very happy they were women because it was the only thing keeping him from beating them bloody, he'd carried Anna upstairs.

He hadn't wanted to leave her, but he needed to feed. She'd sent him away, assuring him she was fine. She hadn't been prepared to consummate this . . . whatever it was, with Luc. Not while she was still so freaked about the episode with the magic downstairs.

That was five minutes ago. Now, she felt a little differently about the issue. She wanted him with her, and if he had to feed to do that, so be it. She got out of the bed and went downstairs, still feeling a little wobbly.

Drawing a shaky breath, she knocked on Luc's door before she lost her nerve. Olivia was visible in the background when he answered.

"Anna, are you all right? Do you need . . . ?" He faltered over the words as if he couldn't quite determine what it was that she needed.

"I'd rather have stolen moments than nothing." Anna turned to go back upstairs. She didn't have to look behind her to know Luc would follow.

24

The door clicked shut, and Anna spun to find Luc standing with his back pressed firmly against it, that predatory gleam in his eyes. Part of her loved that look, and yet . . .

He looked at her as if he was the big bad wolf, and the only weapon she had was a picnic basket. Why couldn't he choose now to be disarming? She longed for petty arguments over bath towels or holes in the wall. Anything to make what they were about to do seem less scary.

Her heart pulsed out of control as he stalked her, crossing the floor so fast it made her breathless. Then his hands were tangled in her hair, and his mouth covered hers until she gasped for air. A moment later, he broke the kiss, his hot breath in her ear.

"God, Anna, it feels like I've waited years for this." His hands skimmed over her arms like he was trying to be sure she was real. "You're trembling."

"I'm scared."

"You know I won't hurt you."

"There's more than one way to hurt someone."

If she crossed this bridge with him, it was over for her. No one else would compare to an incubus. When he inevitably left to go off and do what incubi do, she would be the one with the gaping hole in her chest where her heart had been.

His eyes locked with hers. "I'm going for a change of venue. I need you to relax." He flicked on the small television set. "Sit. Watch. I'll call you when I'm ready for you."

Images flickered on the screen while the water ran in the bathroom. The words coming out of the speakers were meaningless sounds Anna couldn't translate in her head. Nothing could distract her from the knowledge that there was a demon only a few feet away who had plans for her. Ten minutes later, the door swung open.

The light from the bathroom cast Luc in shadow, but she could see he was completely, deliciously nude. She had the crazy impulse to say, *meow*. He was doing strange things to her, throwing her brain off kilter. Nice girls didn't openly gawk at a man's package and make cat noises. Technically, nice girls weren't alone in their bedrooms with sex demons in the first place.

"See something you like?" He waited a moment, watching her blush and enjoying her discomfort, before crooking a finger.

Anna tried desperately to stop looking at his erection. She'd only been in bed with a couple of men, but they'd done it lots of different times. She wasn't a blushing virgin.

She'd also watched porn. And she'd watched it so when confronted with other naked males, she wouldn't react the way she was reacting right now. That plan had failed her.

"Are you sure you aren't using the thrall?" she asked with a little squeak as she reached him.

His gaze heated her from the inside out. "I don't *have* to use the thrall."

She felt ridiculous wearing what amounted to kid's pajamas. The only thing missing were feet with rubber grips on the bottom. Couldn't she have changed into something sexier before she'd gone downstairs to drag him from his meal? Anna shivered. He was going to feed off her. But the part that made her shiver was the fact that she wanted him to. After his brief taste the previous night, she was more than a little eager for more.

As if reading her mind, Luc ripped her top. She'd been so focused on his eyes, she hadn't seen what his hand was doing. He'd kept his form everywhere else, but had brought out his claws. A neat, sharp cut line in her t-shirt left it hanging open. An inch deeper and he would have sliced through her.

She tried very hard to muster indignation over how he played with her life by centimeters. But the way his eyes bored into hers, half challenge and half that lost look she'd only seen men get in movies, caused her to falter. It was as if she were the only woman that existed for him. Intellectually, she knew this was how every woman he'd killed over the centuries had felt, that she was buying into the same seduction. But she couldn't resist him even with that knowledge.

"I liked that shirt," she said.

"We'll get you another one."

Before he could shred the pajama bottoms to match the top, she quickly moved to take them off herself.

"Deep down, I think you're a little naughty," he said, probably in response to her lack of underwear. He pushed her forward into the bathroom, cutting off her very reasonable explanation.

The room glowed with dozens of candles. Candles she'd helped make. Had he been chipmunking them away for his later seduction? Her eyes drifted to the enormous tub filled with bubbles.

"We can't have an orgy, but we'll do what we can."

The blush crept up the back of her neck again. Luc must have been standing in this spot all invisible and sneaky when Cathy had given her the house tour. Had he been planning this since then?

He frowned. "Why are you still wearing that?"

The gaping t-shirt still hung on Anna like a poorly-tailored jacket, the last comforting piece of fabric between her and complete naked vulnerability. Seeing the look in his eyes, she scrambled to take it off.

There had to be thrall involved. She was officially losing her mind. Otherwise the only reason she wasn't a wanton slut was because she hadn't had sufficient opportunities. It was a possibility she didn't want to entertain at the moment.

The water was hot, just barely tolerable. Anna sank onto the bench, the bubbles coming over her breasts. Luc joined her and leaned against the rim, his arms propped on the edge, completely at ease.

Of course he was.

"I went to all this trouble, and you look like you're planning your escape," he said.

"Just touch me." *Just do anything but stare.*

"There's the demanding Anna I know and love."

He'd said it again. Love. She wondered if he was normally so casual with that word. Now, instead of making her want to get as far from him as possible, it made her want to move closer. She inched forward.

When she was close enough, Luc picked her up like she weighed nothing and placed her on his lap facing away from him. His erection pressed against her, driving her crazy as he rubbed the tension out of her neck and shoulders. Anna arched at the gentle strength in his hands, and her head dropped onto his shoulder. Before she could issue a flimsy protest, he lifted her again and was inside her.

She was about to give him a dirty look for the proprietary way he'd just decided to *take* her without further fanfare, but that thought left her mind at the same time the mortifying sound left her mouth.

Her whimper was answered by a rumbling chuckle. They fit together perfectly. The part of her brain that would have reminded her he was a shapeshifter, and perfect fits weren't shocking, had shut off.

Water sloshed over the sides of the tub as she rode him more aggressively, finding a rhythm. He seemed content to let her pick the pace, not pushing, just quietly urging her on with pleased little growls that set off a series of aroused flips in her stomach.

As they made love, she wasn't sure if certain images or feelings were actually happening or were just in her mind. Emotions and tactile sensations blended together until it was hard to separate reality from fantasy.

As soon as her orgasm started to build, he began to feed. She couldn't stop the soft sighs and moans and vowed she'd share this man with anyone as long as he didn't stop touching her.

Anna convulsed around him as he kissed and nibbled the side of her exposed neck. When she slumped, boneless, he lifted her into his arms and carried her out of the tub.

"Luc," she whispered, feeling a little drunk.

"I'm not finished with you yet." He pulled her down to the floor, so she was on top, straddling him, her hands gripping the furry white rug beneath them.

"Come for me again."

"I can't. I just ... "

He didn't have to say anything else; the look in his eyes was enough. She nodded and started moving again. Anna wasn't sure where this sudden stamina came from. She was a *one orgasm per visit* kind of girl and had never understood women who could have four or five in a row. Still, she kept going, and that's when she figured out what the fuss was all about.

A second orgasm built, this one from the inside. Then she felt Luc let himself go, feeding fully now. The tiny tugs suffused her entire body with a pleasant, tingling warmth. If he'd asked for her soul right then, she would have gladly gift-wrapped it for him, too lost in sensation to be able to think past what he was doing to her. She felt as if she were floating when she came again.

S<small>UN FILTERED THROUGH THE WINDOWS, BUT THE WARMTH</small> A<small>NNA FELT</small> came from the male body pressed to hers. He'd pulled her up against him in sleep as if unwilling to ever let her go, his arms wrapped around her in a vice. She couldn't decide if the feeling was comforting or claustrophobic, but settled on the former.

She'd secretly feared the reality of an empty bed at sunrise. How could she feel like anything but his whore if she didn't wake with him beside her? She knew he didn't sleep overnight with the harem and wondered what else would be different between them.

As she contemplated this, she realized she hadn't dreamed.

Well, she'd dreamed. Something about a circus monkey and needing to find Monopoly money so she could buy bananas from a corner grocer with a Haitian accent. But she hadn't had one of the *surround-sound fully lucid but can't control anything or wake up* kind of dreams she'd had every night since Luc had formed the bond with her. She felt him tense.

"Anna, I'm sorry. I didn't mean to . . . "

She racked her brain to figure out what it was he didn't mean to do. Then she remembered she hadn't been there for the afterglow because she'd passed out. The sex had been great, really great. It had been *Anna, you're so stupid you could have been doing this for over a week now* great. But somehow she doubted that was why she'd fainted.

"I took too much," he said, confirming her suspicions.

Anna rolled to face him, surprised by the pain and guilt in his eyes, and even more surprised that she wasn't at all freaked out that she could have died. So maybe she trusted him a little. She ran her fingers through his bed-tousled hair. "It's okay. You stopped."

Luc climbed out of the bed and went to put his jeans back on. Her eyes hungrily drank him in as she watched, causing her to wonder if sex with an incubus had addictive properties.

Finally, he turned back to her. "No. It's not okay. I haven't lost control like that for a long time. If you had been hurt . . . "

For once, Anna was unconcerned with her nudity as she moved to embrace him. Luc's arms went around her, clutching her.

"Maybe it was the spell," she said. "Maybe it took too much out of both of us. Next time it'll be different." She'd officially lost her self-preservation instinct. She was already thinking ahead to *next time.*

He pulled away. "I just wish you would give me . . . "

"No." She'd never give him her soul. Trusting him enough to share his bed wasn't even in the same league as that type of request.

He growled. "Fine. What are we going to do about getting me out of the house?"

The subject change gave her emotional whiplash, and she tried not to feel hurt that he was already concerned with how to get away from her. "I don't know."

The demon was scrutinizing her now, and the nudity that hadn't mattered five seconds before was becoming increasingly problematic. Anna opened a drawer and pulled out the first jeans and t-shirt her hands could close around.

She struggled to cover herself and glared at him. His gaze never wavered from her body. He could at least look away. *Yeah, just like you didn't stare at his ass while he was putting his jeans on two minutes ago.*

"You know you're going to have to burn it down. We've tried everything else."

"If I do, are you going to leave me?" She knew she sounded needy, like she had to keep a man locked in her house for him to want to be with her.

Luc's eyes shot up to meet hers and narrowed. "So, you want to keep me as a pet now? Did you decide Beatrice had a good idea after all? You can have your very own sex slave. Only twice a week, but it's quality not quantity, right? After all, I don't even have to touch you to make you come. I just have to think the right thoughts in your direction."

"Luc, that's not what I meant. I don't want to keep you trapped. I just . . . you've been here fifty years . . . can't you give me a few weeks to work up to the possibility that I might have to burn the house down? Maybe there's still another way."

Anna knew it was unlikely but she wasn't about to set her house on fire if there was even the remotest chance she didn't have to. She wasn't ready to become an arsonist.

He grunted.

The phone on the bedside table rang, preventing her from obsessing about his *I just have to think the right thoughts in your direction* comment. What Pandora's box had she just opened?

"Yeah?" Anna said, grateful for the interruption.

"It's Tam. I just wanted to say I'm sorry about the coven's behavior yesterday. They've never been around an incubus before. I should have prepared them better. And they could sense how much you didn't want them there."

"So it's my fault?"

Tam sighed into the phone. "That's not what I'm trying to say."

Luc leaned against her dresser, his arms crossed over his chest, making no secret of eavesdropping.

"Sorry," Anna said. "I'm just cranky. Is that why you called?"

"Yes and no." There was a pause on the line. "I need you to meet me at the coffee shop. There's something I have to talk to you about."

"There's this wonderful invention called a telephone where you can speak to someone without them being physically present. Oh, hey look, we're talking on one now."

"Anna . . ."

"You can't just tell me?"

Another pause. "I can't talk about it on the phone. It's important."

"Fine. Give me an hour to get ready."

TAM WAS TAPPING HER BRIGHTLY-PAINTED FINGERNAILS ON THE surface of the table when Anna walked into the coffee shop. Her blonde pixie cut had been sharpened into spikes with gel, and there was glitter in her hair.

When Anna reached the table, Tam shot her an irritated look. "You're thirty minutes late. I called you at nine o'clock. You said, one hour. It has now been ninety minutes. Well?"

"Well, what?"

"Why are you late?"

Anna slid into the booth across from her friend. "I didn't realize this was a White House luncheon. I got tied up by Luc." She felt a mixture of indignation and flattery that it had been so hard to get him to let her leave the house. He'd been worried for her safety.

"Really? Maybe my news can wait." Tam perched on the edge of the booth, leaning toward Anna like a scavenger waiting for her to die so she could eat.

"I didn't mean it like that."

"Well, damn. I thought for a minute you might have gotten laid."

"I did."

Tam couldn't reply because the waitress arrived with two chicken salad sandwiches and mochas.

"Chicken salad for breakfast?" Anna asked.

"We're calling it brunch. It's ten-thirty."

Anna didn't miss the accusation, but ignored it in favor of the sandwich. "So what was so important and mysterious you couldn't just tell me on the phone?"

"Oh, I don't think so. You slept with Luc. Spill."

"It was nice. And I'll tell you what I told the harem on my way out this morning. It's personal. Now, once again, what was so important you had to drag me all the way down here?"

The witch had become interested in her own sandwich.

"Tam!"

"Okay, jeez. I think I know why none of the spells and rituals to get Luc out of the house have worked."

She had Anna's full attention now. "You mean besides the fact that we know how to break the curse, but I stubbornly refuse to do it because if I did, it would make everybody's life so much easier, and I've never done anything easy?"

Tam smirked. "Yes, besides that. I hope you know I fully support you on not setting the house on fire. We need that kitchen for the business."

Anna sat with her arms crossed and stared at Tam, not impressed with her stalling tactics.

"Fine. The coven thinks it's possible Beatrice is still in the house."

Anna shoved her plate to the side and dropped her head on the table. "I hate my life. So ghosts are real, too?"

"Remember, originally I thought the house was haunted? I might have been right. It's possible both Beatrice and Luc are trapped."

Of all the things Tam could have told her, a ghost interfering with the magic wasn't one she'd been expecting. "But that doesn't make any sense. Why wouldn't Luc know she was there? Why wouldn't she try to be with him?"

"Just because he's a demon doesn't mean he senses everything. Beatrice may be keeping herself very well hidden. We felt her essence when we were doing the spell, and she may be blocking it. Or she may not even be there. It may just be residue. We'd have to do a séance to be sure."

Séances were just another level of ick Anna didn't want to have to go through. "I'd really rather not."

Tam rolled her eyes. "As to your second question, she couldn't be with him even if she wanted to. As a spirit, she's non-corporeal. And since her soul wasn't tied to him before she died, there's no way they can be together."

"Kind of like Romeo and Juliet, except where you hate Juliet and are kind of glad she got what she got?" Anna said.

"Not bitter are we?"

"Who me? Not at all. I have absolutely no rage against the psychotic witch who made my life about seventeen more levels of complicated than it ever had to be. Why doesn't she just *leave*?"

Tam shrugged. "She may still be trying to punish him. Or she could have become trapped by her own spell. And before you say she wouldn't try to stand in the way of magic that could free her . . . you're thinking like a person not a ghost."

Anna *had* been about to say that. "Huh?"

"Ghosts become shadows of themselves. They can get trapped in a loop and repeat the same things over and over, forgetting they're doing them. She may not realize she's impeding the spell or she may not know she's trapped. Either way, we need to get her out of the house before we can break the curse to get Luc out."

"You couldn't tell me all this on the phone because . . . ?"

"Because if she *does* know what she's doing, it might piss her off to find out we're on to her."

To say nothing of all the women sleeping with Luc right under her nose.

"Won't a séance give that away?"

"Yes, but we'll put up safeguards so once we call her spirit we can bind her until we can expel her."

Tam went back to eating her sandwich. For the first time all week, Anna wasn't thinking about the best brands of lighter fluid. She might be able to save her house after all.

25

*I*t was only a few days until the moon and planets would be in the right phase and positions. Then the coven would return. Anna and Luc had made love another six times since the first night three weeks before. He always slept in her bed, though, after showering to wash off the scent of the others.

When Luc held her at night, it kept the dreams at bay. The bond seemed satisfied as long as they were in some way connected. It didn't matter if she dreamed about him or if his body was wrapped around hers.

She'd started sleeping naked. Luc had threatened to stop sleeping in the same bed with her if she didn't stop tempting him with what he couldn't have every night. But she'd persisted. He'd responded by wearing pajamas to bed.

Anna rubbed her ass against him, and he tensed. So she did it again. His erection pressed into her back, and she couldn't help another little wriggle.

"Anna . . . " His tone was warning.

What was he going to do? Spank her? Hell, at this point she'd take anything. It was getting harder to wait. "Luc . . . please," she whimpered still squirming against him.

He held her still. "I've told you, I can't. Not without feeding. The only way would be if you didn't get anything out of it, then I wouldn't get anything out of it. It would be a pointless exercise and frustrate us both more."

"But it's been two days . . . please."

What had he done to her? There was a time when once a week would have been just fine. She never would have dreamed the hardest thing about being with Luc wouldn't be sharing him, but waiting for him.

"One more day," he said as if she were grounded until then.

Anna ignored his pronouncement and started grinding again. He growled and nipped her shoulder. "I said stop it! Don't you have any kind of desire not to die?"

She rolled to face him. "Can't we . . . just a little . . . It doesn't have to be actual sex . . . "

He jumped out of the bed. "Goddammit, Anna. Sometimes I just want to drain you. Do you understand what you're doing? Teasing a demon isn't one of your better ideas. You're just like Beatrice."

Anna's eyes blazed. There were many things he could say to her, many things he could get away with by offering a wink or caress, but that wasn't one of them. She threw the covers back and stalked past him. The handle of the dresser drawer almost broke as she jerked it open to grab jeans and a t-shirt.

"I'm sorry," he said following after her.

She held up a hand. "No, Luc. It's already out there. You can't take shit like that back." She slammed the bathroom door in his face. Thinking better of it, she opened it again. "Oh, and just so you know, I plan to masturbate in the shower. And you aren't invited to the show." The door slammed again.

When she got to the kitchen, the harem was gathered around the table eating breakfast. She wanted to hurt them. She felt bad about it, but she couldn't stop the feeling. She didn't want to share him. *And you don't have to*, a voice in her mind reminded her seductively. A voice that sounded too much like her incubus.

"Where's Luc?" Anna wanted to know so she could avoid him. She was about to crawl out of her skin.

"He's in the wine cellar, trying to get drunk again," Renee said absently. The remark was followed by a dirty look, as if it was Anna's fault he was trying to turn himself into a wino.

It wasn't that the harem seemed to mind sharing him, they just resented Anna for not taking what he offered and becoming his mate. She had no idea why they cared. Were they trying to live vicariously through her? Or could they actually want him to be happy?

For a couple of weeks now, she'd toyed with the idea of giving him her soul. Would it be so bad? He loved her. He had to, to not have killed her already. If she were him, she would have.

She grabbed a muffin and headed toward the library. When she reached the trap door that led to the cellar, she heard Luc curse and smash a wine bottle against the stone wall below. He definitely wasn't going to get drunk if throwing them was his method. She should be more angry that he'd turned her into this obsessive creature. Instead, she was counting the hours until he'd be inside her again.

There was one of two ways this could end. His Beatrice comment hadn't just pissed her off, it had stung. She was going to prove she wasn't like the last woman he'd loved. She edged closer to the oak table with all the books on it, listening in case Luc came upstairs.

When it seemed he was staying for awhile, she shuffled through the weathered volumes until she found the one she was looking for; then she slipped out the front door into the morning sunlight.

Tam seemed surprised to see her.

"Hey," Anna said.

"Hey, yourself. Come on in." She stepped back to allow Anna into the house. Tam eyed the book.

"I'm considering it." Anna didn't have to elaborate. Tam knew what *it* was. *It* had been the subject of tearful phone calls for the past three weeks.

"I see. You want coffee?"

"That's it? I *see*? This is monumental. It's forever. I've known him a little over a month. You aren't going to give me a lecture about it?"

"I told you I think he's perfect for you. What's with the book?"

"It's about the ritual." Anna sat on one of the bar stools and flipped it open while the music of dripping coffee filled the room.

"Oh," Anna said, dismayed.

"What is it?"

The book didn't just give details of the ritual, it talked a bit about the relationship after. She pointed to the page.

"So?" Tam said. She seemed honestly baffled by Anna's distress.

"You don't see the problem here?"

"Not really. I mean you don't want to share him. What did you think was going to happen? He isn't suddenly changing species."

"But it's not just that he *can* be exclusive. He still has to feed, and he'll only be able to feed from me. There's no, *Sorry honey, not tonight I have a headache.* That's a lot of pressure."

Somewhere deep down she'd known this. After all, that was the idea if you gave a demon your soul. You belonged to them forever.

"And you're honestly complaining? Besides, since he won't be able to kill you, I think you could get out of it on occasion . . . you know if you go crazy and forget how good he is in bed. You got real intimate with the details after that first time. I'm considering hunting down my own incubus."

Anna shut the book. "Do you understand how much control he has already? Do you know what I've become? I don't even recognize myself anymore. I can't give him that. I'm not that girl." She needed to breathe into a paper bag.

Tam handed her a cup of coffee instead. "So what are you going to do? Because I don't see you sharing him forever. This month has been hell on you. And then there's the bond. Can you be tied to him like this for years?"

"I have to get it reversed." Tears pricked at the corners of her eyes, even as she said it. She never should have slept with him. Never should have fallen for him. *Fuck.*

This was all wrong. It had to be the bond. Maybe it affected Luc, too. She didn't want to think he'd been lying to her to take her soul all this time. If it wasn't real, she wanted it to be an honest mistake at least.

He didn't seem to have it in him to lie to her. Then again, he'd spent centuries lying to women. She thought she was above it? Like she was the one woman in all the world who had magic lie-detecting skills? Or that she was just so very special he'd never lie to her no matter his previous track record? There was a word for that type of thought process. Delusional.

The scar started to burn, and she rubbed her palm on her jeans to soothe it.

Anna was tired of being played with. She wanted it over. If she could reverse the mark and let Father Jeffries hide her away some-where, she'd be okay. She'd gain control of her own feelings again. She'd be able to think straight.

Tam's quiet voice interrupted her thoughts, and she realized the tears she'd been holding back had broken free. "If this is what you really want, I'll help you find the ritual to undo it."

"Father Jeffries has a book." She didn't want to reverse the bond, but she had to. If nothing else, she could still save her soul.

26

_P_re-recorded Gregorian chanting infused the sanctuary as Anna waited for Father Jeffries to arrive. Her hand hadn't stopped itching since she'd made her decision.

She was startled to see Caroline Johnson light a candle then sit in the first pew. Anna lit one out of habit and sat beside her.

"I don't know what you did, but thank you," Caroline said.

What had she done that warranted thanks?

"Sara called me. She's herself again, and she's going through the therapy sessions to get released. She said you went to see her."

Anna had forgotten all about Sara in the midst of her soap opera. She'd meant to visit again after having the dream to let the girl know it was safe to leave. That had been the turning point, when she'd decided she'd been wrong about Luc.

Why was she here again?

"Father Jeffries called me," Caroline continued. "He said you might need support, and I know a bit about the situation, how . . . seductive he can be . . . "

Dreams or not, the woman had no idea how seductive Luc could be. She wondered what Caroline would think if she knew Anna had been the favorite wife in his harem for weeks now. She doubted she'd be sitting so close.

The clock chimed the hour, announcing Father Jeffries' arrival. He stepped solemnly into the room, his cardboard box with supplies in tow. "We're going to do the ritual in here," he said. "It's the most holy place in the church."

Anna wondered if it had been determined to be the most holy place because it was the sanctuary or because it was the only room he hadn't fornicated in. God, she felt dirty. She wanted to leave, but the expectant looks on the faces of the priest and Caroline made her stay.

Cain and Jackson hadn't been back, but there was no guarantee they'd never return. Soon Luc would be out of the house, too. It wasn't that she felt she needed protection as much as she needed help resisting him. She wondered if there was any magic on earth that would make such a thing possible.

The priest unscrewed the lid of the olive oil and set about putting a small drop on Anna's forehead and hands. When the oil touched the scar, it burned with a new fervor. She flinched but didn't cry out. He repeated the process with Caroline and, finally, himself.

He began chanting in a language she didn't understand but didn't recognize as Latin. She guessed spells didn't translate over when the books hopped dimensions. Maybe they were too specific and something got lost in translation. He took loose herbs that he'd ground into a fine powder with a mortar and pestle and held his hand out for her.

She joined him in the center of the circle and he sprinkled the herbs over the mark. The scar burned more intensely as it tried to resist the spell, fighting for survival. A small part of Anna rooted for it to succeed.

Caroline grasped her other hand, telling Anna to fight it as if she were actively resisting the ritual. She wasn't, but it hurt worse than any fiery hell she'd imagined. The chanting became louder and more forceful. Then, when she thought she'd pass out from the pain, the scar glowed bright red for a moment and faded to nothing.

Anna fell to the floor in the middle of the circle and sobbed, not knowing where the tears came from or why. She only knew that she felt nothing but bone-crushing loss. As if someone she loved deeply had just died.

She hadn't understood how strong the connection would be or how abandoned she'd feel when it was broken. She realized then that she hadn't felt alone in weeks; she'd felt . . . connected, pulsing with life. And now it was gone. The sharp starkness of reality pushed in on her faster and harder as she struggled to make sense of it.

Until that moment, she hadn't known that she didn't want to be free. Not from Luc. Laughter bubbled out of her. A loud, incongruous noise in the silence of the church.

"Now, don't you feel better?" Father Jeffries said.

She couldn't stop laughing. The priest and Caroline seemed to think she was laughing in relief because she was free. But it was the irony. She'd thought breaking the bond would solve her problem, make her not want Luc anymore. But her soul cried out to him stronger than before, and all she could think about was getting back to the house.

He'd be angry with her for taking her safety so lightly to escape him. She didn't know if he'd renew the bond again now that she'd broken it. She didn't care; she just wanted to be back with him. The rest could be sorted out later.

Suddenly, waiting and sharing seemed like silly reasons to leave when he was everything she'd ever wanted. It wasn't like he wouldn't wait for her. She could take her time, and when she was ready, they could be together in that forever she'd so feared. She didn't have to run from him. Too bad she hadn't figured that out before the bond was broken.

Anna managed to compose herself and wipe away the tears still clinging to her face. "I'm sorry I wasted your time, Father."

"What? No! You can't let him get to you. It's a residual effect," the priest said, now frantic. "We have to take you to another dimension and hide you."

Anna shook her head. She knew now she'd never do that. She'd return to Luc and beg him to forgive her. She belonged to him, and he belonged to her. Mystical bond or no.

"I'm sorry." She turned to leave, but Father Jeffries and Caroline were behind her.

The priest grabbed one of her arms, and Caroline grabbed the other. "We can't let you leave. I have a duty to protect you," he said.

Caroline's hand encircled Anna's arm, and rage like Anna had never experienced rose within her. She jerked free, jabbing the woman with an elbow.

Caroline landed on the ground. Her eyes held betrayal as she touched a finger to her bleeding lip. "I can't believe you'd go back to that monster."

The priest tried to restrain Anna, but she spun and punched him in the nose. He released her, more from shock at the action than anything else. Her hand flew to her mouth, surprised at what she'd just done. Then she ran.

It was a couple of blocks before her pace slowed. Then headlights shone around the corner as a car came nearer. She didn't have to see the face behind the wheel to know it was Father Jeffries with Caroline.

Small towns didn't allow for much in the way of a night life, and all the shops on main street had closed their doors hours before. She ducked between a couple of buildings to force them to pursue her on foot.

She knew now that she would always run to Luc. She just hoped she could get to him this time.

Anna panicked for a moment, realizing she'd backed herself

into a corner. The only freaking dead end alley in the whole of Golatha Falls and of course she had to be in it. That meant climbing.

She shimmied up the fire escape onto the roof of the Java Junkie. The roof sloped down in back, making it not quite a one story drop. A cluster of bushes below could break her fall. It was only one story after all. How bad could it be?

She dropped into the bushes and stifled a cry. It really *did* work out better on TV. She wasn't going to be able to suspend her disbelief if she ever watched another action flick. Her ankle was hurt, maybe sprained.

Dry leaves crackled under Father Jeffries' boots as he rounded the corner. "Anna?"

She maneuvered herself behind the bushes as quietly as possible. It was too open here.

"Anna?" The flashlight blinded her momentarily, but the foliage was too dense for him to make out her shape. It didn't matter if he found her; she'd claw and fight him like a wildcat to get home.

"Call the rest of the parish. We need to find her. Get them to her house. We'll head her off," he said. Caroline's footsteps trailed off as she tried to find a spot that would pick up her cell phone signal.

There was no way Anna would be able to fight them all off if they got to the house before her, and with cars she knew they would. She was still several blocks from her house with a hurt ankle. Why not hail and lightning next?

She felt around on the ground and found a tree limb that had fallen in the last storm. Some god was smiling down on her. Maybe not the one from this dimension, but one of them at least. She watched Father Jeffries through the bushes and felt the feral grin light her face.

When the branch struck his head, he crumpled to the ground. She was oddly pleased with herself. Then her eyes met Caroline's.

The woman was too frightened to move. She still held the cell phone stiffly, not yet having made a call.

"Give me the phone, Caroline. I don't want to have to knock you out, too." She raised the branch like a baseball bat and readied her stance.

Caroline's hand shook as she held the phone out. "Why are you doing this?"

Anna slipped it into her pocket. "You can find a pay phone and call whoever you want once I'm safely back inside my house. Then you can bring whoever you want to try to drag me out of it. I dare you to."

"Why would you do this? You must be possessed after what he did to Sara," Caroline said.

"It's not what she thinks. I saw it . . . in dreams."

"Then he tricked you."

"He didn't." Anna had never been more sure of anything.

Caroline was flustered. "Still, that's no reason to go to him. You don't owe him anything."

"I love him." It was true. She wasn't falling in love with him; she *did* love him. And now that the bond was gone she couldn't say it wasn't real.

The priest was starting to come around. As satisfying at it would be to hit him in the head again, she didn't feel like pressing her luck. She ran, ignoring the pain in her ankle and didn't stop until she was safely locked inside the house. Her weight pressed against the front door as she panted, catching her breath.

The harem was clustered around the television in pajamas, all of them but Susan. They turned to stare at her.

"Where's Luc?"

Renee smirked. "Where do you think? He's having dinner with Susan."

"Cute," Anna said with an eye roll.

When she reached Luc's room, she could hear soft moans

coming from the other side of the door. She steeled herself and took a breath.

In about fifteen minutes they were going to be under siege by a religious mob trying to save her from herself and from Luc. Now wasn't the time to be squeamish. But she couldn't bring herself to turn the knob. It was bad enough to hear it, to know it was happening. She wasn't sure she'd ever recover from *seeing* him with another woman.

He'd be angry with her for doing the ritual and causing the trouble in the first place. Very angry. Wouldn't it be better for him to be mad on a full stomach, so to speak, than on an empty one? Anna ignored the voice in her mind that said she was a coward for not facing him.

She still felt dirty from her encounter in the church and needed a shower to wash the feeling off. It also might be good if Luc couldn't smell the priest on her. She didn't want him to know what had happened before she could break it to him gently, assuming the parish didn't arrive first to beat her to the punchline.

A few minutes into her shower, the bathroom door clicked open. "Luc?"

Great. He'd heard her downstairs. So much for stealth. She finished cleaning up and grabbed a bathrobe. She was still tying the robe around herself when she walked into the bedroom.

"Luc . . . I . . . " She looked up.

Cain sat on her bed with a self-satisfied smirk on his lips. "You're a very stupid girl, Anna."

"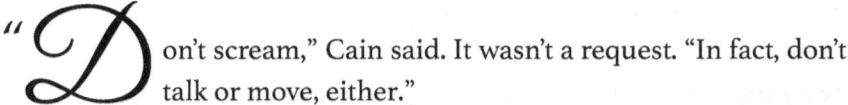on't scream," Cain said. It wasn't a request. "In fact, don't talk or move, either."

Anna stood like a great oak tree whose roots had burrowed underneath the floor while the demon prowled around her, looking at his prize. He trailed a hand over her back and across the nape of her neck. If she could have moved, she would have cringed away.

She was painfully aware that nothing more than a flimsy bathrobe shielded her. *Note to self: showers in the middle of a crisis? Not the best plan.*

"I bet you're wondering how I happened to be here at just the right time."

She stifled the urge to say, *Not really, I was more wondering about my current choice of outerwear.*

"How do you think Father Jeffries got the book to do the ritual? Never trust a book from a neighboring dimension. You never know the motives of those who wrote it or those who chose to share it.

"Not that you're much brighter. Though you are a stubborn one. I had to put a suggestion in some of the witches to get them to scare you enough to break the bond. I see it finally took."

No wonder Anna hadn't liked the coven. They'd had Cain's evil dripping off them. Tam was the only one of the group who'd taken the situation seriously enough to shield properly.

"Turn around and look at me when I'm talking to you."

Anna turned like a zombie to face her captor. Cain had moved to sit in the chair beside the dresser. How poetic that she was about to die with an incubus sitting in the same spot she'd first seen Luc.

Cain smiled and his form shifted. He was handsome still, ruggedly so, but his eyes were harder, darker, his face more gaunt. Anna realized this was his human form underneath the illusion he created to lure women to their demise. There was a strange mark on his forehead.

"Come on, Anna. Let's put that Catholic school upbringing to good use. Who am I? You aren't the only one who ever had a mark of protection put on them. The difference is, I was smart enough to never try to get mine removed."

Not possible.

"Oh, that's right, I told you you couldn't speak. You may whisper. We wouldn't want Luc to hear and come up, now would we?"

Anna found her voice, and true to his word, she could only speak softly. "I hope you aren't planning on doing the whole evil villain soliloquy now. That's so tired." She'd gained a bit of courage since he didn't seem about to attack. He might rant and rave forever. She had some time.

"Is it? Well, I'm old. I don't always keep up with what you humans find trendy."

She wanted to say he was lying about his identity, but maybe he really was *that* Cain. "How old are you?" she asked instead.

"Now that's rude, Anna." He rolled his eyes. "Oh all right. I'm about eight thousand. Give or take a few."

"The earth is billions of years old." She wasn't getting into an age-of-the-earth debate.

"Yes. Your point?"

"Your parents can't be Adam and Eve," she said as if she were talking to a crazy person standing on a ledge.

"Why not?"

Anna gave him a *duh* look.

"Adam and Eve aren't the first people ever. They are the people the Hebrew god created when he did his little botanical garden experiment. The talking snake was his idea. The other gods found it silly.

"The Hebrew god is the youngest of the gods. Still, he had fervent followers and managed to take control of this dimension. I'm the first murderer of his children, so he made me the first incubus."

"That doesn't make sense. Incubi are all about sex." She didn't know why she was arguing with him, aside from buying herself time. If she could keep him talking, maybe Luc would come for her.

And Father Jeffries would have people banging on the door soon. She might just have to keep the demon's jaws flapping for another ten minutes. She could do conversation with a complete psychotic for ten minutes. *That's right Anna, save the day with your conversation skills.*

"No," Cain corrected like he was talking to a small child. He stood as if what he had to say was so dramatic it couldn't possibly be said from a seated position.

"Incubi are all about betrayal. Gain someone's trust, betray and kill them. The gender or method doesn't matter. Of course, my brother wasn't the only one I betrayed. Betrayal isn't something you outgrow. When I moved to a new town, one run by one of the other gods, the people took pity on me. I found a wife . . . and slept with everyone but her."

He shrugged and grinned as if his behavior were cute. "I was a huge disappointment to the Hebrew god, so my punishment had to be something extra. He created a new demon breed just for me. I was special."

"Yeah, real special," Anna said. It wasn't like he'd accomplished anything that you couldn't find on a daytime talk show. Philanderers were a dime a dozen.

He'd returned to his more seductive form, and she found herself wanting him even as she knew what he was doing. She leaned into his touch, her heart hammering in her chest. A whimpering mewl escaped her throat as he stroked her skin.

"It's a pity I don't have more time with you. Oh well."

Cain turned from her and sank back into the chair. Anna felt the sexual desire ebb, and she could breathe normally again.

"Everything in this dimension is about punishment, you know. There is no redemption. Not for anyone. Not even you. You'll go to Heaven, you'll be there for awhile, and then you'll be sent back. You'll never escape the loop. But I'm above it. You see, to be punished, you must have some humanity to begin with. They trapped me in my sin for eternity, but I can't start suffering until I allow humanity to taint me like Luc has. He suffers now because he's allowed his punishment to catch up to him. I've eluded mine for thousands of years. He feels remorse and has become an unhappy whore instead of the predator he was meant to be. My brother is only a shadow now."

"You mean your clan brother." Anna was bothered that he insisted on affecting the illusion of family when he had none.

Cain's mouth twisted in a grotesque grin. "Is that what he told you? See, little girl? Even Abel can lie on occasion. I'm not the only bad seed. No, he's my brother, brother. From when I was human. When I get Luc out of this house, I'll help him remember who he was. He'll forget about you, and he'll forget about the witch who put him in this situation to begin with. Unless I can save him, his punishment will be eternal. Do you understand? Your life is a small price to pay for his freedom."

"My life?" Anna wasn't as good at stalling as she thought. He seemed to be getting to the climax of his PowerPoint presentation of evil.

"Do you know why we consider humans one of the lower life forms?" He didn't wait for her answer. "Because you haven't figured out how to attain physicality and immortality at the same time. When you're immortal you aren't physical. While you are physical you aren't immortal. You want to live forever, and when you have that you want to come back so that you can feel. But you *are* immortal. You just forget and have to rediscover it each time. This is your punishment .. . this constant loop and forgetting. You'll never escape it."

Anna's eyes widened as Cain took a jug of kerosene and started dripping a trail of it around the room. "You can't light the house on fire. It won't work," she said, recalling Luc's words about the magic.

"I know. That's why you're going to do it. Luc is too nice to push you, but you've always known this was what had to be done. You'll have to burn down your beautiful house. Just think, if you'd done it sooner, you might have lived to tell the tale." Cain put the jug of kerosene down and placed a matchbook in her hand.

She waited like a robot for the command to strike the match. "You don't have to kill me to do this."

He laughed. "I told you, you're immortal. Scared of a little death? You've probably done it hundreds of times already. Now be a good girl and light the match, then toss it over there on the bed."

Her hand trembled as she fought not to follow his command, but how could one fight someone who'd spent thousands of years perfecting hypnotic suggestion? "Please, don't . . . " she said, even as the fire came alive in her hand. She flung the match onto the bed and the flames began to engulf the room.

"This has been fun," Cain said. "As soon as I'm gone, you can move and scream and run, and whatever else you silly humans do in a crisis situation. I'll stay out of the way until it's time for me to pop back in and say something insightful."

As soon as he dematerialized, Anna found her ability to move, and scream. "LUC . . . LUC!"

Smoke streamed out of the bedroom into the upper hallway as she raced down the stairs.

Luc was called out of his room by the pounding on the door. The parish had finally arrived. "Anna, what's wrong? Are you okay?"

Tears were streaming down her cheeks. "Cain made me set the house on fire."

Scarlett and Rhett ran through the foyer, while the harem darted after them. "Get the cats!" Anna shouted to no one in particular.

The door opened to reveal the entire parish standing on the lawn with flashlights. Somehow it was upsetting, even without torches.

The harem rushed out the door, taking what little of their belongings they could carry. Anna could hear the din of voices outside as they shouted for her to come out. Luc turned her in his arms, lifting her hand to inspect the unmarred flesh where the scar had been.

"I'm sorry." Tears streamed down her face. "I got scared. I didn't want to share you, and I was too scared to give you forever. It was the only way I knew to be free."

Luc sighed. "We'll talk about it after this is over. You have no idea how pissed off I am that you would do this. You knew your safety was at stake. The mark was to protect you. What if Cain had done more than just make you set the house on fire? Do you know what that would have done to me?"

"I'm so sorry, but we can't do this right now." She tugged on his hand. "Come on, we have to leave."

"I can't yet. The spell was very specific. The house has to be burned to the ground."

"But . . . it'll hurt you. You'll burn."

"I'm strong enough to change my form. I don't have to be physical. I won't feel anything. It'll be fine. Go on, I'll be out there as soon as it's done." He shoved her toward the door.

"What about them?" Anna pointed out the window at the angry mob. "They'll try to take me away. There's too many of them. I'll be in another dimension somewhere. You won't be able to find me without the mark."

"I'll find you." He pulled her to him for a kiss. Hungry. Desperate. As if he wasn't actually sure he could find her again without the bond.

"I'm sorry," she repeated, pulling away from his mouth enough to speak.

"I'll yell at you later." His lips moved over hers again as if he were memorizing the taste of her. He finally managed to tear himself away. "Go!"

Anna took one last look at him before turning to leave. Sirens blared as the firemen dragged hoses around the back. Someone must have called as soon as the flames started.

"What if they put out the fire?" she asked, pausing in the doorway.

"Anna . . . "

She put her hands on her hips. "It's a legitimate question. How can someone burn a house to the ground in a nice neighborhood where the firemen will get to it to put it out? It's a lost cause. You'll never get out of here."

Cain materialized beside the staircase. "The reversal spell has started. They can pour water on it until Armageddon. It's not stopping the flames."

"You!" Luc growled.

"Me." Cain smiled. "Anna, darling, you should probably go on outside. You wouldn't want to burn alive, now would you?"

She looked uncertainly between the two.

"Go, Anna, I'll be fine. As much as I'd love to, with our abilities, we can't really hurt each other. It's hard to get into a fist fight with someone who keeps dematerializing," Luc said, disgusted.

Anna moved to step across the threshold and bounced off the barrier. Her eyes widened. *Oh, Fuck.*

Cain laughed. "I love this part. Do you know how long I've waited for this part? I've been like a kid waiting for Christmas with one of those stupid advent calendars with the candy. You can eat the candy early, but it doesn't make the holiday come faster."

"What did you do?" Luc ground out.

"It isn't what I did. It's what your little Beatrice did. You see, the seer discovered the owner of the house had to burn it down to break the curse. But once they set the house on fire, they'd be trapped, too." He turned to Luc. "I'm sorry I couldn't tell you. I knew you'd never sacrifice an innocent to save yourself. Not now with your pathetic guilt complex." He paused to admire the carnage. "I think I've wrung all the fun out of this event. I'm sure once the house is down you'll be back to your old self. We should hook up and have drinks."

Cain dematerialized.

"Dammit!" Luc said, smashing a lamp over the mantel.

Anna stood numbly by the door, her arms wrapped around herself, so close to freedom but unable to get to it. The smoke was drifting down the stairs.

"Luc?" she said quietly, tears threading her voice.

"Yes?"

"I don't want to die like this."

28

*L*uc had something like pity in his eyes. She hated that. After all she'd done, dragging his emotions all over the place, and he still cared. He took her hand and led her down the hallway to the library and shut the double doors behind them.

Anna sat huddled against one of the bookcases, shivering. That stupid gypsy. *Long lifeline, my ass.* And then there were the tarot cards. Tam's voice sing-songed in her mind. *The death card doesn't always mean death.*

"I don't want to die like this. I don't want to burn to death."

Luc gave her a strange look. "You wouldn't burn to death. You would die from smoke inhalation." He must have seen her face pale because he continued. "But you aren't going to die like that either."

Her knees were pulled up to her chest, her arms wrapped tightly around them. "There's no way to stop it. It's going to burn, and I'm going to go with it."

Luc pried her arms away from her body, and settled her on his lap. He brushed her hair away from her face. "I know. But you don't have to die, *like that.*"

Anna's eyes widened as his meaning sank in. She was trapped in a burning house with an incubus. Of course she didn't have to die like that, but it was hard to think straight in all the panic. Being trapped in a burning house was one of her greatest fears. Living that fear didn't make for great emergency planning.

"You'd do that for me, after . . . the others?" She knew it had to be hard for him, to willingly and voluntarily kill someone when he'd vowed to never do it again. It was only a reminder of what he was and who he'd been.

"Of course." He wiped a tear from her face. "If you have to die, you'll die in my arms and not in pain."

"Bit full of ourselves, aren't we?" she snarked.

He smiled a sad smile. "You know I'll get the job done." He was getting choked up himself.

"I don't want to," she said.

"For God's sake, Anna! Now is not the time for you to be getting common sense where I'm concerned."

"I don't want to leave you." If anything, the events of the last few hours had crystallized the decision she'd been hedging on. She didn't want to leave him, ever.

"You don't have a choice."

"Yes, I do."

Luc cupped her face, turning her toward him. "So help me, Anna. If you are playing with me . . . "

"I want to do the ritual. I want to give you my soul and stay with you. I can still do it, right?"

He jumped up, sending her toppling, and went for the door.

"Where are you going?" she asked, her voice rising in panic. This wasn't the time for him to get cold feet about eternity.

"We need a knife. I'll be right back."

She cringed when he returned a few minutes later with a sharp-looking kitchen knife. There was always blood.

"The sharper it is, the less it'll hurt."

"Okay."

Ordinarily, he wouldn't have to kill her right away. But with the fire coming closer, there wasn't time for a long engagement.

Luc laid her gently on the floor. She was still wearing her bathrobe, the belt tied around her.

"I hate this. I hate the ritual is so specific. There's no sense in scaring you more," he said.

"It's okay, I read about it. I'm not scared of you." She laid her arms out over her head, the backs of her hands resting on the floor.

He straddled her and cut a thin line down the center of each of his hands as well as hers, then clasped their hands together. "Anna, close your eyes."

"Why?"

"Just do it."

"Not before you tell me why."

"I have to change forms completely. The transfer can't happen in human form, and I don't want you to see."

"Oh my God, Luc! I'm fucking giving you my soul. I should be able to see what I'm giving it to. And don't go invisible for it, or it's no deal."

"Anna . . . "

She stubbornly shook her head. He sighed, a look of resignation on his face; then he shifted. Anna couldn't help struggling to get away. But he held her still, and she instinctively understood it was to keep from breaking the magic that had started flowing between them.

Nothing could have prepared her for his demon form. It wasn't so much the way he looked; since the dreams, she wasn't shocked by the reddish brown skin and scales. His hugeness, and the horns popping out of his shoulders weren't that horrifying either, as scary things went. He had sharp teeth, and in the demon form, his eyes glowed red like two burning embers.

But it wasn't any of that. It was the palpable, suffocating feeling of evil, fear, hatred, anger, and betrayal swirling all around her, pushing in on her senses. She felt undiluted, pure bad. She'd never felt emotions in such a strong and solid way. But she could feel them now so intensely she could almost smell them. Each negative emotion and feeling swept over her and through her. The last being her own terror.

"Anna, it's just the form." His voice came out a harsh growl, so different from the seductive purr of the voice she was used to.

She knew now without any doubt why the soul ritual was so rare. If anyone actually got to the point of agreement . . . if they saw or felt what she saw and felt, they'd believe they'd been tricked and turn back, knowing they couldn't save their life, but at least they could save their soul.

"If you want to back out now, I won't hold it against you."

His thumb stroked gently over one of her hands, a contrast to everything else she saw and felt. She looked into his eyes, and she could see him. Somehow underneath the terrifying form looming above her, there was Luc, the man she loved. The one who'd protected her and been patient through everything.

Cain had told her there was no redemption for anyone. He was very wrong about that. The form and the ritual were meant to scare people away so Luc would always be punished. Anna believed he'd been punished enough. She was no longer concerned about her own soul, only Luc's. Though it was no longer human, it was still there, and it had been tormented enough for one eternity.

"No, I'm doing it."

He spoke the words of the ritual over her in a language she didn't know that felt older than time. When he was finished he waited, expectantly, for her acceptance or rejection.

"Yes, I'll give you my soul."

The simple language seemed so lacking, but the magic required nothing more elaborate. It swirled around her as the connection that had once been between them wrapped even more tightly into a bond that could never be broken by anyone's magic: human, demon, or god.

He shifted back to his human form. "I love you," he said. He collapsed on top of her, nuzzling her neck. She felt the warm wetness of tears against her skin and realized he hadn't believed she'd do it after seeing him.

"I love you, too." She squirmed under him. "Luc, as touching as this moment is, don't you think we should finish? The fire is getting closer."

He lifted off her and smirked. "You're getting it for eternity, and you can't wait two minutes to let me bask in the fact that I have you forever?"

"Nope," she said grinning up at him.

"Fine," he snarled. But there was no anger. He stripped his jeans off and fiddled with the belt on her robe. He finally got frustrated with the knot and ripped it off her.

There was no foreplay or teasing; there wasn't time. And Anna didn't need any preparation. She'd waited three maddening days for him to be inside her again. He was gentle and sweet, cradling her body against his own as he thrust slowly into her. He whispered endearments into her skin as if to apologize for what she'd just been through, to reassure her she was with the real Luc, and the other had been only a passing illusion. What he was, but not who he was.

Not anymore.

The warm, tingling sensation started along her body then. She had a moment's panic, knowing he wouldn't stop this time, that he would feed until there was nothing left. But then her orgasm came cresting over her, and she relaxed again.

As the last of her life slipped away, her soul was ripped from Luc's arms. She floated behind him. Then she was huddled in the corner, sobbing, rocking back and forth as well as one can in a nonphysical form.

The memories of her previous lives flooded through her, but it was the most recent incarnation that had her crying uncontrollably. Luc was still turned away from her. The muscles in his back tensed, and she knew he knew. Somehow when her soul had been ripped from her body and gone through him, he must have gotten a flash of her memories, and he knew.

He rounded on her, snarling, his eyes glowing that eerie red again. "Beatrice!" he roared at her.

Anna couldn't stop crying as she looked up into his eyes. "Don't call me that! I'm not her anymore."

He stalked over, menace pouring off him. This was what she'd been afraid of all along. She just hadn't known it. The truth had been buried too deep in her subconscious.

This was why she couldn't give him her soul, why she'd fought him and burning down the house every step of the way, why she'd been afraid of witches. Some part of her had to have known. She kept repeating to herself, *he can't hurt me, he can't hurt me.* How could one physically hurt a ghost?

But then he gripped her shoulders hard, and she had solid form again. He laughed the kind of laugh she never wanted to hear from him as he watched her realize he could make her physical.

"Oh yes, Anna. How do you think I'd be able to feed from you for eternity if I couldn't give you form?"

"Please, Luc, I'm sorry. I didn't know I was her. I swear."

He growled again but stepped back, trying to reign in his anger. "Why? Why did you do it?"

Anna looked miserably down at her hands. He'd let go of her, and she was once again in ghostly form. She just wanted him to touch her again, even if in anger. So she could feel real.

"Where do you want me to start?"

He scrubbed a hand through his hair, pacing and backing away from her even farther, as if he feared he might strike her if he didn't put enough distance between them.

"I can understand parts of it. What I don't understand is . . .

knowing what I was, why did you put a spell on me to make me love you?"

"I didn't."

His eyes glowed brighter. "Anna, do not lie to me."

"I'm not. I did a spell, but not that."

"Tell me."

She took a deep, steadying breath that suddenly she didn't need, but that felt comforting all the same. "When I met you, the first time, as Beatrice . . . I didn't know what you were. If I was any kind of decent witch I would have known, but I didn't. It wasn't until we were in bed together and I felt you feeding from me that something clicked in my mind, and I knew what you were.

"I realized you were going to kill me. I was scared. I didn't want to die. I whispered the only spell I could think of into your ear. I was always good with incantations. I just wanted to unlock your humanity so you'd feel enough compassion to spare me. I just wanted to live." She looked up at him, begging him to understand.

The glow faded from his eyes, replaced with guilt. "Go on," he said, his voice more controlled, much of the anger seeming to dissipate.

"Then you kept coming back to me. And I could never resist you. Before I knew what had happened I was in love with you. Months passed, and I couldn't handle it anymore, you being with others. I wanted to be with you, but I didn't know if my spell would hold. I was afraid that as soon as I gave you my soul, you'd revert to what you were, I'd be tied to you forever, and you'd never stop punishing me for making you feel human. I was so angry, at you, at myself . . . I don't know. I knew I'd never have the strength to leave you, and I couldn't stand watching you walk away from me."

Moments later, Luc was holding her. "How could you make me kill you? You selfish little . . . "

"I'm sorry. I know it was wrong. I was only thinking of myself. I didn't think about what would happen to you after I was gone.

What are you going to do now?" She tensed in his arms. She was tied to him forever now, and she didn't know if she could forgive herself, let alone if Luc could forgive her.

He pulled back, his expression softening before he sighed. "I expected you to either forgive or forget all the awful things I'd done in my past. To hold one mistake against you, no matter how bad . . . "

"I don't deserve forgiveness."

"Does anyone? Why did you do the last part of the spell, the part about the house?"

"I wanted a fail-safe, so I wouldn't back out. I couldn't leave you, and I'd decided I'd die in your arms and then go to Heaven and forget about you. But I couldn't." She was crying so hard she could barely get the words out. He held her hand as she continued.

"Cain told me everything is a loop and you never break free. But I could have stayed there if I'd wanted to. If I'd been content to be without you, but I wasn't. They let me come back. They could have sent me to Bangladesh, but they sent me back here. Some part of me always knew. I had to. But the memories were all locked away, and I couldn't get to them. I'm so sorry. I said I loved you, and then I just left you in the house to rot."

Of all the things she'd done, all the stupid mistakes, leaving him there was her worst. She should have burnt the house down first, so he'd at least have been free once she was gone. She didn't know how he could look at her with anything but loathing. Yet all she could find in his eyes was calm acceptance.

"Why?" she said finally. "How can you forgive me?"

He held her hard against him as if she might disappear. "How can I not? I'm not saying I'm happy about the way it happened, but you've freed me."

He didn't have to tell her he wasn't talking about the house. She'd freed him from the hunt, the hunger, the loneliness.

"And I loved you so much," he said. "It killed me to lose you. No matter how mad I am at you, I can't help but be grateful you're back, and I'll never lose you again."

She pulled back and smacked him on the arm. "Hey! You love her more than me!"

Luc laughed. "You are so infuriating, Anna. I've loved two women and both of them are you. I don't love one incarnation more than the other."

"Luc . . . "

He looked up to see the smoke seeping under the door. "Right." He took her hand and led her down into the wine cellar to wait while the house finished burning.

LUC LET GO OF ANNA'S HAND FOR THE COUPLE OF HOURS IT TOOK SO she wouldn't get smoke fumes. Despite his reassurances, some part of her had feared he'd hold her into the flames and let her burn to punish her for what she'd done. She wouldn't have blamed him.

Had their positions been reversed she couldn't say with certainty she wouldn't have done the same. He'd forgiven her much more easily than she would forgive herself.

Once the fire died away, he made love to her again. It wasn't about the feeding. It was comfort, reassurance that nothing had changed about the way he felt. He still loved her. They'd be okay.

They were about to go up to the surface. "Luc . . . I don't think this is proper attire." All their clothes had burned away in the library.

He arched a brow as if it was incredibly stupid for her to think he'd let her go cavorting on the surface naked. The possessiveness in his eyes said he was the only one that would ever be looking again. As he held her hand in his, he went invisible, and she found she did as well.

"Nifty," she said, but she was disturbed by the fact that she was, in some sense, not there anymore.

"You'll get used to it. You'll get a lot of my shapeshifting powers over time. The longer we're together and the more I feed from you. It'll make you stronger now that you aren't tied to a human body. You can't do any of it by yourself just yet, though. It might take a couple of decades before you can hold a solid form without me touching you."

"A couple of *decades*!" she said turning to where Luc should be. "Luc, materialize when I'm talking to you!"

He did as she asked, shaking his head and laughing. "You get upset over the weirdest things. You just gave your immortal soul to a demon, and you're upset I'm invisible while you're talking to me? Eternity with you is going to be fun."

"Shut up." She punched him in the arm, but there was no malice behind it.

He made them invisible again, and they went to the surface.

EPILOGUE

The people of Golatha Falls never knew exactly what had happened at the house on Cranberry Lane, or for that matter what had happened to Anna Worthington and all her money. Luc spent weeks systematically going through the town erasing memories. But people kept talking, as people are prone to do.

Bits of legend built up about the strange happenings at the house. Still, most remembered what they had witnessed as dreams. And if it was weird that everyone in the town seemed to have had the same dreams, no one was talking about that part. Denial is a strong survival skill.

Bitsy and Mimi were the only two people in town who didn't seem able to be enthralled. If anyone could resist the mind control of a formerly evil incubus it was those two stubborn old biddies. The old women spent a couple of weeks talking about being camped out on Anna's front lawn with flashlights waiting to rescue her from the devil. Luckily, most of the people in town decided that the Baker sisters had finally hit senility, and they were shipped off to a retirement community in Florida.

The people at the bank were probably the most confused by what had happened. They seemed to remember Anna coming in a few days before the house burned down and withdrawing all her money, but that sort of thing usually took more time. There was paperwork to go through. Paperwork which didn't exist. But it couldn't be denied that the money was gone, and there were no signs of a robbery.

Anna's anger at the harem had dissipated now that they no longer posed a threat. In hindsight, her jealousy made more sense in light of her previous life as Beatrice.

The harem continued to work with Tam on the business. They opened a candle and occult shop next to Sally's. The town was really freaking out over the occult part.

Anna had a hard time maintaining anger at anyone, since her stupid spell had been the thing that started everything in the first place. Karma was seriously a bitch, and she wasn't going to forget that lesson in the foreseeable future.

She transferred a large sum of money to Sara Johnson. The girl was confused by the sudden increase in her account when she got out of the institution, but the letter left for her in a safe deposit box explained things. Well, most things.

Anna had wanted to visit Cecelia Townsend, the one constant and close friend in both lives, but she'd been afraid the shock would kill the poor woman, and Cece, being who she was, would just haunt her forever. So, like a coward, she left a letter instead, watching outside the window as the woman read.

Cece would never see the inside of the house she'd spent that one evening in, but she deserved to know the truth. In the letter, Anna apologized for the spell that started it all, and heard Cecelia forgive her.

There was one person she did have to see. Tam was going to be pissed that she'd waited so long to come by. But she'd had things to take care of. Plus there was that whole avoidance thing she was still doing.

"Oh my God, Anna. I thought you were dead!" Tam said when she opened the door.

Anna had momentarily let go of Luc's hand, and Tam went through her when they tried to hug. "Well, I sort of am." She grabbed hold of Luc so she could hug her friend properly.

Tam pulled back and glared at her. "You know what I mean. I mourned you. And you're not gone."

"I could leave," Anna said, only half serious.

"Get in this house."

Anna and Luc went inside and spent the next two hours telling Tam the entire story. Tam burst out laughing at the end.

"Whatever you do, don't tell me about it," she said in a high voice, mocking Anna's response to witchcraft.

Anna rolled her eyes. "What about you and your, *the death card doesn't always mean death*?"

"It doesn't. I was just in denial that time. The rest of the spread really did look pretty good. And I knew you'd get together with Luc. But you said you didn't want to know . . . so I didn't say anything."

"Gee, thanks."

"No problem." Tam got serious then. "I guess I won't be seeing you anymore."

"I have to keep a low profile, and all, since people think I'm dead or at the very least a missing person, but it's not like I'm banned from the planet or anything. We're probably going to Europe for awhile, and then there are other dimensions to check out. But we'll visit."

"You better."

Cain had disappeared soon after making Anna set the house on fire. She had mixed feelings about that. Sure, he was evil and couldn't seem to stop betraying people, but if not for him she wouldn't have Luc. And really . . . it *was* her spell. Still, she wished he could be punished.

Luc wasn't any happier about it, but what could you do? Cain was the first incubus and their leader. The buck kind of stopped with him. And she knew no god would be intervening.

Her karma had caught up with her. Someday, so would Cain's.

I HOPE YOU ENJOYED INCUBUS AWAKENED. TURN THE PAGE FOR the first chapter of book 3 of Fated Mates, HUNTED.

29

HUNTED PREVIEW

Just have to make it to the mailbox. Everything will be okay. Fiona Patrone stared out the window at the lonely box at the end of the driveway. Her house was surrounded by trees in a heavily wooded area of Golatha Falls—so far out it was amazing the mailman delivered. And yet it felt so open and unknown out there. It was safer inside.

There probably isn't any mail. Just check it tomorrow. Nothing important. Not worth going out. The thoughts tunneled through her mind like vicious moles. If she didn't venture out, she'd be even more a prisoner of her own mind and fears. She couldn't remember the last time she'd gone past the mailbox. If she got to the point where she couldn't even get that far...

The birds outside screeched then, chattering warnings, screaming the same awful things they screamed at her every day. *If you go out there, something bad will happen.* She believed them. Birds had no reason to lie. They were excellent seers, so much so, that for centuries people had read bird entrails, not realizing you needed a live bird to get any knowledge of value.

Something bad.

They could at least give her a little detail, some clue as to what she should fear, but the threat remained the same—vague and foreboding as ever.

Fiona had been able to understand the language of animals before she could understand that of humans—a rare and special gift for a witch to inherit. She'd gotten it from her grandmother. Though she'd always seen it as a curse. If not for those damned birds, she'd be outside living her life. Maybe she would have found love, a job, something.

Well, she had a job on the Internet. Her money was direct-deposited. She ordered her clothes online and had her groceries delivered. Thanks to the web, agoraphobia had never been so easy. At least from a logistics standpoint.

She took a slow, measured breath, her hand poised over the doorknob. *You can do this. You can do this. You can do this.* Fiona mentally repeated it like a subliminal message she prayed would take hold. The doorknob clicked in her hand. She moved through what felt like invisible molasses as she forced herself out the door and into the throng of screeching, angry birds.

The wind had a new crispness. Almost Halloween. As a witch, shouldn't she be in her element right about now? But the idea of ghosts and goblins and veils thinning served to make the whole ordeal seem more dangerous.

Fifty-five steps. She counted them every day because counting them was the only way she could make herself get there. It wasn't far. She could run back into her house if the birds were right.

The mailbox held nothing of interest: an electric bill that could have waited until tomorrow. On her way back, step twenty-four, she became aware of the eerie silence. The birds had stopped their squawking, and a stillness blanketed the yard. She would have run straight for the front door except for the plaintive cry coming from the yard.

Ignore it. It's not your concern, she told herself. *Thirty-five.* But the noise happened again. So sad, scared. She'd want someone to help her if she were in distress. She tucked the electric bill into the waistband of her jeans and struggled through the wild growth of the front yard. She hadn't worked on the garden in five years, and it showed.

When she reached the side of the house, she found a wolf pup with wide, brown eyes, crying. He was old enough that he should have started learning the language of his kind, but he hadn't. There were no words to pick up and decipher. She could still get emotions and basic information, especially if those emotions were strong. In some circles, this made Fiona dangerous; in others, it would make her a pawn of those who might want to capitalize on such information.

The pup was lost, hungry, scared.

She didn't sense a mother wolf nearby. Had he been abandoned? Her mind screamed at her to leave him there. But he was so hungry and pathetic. She couldn't stop herself from scooping him up and taking him in the house.

She sat him on the kitchen counter, and he stared curiously at her, turning his little wolf head to the side. He was reddish-brown and white, the cutest thing she'd seen in forever. At least he seemed old enough to be weaned.

She cut some meat from a leftover roast and put it on the counter. The pup's tail wagged as he gobbled up the food. She placed a bowl of water down, and he took care of that, too.

He stared at her from the top of the counter as if to say *What next?* Oh wow, yeah. She hadn't thought through that part. If he was just lost, his mother would be coming soon. If he was all alone, she couldn't have a wolf in her house. Even understanding what he needed, it was just insane. And probably illegal.

He positioned himself on the edge of the counter, shifting his weight from paw to paw, negotiating the drop to the ground. His full concentration was on the jump. When he made it to the linoleum, he looked up at her, all pleased with himself, and she melted. So cute.

"Well, maybe you can stay for a little while until I figure out what to do with you." Those words had barely tumbled past her lips when the window over the breakfast nook shattered, and a large ball of black fur leaped into her kitchen.

It must be the mother. But no. As her confusion cleared, she saw it was a large, angry black panther.

Fiona edged back, afraid he'd pounce if she made any sudden moves. What she wouldn't give right now to have a few handy incantations at the ready. For spells, she needed all the proper tools: sage stick, herbs, candles, salt, etc. She could incant a little if she was very focused, but now, with her heart pounding so fast, wasn't one of those times. Her own name was a blank—forget coming up with a snappy protection chant.

She grabbed at stray pots and pans and emptied a whole drawer of utensils as she threw everything she had at him. He batted the objects away, prowling closer, his growl low and menacing. Within seconds, he had her backed into a corner, claws out, swiping at her.

She screamed and grabbed her bleeding arm. Her side burned as well. All at once, her brain snapped into sharp focus. She was going to die in a matter of seconds if she didn't figure something out right now.

He'd stopped clawing at her for a minute and was growling, something about her taking the pup, wanting to hurt him, people after him. Oh, wait. Wait! She felt the magic crackle around the panther. Therian! That meant there was a person in there. Somewhere.

She called on every reserve of courage she had to form words. "I wasn't trying to hurt him. He was lost and hungry. I brought him in to feed him. That's all. I'm not whoever you think I am."

The panther stared at her hard and growled again.

"Yes, I understand you."

How is that possible? He growled.

"Rare gift. I meant the pup no harm. I swear." She held her hands out defensively, hoping he believed her. An animal attack wasn't how she wanted to go out. Blood dripped in a steady flow down her arm; her shirt was torn near her ribcage where more blood was pooling. Oh God. That swipe alone could have killed her.

Breathe, Fiona. He's calm now. Everything will be fine. Thank God he was a therian and could understand her as well as she understood him.

She still couldn't figure out what a panther's concern with a wolf pup was. But really, all she wanted was to get the both of them out of her house and call a window repairman. She was trying to forget the bleeding part. She vowed she'd listen to the birds next time.

So you can understand him? The panther's gaze shifted to the pup who gingerly stepped around the broken glass, sniffing things.

"Well, he doesn't have language like you have yet, but I know what he needs. My gift runs a little deeper than just speech."

He shifted—right in the middle of her kitchen. Her eyes didn't know where to go. Tanned, muscular legs. And... oh dear, skip that, skip that! But her brain had already processed parts of a man she'd never seen outside of television or the Internet, due to her phobia. There weren't a lot of opportunities to hook up with men when you never left your house.

Farther up, were very nice abs and pecs—and those arms. Oh boy. She swiped the back of the hand that wasn't bleeding across her face, afraid she might be drooling. She wanted to lick him, but under the circumstances that seemed a little weird. Her arm and side burned like fiery hell, but damn, he was pretty. So sleek and lithe, just like what he shifted into.

When her gaze made it up to his face, a boyish smirk graced his lips. There was a twinkle in his brown eyes. His dark hair was longish, but somehow still masculine. Oh yes, there wasn't an unmanly bone in his body.

"So," he drawled, moving closer by mere centimeters, "should we just get it on now?"

Her mouth dropped open. He couldn't have just said that.

A strange look crossed his face. "Sorry. Wild animal here. A little amped up. That was inappropriate." He extended a hand, attempting to move past the new awkwardness. "Let me look at you."

The pain in her arm and side flared fully to life as she processed everything that had just happened in her kitchen. When she didn't respond to his request, he pulled her to him and lifted her shirt to inspect her side.

He frowned. "Not as bad as it could have been. Nothing major harmed."

She was about to get angry and indignant about his flippant attitude, but then his eyes met hers, warm and honest.

"I'm very sorry about your injuries. I was afraid for the pup and sensed the magic on you. I thought you were one of the ones who tried to take him. I'm all he's got."

The pup, as if sensing he was being talked about, clomped through the debris to sit between them, his little wolf gaze going back and forth.

Fiona looked back at the man standing in front of her, so sincere and intense... and attractive, and then the waterworks started.

"Oh, no, don't cry," he said, almost in a panic.

It wasn't pain that had brought forth the tears; it was the fact that *this* was what it took to get near a hot guy for her: a near-death experience, and him breaking into her kitchen: the idea that he was going to take the pup and go on his merry way, and she'd have the memory of him emblazoned on her brain, but that would be all. Her close brush with maleness. Inches from her, but no dice.

It wasn't that she wanted to take him up on his carnal offer. He was a stranger. And, as he said, a wild animal. And she wished he'd cover himself with something, because judging from outward signs, he was all raring and ready to go. Like most therians, he was unaffected by his own nudity or arousal. It was something she wished humans shared in common with them, so she wouldn't feel so freaked out by his nearness... or so much longing for something she wasn't going to ever have since she couldn't make it past her own mailbox.

His smooth, deep voice interrupted her mental hysteria. "Do you have bandages?"

"Bathroom, down the hall," she croaked, feeling stupid for going all blubbery on him. Thank God he couldn't read her mind and know why she'd been crying. That would have been too mortifying for words. Better for him to think she was a big wimp who couldn't take surface abrasions than to know the truth.

Z AMBLED DOWN THE HALLWAY, TRYING TO REMEMBER HOW TO ACT like a person. He wasn't good with people. He lived alone and hunted alone. It was how he liked it. Women were a complication he tried to stay away from, except when he had a quick roll in the hay—or cave, with another of his kind who was equally allergic to relationships. Occasionally, he had sexual liaisons with human women or other therian breeds, but on principle he tried to avoid those who wouldn't understand his solitary nature.

A confirmed bachelor, he had everything he wanted, exactly how he wanted it. Total freedom. That is, until he'd stumbled on the pup. Panthers didn't raise babies—their own or anybody else's—which was obvious from the mess he was making of it.

The little wolf had been sitting in the forest in the middle of Z's hunting ground, staring at a spot in the dirt where there had been a struggle. There was evidence a body of some sort had been dragged off, probably the mother.

Z had immediately known the pup was a werewolf, but there

wasn't a pack in Golatha Falls, so how the little guy could have gotten there, he didn't know.

He should have just walked away, but he couldn't. After a lot of frustration, he'd managed to get the pup to drink human formula until he could start eating meat, but now instead of getting easier to raise him, it was getting harder. Every day Z was more aware of how difficult it would be for the pup when he shifted to his human form and couldn't speak the language of his own kind. When did the ones born in their fur first shift? Age five? Six?

The bathroom the woman had pointed out was the most organized he'd ever encountered. Her perfectly folded towels were arranged by color. Her medicine cabinet looked like a pharmacy—preparation for every potential contingency. Her first aid supply left something to be desired, though. He didn't imagine she had a lot of accidents as cautious as she was. He could patch her up okay with what she had. At least until she could see a doctor or something. She might need some stitches.

He felt a twinge of guilt at that. She'd been at least five kinds of terrified when he'd busted in the house. Z shut his eyes against the image of her pressed against the wall, her lower lip trembling. In truth, it was her smell that had startled him out of the mindless clawing. She smelled so good. He'd looked up and seen those golden curls cascading down her back, those light green eyes, and the dusting of freckles on her nose.

He'd switched from violence to growls, not expecting her to understand a word of it. But she had. Now the wheels in his head were turning. If he ever wanted his bachelor cave back, he needed her. Though he felt guilty about her injuries—and her window—he had no intention of negotiating with the woman. Z operated on the law of the jungle, and she'd stumbled into his jungle. Sort of.

The pup was cute, but the kid cramped his style. He was losing sleep, not getting laid. It was making him grumpy and unhinged. He wasn't cut out for this parenting gig, and he was willing to do anything to fix the situation, up to and including felony.

Basket of first aid supplies in tow, Z sauntered back into the kitchen to find the woman sitting at the table, cradling her arm, so quiet he feared she'd fallen into some kind of fugue state.

"So I've decided you're coming with me," he said without preamble.

"W-what?"

He chuckled when she averted her gaze from his nakedness. She should be glad he was a gentleman—more or less—because she sure was a sweet little thing. It had been a few weeks since he'd scratched that particular itch. Having the pup around all the time made prowling for women low on the priority list. He wondered for a moment if he could convince this one to have some down and dirty, no-strings-attached sex. Maybe after he found the pup's family. Before that would be too much complication with them in such close quarters—since she was coming with him.

Z cocked his head toward the pup who sat on the table with his nose pressed into the crook of her elbow. This was perfect. The pup even liked her. It was like a nanny had fallen out of the sky. A multi-lingual nanny. Praise the gods.

"You understand what he needs. I need you to help me care for him. And I need you to stay with him at my place while I find his family. It's more secure there. We'll take you to a doctor first about your injuries."

He knew she probably had a life of some sort. Maybe a job. Probably a boyfriend. But he didn't care. He was desperate to get this kid out of his hair. The only way it was happening was if he got some help, and he couldn't bring himself to ask another panther. They'd laugh at him for his foolishness in taking the pup in the first place.

She sat frozen for a moment as if she were processing all of that. When she spoke, her voice came out calm and even. "I'm not going anywhere with you. I don't *know* you. And I don't need a doctor. I just need my magic books and tools. I can heal myself."

Z had been surprised when she hadn't started shouting spells at him and throwing balls of energy. Some witches were kind of intense. Different magic users had different skills and gifts, and he was thankful that didn't seem to be part of her repertoire. Aside from the skill she had that he needed, she seemed to need a lot of prep work for magic, which was good. It kept the balance of power in his favor, exactly where he preferred it to be at all times.

He pulled her to him, setting to work bandaging her arm. "I'm Zane Trent, but you can call me Z."

"I need my books. I can heal this if you'll just let me get my books," she said, ignoring his introduction. Poor girl probably wasn't yet prepared to see him as anything beyond the crazy naked man in her kitchen.

He snorted. "Sure, I'm that stupid. I get you your books, and you hex me into a sealed magic jar or turn me into a frog. No can do. Besides, don't self-healing spells take a lot of energy out of a witch?"

"Yes, but..."

"I need you with full energy to help take care of this pup."

"You're insane."

"Only moderately. This kid is driving me crazy. I need help."

Her expression softened. "Still. I-I can't go out there."

"Out where?"

Her gaze went to the door.

"You went out there to bring the pup in."

"I know but... I try not to go outside."

Z moved on to her torso, which was just grazed, not as bad as the arm. He was beginning to think he had a nut job on his hands. "Why?"

Her voice lowered to a whisper as if she didn't want to be overheard. "The birds told me something bad would happen."

Fucking great. All he needed was a mentally unstable nanny he couldn't bring himself to leave the kid with. What good was that going to do him?

"I'm not crazy," she said, as if reading his mind.

She'd probably just read his facial expression. Unless she could read minds. Could she read minds? *Hey, I think you're real pretty. If you weren't so pretty I'd eat you for dinner*, he thought at her. But she didn't react; she was still on about her birds. At least his mind was safe from her.

"They *did* warn me," she said, "I heard them just like I heard you when you were in your other form. And just like I understood what the wolf needed."

She had him there.

"Come on, it's only a few miles from here," he said. Despite his intention not to negotiate with her, he found himself negotiating. If he could get her to come to his cave of her own free will it would be so much simpler. Maybe her weird outside phobia was minor, just a blip on an otherwise sane human being.

"Miles? Miles! No. Oh no. Miles are too far. Way too far. That's just impossible for me. I'm sorry."

He'd known it was too much to hope for.

"Nothing will get you out there. I'll protect you," he said, standing and offering a hand like he was about to sweep her up on his white stallion and go riding off into the sunset. Was he about to do that?

She held her bandaged arm up and raised a brow. It was still dripping blood. "That makes me feel safe."

He tried again, willing himself to be patient and not shift and chase her out of the house. He was betting her fear of him would dwarf her fear of the nebulous *outside* if push came to shove. "What's your name?"

She looked away. "I wish you'd put some clothing on."

"No problem, ma'am. Let me just step outside where I keep my traveling walk-in closet." Ordinarily her shyness would entertain him, but right now it was annoying. "Stop acting like a virgin."

The attractive flush that came to her cheeks confirmed the suspicion that had been building in the back of his mind, the suspicion he'd hoped he'd been wrong about. "A girl as pretty as you? You had no opportunities? No interest?"

Her hands were in her lap, and she'd gone to staring at them, he guessed because clothing wasn't about to magically appear on him.

"I don't ever leave my house. So, no. You're the first adult male I've ever..."

"Seen naked?" He'd softened his voice because now he just felt like an ass. He'd destroyed her kitchen, injured her, and now this. He disappeared back down the hallway to the bathroom and returned, wrapped in a towel for her comfort more than his. "Better?" he asked.

"Yes, thank you."

He sighed. "If you won't come with me, I need you to watch the pup for a while. Can you do that?"

She nodded, and he shifted back into his panther form and jumped out the window. By nightfall she'd be in his cave with him where it was safer. She just didn't know it yet. Sometimes these things took finesse.

END PREVIEW

To be notified of new releases, subscribe to my newsletter at http://www.kittythomas.com you'll receive a free ebook as a thank you!

To see a full list of all the books I have available, you can check out my downloadable reading list PDF:

https://kittythomas.com/reading-order-for-new-readers/

If you represent a company interested in licensing sub rights for this book or any of my other work, please fill out the sub rights inquiry licensing contact form here:

https://kittythomas.com/rights-inquiries/

Thanks again!

ACKNOWLEDGMENTS

In no particular order, thank you to the following people who helped bring this book and the surrounding promotional material into existence:

- The ever lovely and hilarious Robin Johnson for kickass cover art.
    - Lindsay Carruth and Andrew Mocete for music brainstorming for the Save My Soul (previous title) book trailer.
    - Susan Bischoff, Kait Nolan, Michelle Davidson Argyle, Natasha Fondren, Lainey Bancroft, and Catherine James for critique, editing feedback, and beta reading.
    - Cathy R. for proofreading.
    - Cara Wallace, my stealth ninja beta.
    - Michelle Davidson Argyle for her awesome book trailer skillz. Without her to put the trailer together for me, I would have probably spent a whole week crying about how making a book trailer is too hard! Also, thanks for the Photoshop skillz.
    - Random grammar and punctuation expert: Jackie Barbosa who always fields my random: "Are you SURE that comma isn't right?" questions.

- My parents for always believing in me.
- M for all his love and support.
- My fellow indies for being there for me to whine and cry on, and for being there when I had awesome news to share.
- And finally to the readers. Without you guys, I'm just talking to myself. Thanks for reading and wanting more.

I would also like to acknowledge that I understand "counter-intuitive" isn't supposed to have a hyphen, but it looks stupid without one. Also, Susan Bischoff supports my hyphen rebellion. We are starting a movement, bitches!